Sophia Watson

Sophia Watson was born in 1962, the daughter of
Auberon Waugh, and educated at Durham University.
She has worked in publishing, as a feature writer for
the *Daily Mail* and as a ghost writer. Her previous books
are *Winning Women*, published in 1989 and *Marina*, a
biography of the Duchess of Kent, published in 1994. She
is married with three small daughters and lives in West
Somerset.

SCEPTRE

Her Husband's Children

SOPHIA WATSON

SCEPTRE

First published in 1995 by Hodder and Stoughton
First published in paperback in 1996 by Hodder and Stoughton
A division of Hodder Headline PLC
A Sceptre Paperback

A CIP catalogue record for this title is available
from the British Library

ISBN 0-340-64041-3

Typeset by Hewer Text Composition Services, Edinburgh
Printed and bound in Great Britain by
Cox & Wyman Ltd, Reading, Berkshire

Hodder and Stoughton
A division of Hodder Headline PLC
338 Euston Road
London NW1 3BH

For my niece and god-daughter,
Mary Eulalia Waugh, with
my love

Laura and Robert's car had become tied up in traffic on the fifteen-minute journey to her parents' house, so they arrived at Foxways Barton at the same time as the first of their guests. Laura's brother-in-law James was chauffeuring them, and as he eased the car down the lane, ignoring the red-faced car-park attendant's manic signals to turn into the field, Laura had the sense of being a guest at her own wedding. Impressions of people she barely knew who had come here to celebrate with her flashed in front of her like scenes from some half-forgotten film. Who was that woman in the broad-brimmed blue hat looking so anxiously up at the sky? Laura watched as she shrugged, slammed the car door shut and made her way across the field, staggering slightly on her high heels.

A green Peugeot crawled along the lane in front of Robert and Laura, and was waved to a halt. "Car in there, sir, ladies out now." Two women, one elegant in grey, the other dragged together in last year's Laura Ashley, got out of the car and paused. "We'll wait here, darling," said the elegant one, while the other began thanking the driver for the lift. Laura and Robert sat back in their seats, not ready yet to begin the greetings, to acknowledge the good wishes.

They saw a fat man in a well-cut suit and military moustache come out of the field and half-bow to the ladies before taking a handkerchief from his pocket and bending to wipe the red dust from his shoes.

James stopped in front of Laura's parents' house and leapt out of his seat to open the back doors for them. "Full chauffeur service!" he said with a bow. Laura smiled at him but her thoughts were for Robert, as she reached out a hand for his. She looked back at the steady stream of cars now arriving, decant̶ ̶ passengers at the gate and bumping up the field to p̶ ̶ ̶ unnecessarily orderly rows. Women checked their lipst̶ ̶ ̶ and kissed the air next to each other's cheeks. The older men greeted friends heartily, while the women eyed each other's dresses. Then, as though by common consent, they began to move towards the house.

For a moment Laura wished she had done this differently. Why had they not just married secretly, told everyone afterwards, maybe given some sort of party then? Her mother would have hated it, called it furtive or (more likely) common, but it was not her mother who was important. Robert was important. She had Robert. She held his hand and looked at her guests and knew what mattered. Laura turned to find Robert's eyes on her, quizzical, faintly concerned, very green. "All right, my love?" Laura nodded, took his arm, squeezing it tightly to let him know she loved him, and they walked through the front door together.

The Sawyers' house lay long and low at the foot of a Devon valley. More substantial than a cottage, it did not have the self-assured squareness of a "gent's res." but its position, with the hill rising green and steep behind it, the small river a hundred yards from the door and the view of gently sloping hills across the narrow valley, was idyllic.

It was a seventeenth-century cottage, higgledy-piggledy at the rear with endless steps and different levels, but with an early eighteenth-century front addition of two well-proportioned rooms and a hall. The hall was grander than the house deserved, reaching up two storeys and dominated by an elegantly curved staircase.

Although it had been raining fitfully all morning, the front door was wide open. A neatly dressed middle-aged woman stood just inside carrying a tray of glasses of orange juice and champagne. A few of the guests were already waiting for the bride and groom to join the receiving line. As they took their places the procession past them began.

Laura's father Michael Sawyer was first in the line. Small and handsome, with a beaky nose and deep-set grey eyes, he did not say much, but shook hands with warmth, promising to catch up with people later. His wife Rosalind, pretty in a pale torquoise dress that reflected her eyes, shook her guests' hands with both of hers, looking at each person earnestly, as though longing to ask a deeply personal question.

Laura was in a pale apricot silk suit. Some of her friends thought she seemed tense as she greeted them briefly, introducing older relations to her new husband and accepting congratulations with a sweet, faintly blank smile. Robert stood beside her, an ordinary-looking man apart from his strikingly green eyes. He was every inch the city lawyer, his suit from one of the best London tailors, his shoes hand-made and gleaming like patent leather. Six foot four, he was in good physical condition although his waistcoat contained the first hint of a paunch. He laughed and talked without restraint, but although he barely exchanged a word with his wife, his hand was more often than not at her elbow, and his eyes returned constantly to her face. Some of the older guests noticed this and smiled sentimentally; his own friends joked coarsely at his being trapped, hooked. Laura's friends watched him closely, speculatively. And then turned back to the champagne and jokes.

Laura shook the sixtieth hand as firmly as she had shaken the first and smiled as warmly at the face above it. A powdery cheek pressed against her. "Muriel Lampett. I'm Robert's aunt, my dear. I do hope you'll be very happy."

Looking around the room, Laura was touched by how happy everyone was – for her. Her mother, talking eagerly to Charlotte (she must go and rescue her friend soon) was frankly relieved at Laura being taken off the shelf. Particularly by so personable and successful a man as Robert, although it was a pity there could be no church wedding. Her father, who so loved a party and was really happy because his wife told him the marriage was a Good Thing. Her aunts and Uncle John, even her Grandmother Sawyer who had decided she approved of Marriage more than she disapproved of Second Marriages – they were all happy. I've given them a chance to join in. Perhaps weddings just shouldn't be private. You have to show everyone how happy you are for one day before you can really be happy together in earnest.

So I must have done the right thing, Laura thought. Then she saw Melanie making an entrance.

Melanie Freeway was Laura's oldest friend. They had been at school together – a middle-range boarding school in Dorset – and had fallen in with each other from the beginning. No one ever understood why, least of all the two girls themselves. Teachers, applauding Laura's hard work, her neat stitches, the way her pies came out of the oven as perfectly golden as Mr Kipling's, worried as they saw her walking round and round the cherry blossom trees deep in conversation with Melanie.

Melanie's mother was dead, her father worked for an oil company abroad and her older brother was not encouraged to spend time with her. Melanie's thick black curls were the envy of the girls and the despair of the teachers. Her lashes needed no mascara, but school rules forbade using it so she spent ten minutes every morning thickening them into black spikes. She was clever – much cleverer than industrious Laura – but lazy. She worked for two weeks before school exams and was among the top five in the class. Laura worked all year round and was always somewhere in the middle.

In their fourth year, Melanie came back from Abu Dhabi with a bicycle and a bottle of Valium she had stolen from her stepmother. "Mad as a snake, poor thing. Can't stand the sun," she said airily. "She says it's these or drink. I reckon she'll be more fun with gin inside her, so I'm doing Dad a favour really." She used the bicycle to visit the captain of rugby at the boys' school on the other side of the town. Before very many weeks she had discarded both the Valium and the rugby supremo in favour of grass and a "musician". "He's getting a band together," she told Laura in an awed whisper after lights out. "After his A levels we're going on tour." They did not, of course. By the summer she had moved on to a boy who was going to make a lot of money out of cars, and her father had roused himself enough to frighten her into staying on at school until after her O levels at least.

Melanie was never caught. The teachers watched her, and congratulated themselves on their vigilance. When her clothes were heavy with the smell of marijuana they reminded her that scent was forbidden. Laura lectured her, but protected her fiercely. Melanie tried to persuade Laura to come out with her, but Laura shirked the Saturday afternoon excursions to meet the boys at the town shopping centre as much as she did the Tuesday night ones to meet them at their school gates. She would not touch the Valium, although Melanie promised her it would be good for her pre-exam nerves (Laura genuinely did not know what her friend meant by that) and even Melanie knew better than to offer her friend a joint.

Their friendship survived all this. Perhaps Melanie somehow admired Laura's straightness, her moral sureness, her ability to be right without being priggish. And at the same time she loved having a foil, someone who she knew was having less fun, someone who could not even be taught how to have a good time. Someone who did not compete.

Laura's friendship with Melanie established a pattern that was to repeat time and again through her life. She was constantly drawn to more glamorous, slightly wild girls while her men friends were always wholly conventional, occasionally prudish. When she grew up, her dinner parties were more often than not total failures.

Laura often felt that boarding school had been the making of her. Much as she loved her mother, she needed to be away from her. There was something about Rosalind – pretty, garrulous, overtly affectionate as she was – that made Laura clam up. For years she could never be with a boy or man without carrying a subconscious picture of how her mother would have been at her age. She would have been able to make men laugh, to flirt innocently, be at the centre of any gathering. The trouble, Laura would think sadly, is that I don't know how to flirt. If I try I only feel stupid. Although she had a brother, Laura was not used to being with men as an equal. Nor was she with women. So she did not mind that her girlfriends were usually racier than she, better at expressing themselves, more willing to take risks. Laura was not competitive, and she had a sense of humour. And so although many of her friendships began on an unequal basis, they did not remain so for long. Laura did not know it, but she was deeply appreciated by those who had penetrated her quiet outside. Laura was something many pretty women do not have – a true friend. Even Melanie knew that, and loved her for it.

Melanie passed her O levels with nine As and two Bs. Laura passed hers with one A, six Bs and a C. Melanie, with minimal talent, no application but occasional flair, left school and went to art college because it sounded fun. Laura stayed at school and took two A levels, then went to London where she shared a flat with two girls, learned to drink gin and found a job as an editorial assistant in a publishing company. Melanie had meanwhile learned to use a needle ("but I've got it under control") and left art school.

Laura's chief quality was loyalty. With no understanding of "the habit", she finally bullied and cajoled Melanie into Broadway Lodge. It did not work the first time, nor the second. Melanie's father kept sending cheques for her treatment which she diverted into pushers' bank accounts. It was not until her boyfriend's brother died in his own vomit that she went to Broadway and came out clean. "He was so talented, he was just about to make it," she wept. "This tour would have done it . . ." After her failure at art college, her boyfriends were once again musicians or "something in films".

And so it had gone on. Laura, hardworking, moderately happy and Melanie living off cheques from her father and the odd job with a film studio or photographer. Laura had barely noticed that she was young in the late seventies, Melanie threw herself into the decade with zest, great joy and occasional great unhappiness. Laura saved Melanie from her two biggest mistakes – a near-marriage to a man needing a passport, and heroin. Melanie stopped Laura from becoming a chalet girl and wearing suits to work. Melanie never took drugs again, but did go back to drink. She took Laura to parties which were more joyous than publishers' launches, and Laura introduced her to young men she thought were on the arty side. Melanie flirted, seduced, shocked and mocked them.

They now only saw each other about once every six weeks, but Melanie had been one of the first people Laura had told about her engagement. She had been hurt and surprised at Melanie's reaction.

"Oh, well, congratulations, I suppose," Melanie had said, pushing her unfinished mozzarella salad away from her. "But

I hope you know what you're doing. I mean he's such a – well, does he make jokes?"

"Yes, of course."

"What was the last joke he made? I mean when did he last make you laugh?"

Laura looked at her avocado and prawn unhappily, her mind a total blank.

"Well, what was the last joke *you* made?" she countered feebly.

"Oh, it doesn't matter. Here, I'm sorry." Melanie leaned across the table and kissed Laura, her green beads dragging in the olive oil on her plate. "I hope you'll be very happy. A big house and a big dog and lots of children. Although you'll have some of those anyway."

Laura watched as the oily beads left a smear on Melanie's cashmere jersey. She couldn't help feeling pleased that the jersey would be stained. Why was Melanie sometimes so foul?

Melanie tried hard to be more enthusiastic through the rest of lunch, but the damage had been done and Laura could only pick moodily at the overcooked spaghetti bolognese as she answered Melanie's questions and tried to remember Robert's last joke. She did not really count the one about the hedgehog and the Porsche. Too many other people had told it to her and it wasn't all that funny.

Over the five months' engagement Melanie relaxed towards Robert and Laura was touched to see that her friend was really trying. She even invited them to dinner, an evening doomed to failure from its inception. Laura tried to warn him, but there was no hope Robert would like or understand Melanie's odd mixture of friends gathered through the years and thrown together anyhow.

A week before the wedding, Melanie brought Laura her present, an exquisite nineteenth-century oil of a small church with a cow grazing by the gate. Laura loved it the more for knowing how much Melanie disliked that kind of art, and how hard she must have had to swallow before buying it.

And so Melanie had tried to overcome – whatever it was, disapproval? envy? – and was here at the reception.

Making an entrance.

Dressed in black and silver.

Laura laughed at her friend and gave her a quick hug. Melanie was true to form. "Get yourself a drink and I'll introduce you to some people." She wondered if Melanie had not already drunk quite a bit, but decided not to worry, not today.

"Oh, I only really came to see you. You're looking nice," she added off-handedly. Laura revenged herself by introducing Melanie to Simon Eustace whose film-star good looks did not compensate for his humourless stupidity.

Time to "mingle". "Remember, darling, you're the bride and everyone will want to have a word," her mother had told her a hundred times. "I still remember every single person at our wedding. I tried so hard to smile at them individually as I came down the aisle. Although, darling, of course . . ." Had she done it on purpose? Were the constant reminiscences about her own wedding intended to wound? Laura suddenly realised that although her mother had gone on and on about her own flowers, bridesmaids, hymns, kind Reverend Love's lectures, jokes and sermon, she had never once mentioned the party after the wedding. Laura had been brought up on the details of her mother's wedding day, she knew them by heart, but from the day of her engagement her mother had never said a word about what happened after they walked away from the church. The lunch for three hundred, the ball for six hundred, the honeymoon in Capri – not a breath about any of that. Only the service.

Rosalind Sawyer was very pretty, very vain, fairly intelligent and totally uneducated. She had bullied her husband subtly for thirty-six years and her children since they were teenagers. She had discovered Proust, T. S. Eliot and the South of France during her menopause. Before that she had been interested in interior design, an interest that resurfaced whenever one of her three children was decorating. Although supremely selfish, she was not entirely motivated by self-love and her relief that Laura had "found a husband at last" was for her daughter's sake as much as her own. Her face lit up as she saw Laura crossing the room towards her.

"Darling, I was just telling Charlotte about that little restaurant Daddy and I found in Peyrens last year. Do you remember? She says she's going to the Dordogne next month, but I told her that really the *paysage* is so much more *au naturel* further south."

Laura was genuinely impressed at how her mother had picked up French in her middle age, but wished she would not scatter French phrases through her conversation.

Bilingual Charlotte smiled. "I have cousins in the Dordogne," she explained.

"Then *bien sûr*, you want to see them." It looked as though Rosalind were about to transfer the entire conversation to French, but Laura stepped in.

"Mummy, I've promised to introduce Charlotte to Richard Tolley. Do you mind? She's thinking of changing jobs and . . ." she led a relieved Charlotte away.

Oriana came and kissed her sister. "Laura, I'm sending Poppy home with Nanny now and she wanted to kiss her Auntie Lala goodbye." Poppy, a pretty two-year-old, pushed her fists into her eyes and showed no sign of wanting to kiss her aunt, but Laura took her into her arms and kissed the sticky cheek. The child whined for Françoise, the au pair girl who Oriana and James insisted on calling Nanny. "I'm afraid someone thought it funny to feed her champagne," Oriana said brightly. "So she really must get her afternoon nap."

That meant James had reverted to the rugby-club sense of humour which was the only one with which he ever felt at ease, and there would be a "marital ding-dong", as he uneasily put it, on the way home in the car. Oh, well.

Laura had not wanted the children at the reception and had flatly refused them permission to come to the wedding. Really she could not have borne Robert's children to be there. She did not want them to witness their father's second marriage, she just could not feel it was right.

Ferdy and Aimée, Laura's brother and sister-in-law, had understood completely and had arrived with no children but a collection of splotchy "artwork" from them as presents. Alexandra, aged six, had painted an elaborate wedding scene. A yellow-haired bride in white, bells and butterflies. Laura shuffled it to the bottom of the pile and sent the children her love.

Oriana on the other hand had insisted that Poppy should not be left out of "Aunt Lala's big day" and had made Françoise bring

Poppy to the party. As though Poppy knew the difference, Laura thought, giving the child a last hug and kiss before handing her to Françoise. She only hoped she would not be as silly with her own children when the time came.

"Good husband material maybe but not my type I'm afraid," Charlotte appeared at her shoulder. "I know it's bad form but I've left your present in the hall. There's Tim – you didn't tell me you'd asked him," and she disappeared again.

Laura always felt comfortable with Charlotte, who she had met through work. She was more her type than Melanie; they had been brought up in the same cheerfully conventional way. But it had to be admitted that she was not as funny or exciting as the wilder girl. Until a week ago they had shared a house. "So now I must find another house or a husband," Charlotte had said on being told of Laura's engagement. "Oh, well, I'm getting on, I suppose. Time I started hunting. You are lucky having a dish like Robert fall into your lap. 'Specially after that brute Frankie."

Frankie was not at the party. Neither was Christopher. Nor were any of the few other boyfriends she had had in between. That was another rule she had insisted on. No children, to keep out Richard and Helen. No ex-lovers, to rule out Camilla. If Robert had a fault it was that he verged on insensitivity about his ex-wife and Laura. He had even thought they might be friends at one stage. The innocent.

"Where are Richard and Helen?" asked Robert's Aunt Muriel.

"With Camilla," Laura answered.

"Oh? Well, give them my love."

"I haven't seen the children," said Simon Eustace.

"They're with their mother," Laura answered shortly.

"You were quite right not to bring the children," Robert's father assured her as he passed in search of a drink.

"What a pity the children aren't here. They could have got to know their new cousin Poppy," Oriana gushed as she put a bottle of champagne out of James's sight.

"They've met," Laura snapped.

"All we need is the children and we'd have the whole family," Rosalind sighed.

"Nonsense, Aimée's left hers at home," said Laura.

She went to the bathroom and locked herself in.

Laura combed her hair, looking at herself seriously in the mirror. She was sure she was right to have insisted they stay away. *Sure.* They seemed to like her, and there was nothing wrong with them, but it was just not right that they should be here. Richard, at three, was at the question-asking stage. Helen, six, was at the put-you-to-rights and knowing-best stage. She could not have borne the questions and answers.

Laura wiped her lipstick off and put more on. Melanie always added layer onto layer. Funny, that. The children were coming to stay when they returned from the honeymoon. She would work at it, they were young enough to learn to accept her. She hoped she would love them. She would try.

There came a rattle at the door, then a giggle. "If there's a coke party going on in there let me in." It was Melanie, the worse for drink.

Laura opened the door. "Sorry, I'm just taking a break from the crowd."

Melanie came in, lifted her skirt and flopped onto the lavatory. Laura always found this embarrassing, but Melanie said she was hung up, so she leaned against the door and looked up vaguely at the ceiling lamp.

"Shit, I've drunk too much," said Melanie. "Who's going to look after me now you'll be keeping an eye on Robert?" She flushed the lavatory and smeared lipstick onto her caked lips. "God, I look a mess," she said truthfully and swung round, narrowing her eyes to focus. "Laura, you are going to be all right, aren't you?"

Laura paused, looked at her friend thoughtfully. "Of course," she said. "And so are you."

Laura had succeeded in keeping the children away, had succeeded in not wearing white or having bridesmaids, but she had not succeeded in stopping the cake and speeches. The "friend of the bride" speech was made by Colonel Johnson, her father's best man and her godfather.

". . . when, as a little girl in a Heidi dress, Laura sat on my knee, and said, 'Godfather Christopher, I'm going to have ten children,' I explained to her that as the chap in charge of her moral welfare I would see to it that she was married first. I'm pleased to tell you all that there was no need for a shotgun, which is just as well for young Robert as they do say I'm something of a crack shot." There were a few sniggers and James inexplicably wolf-whistled. "Well I've seen that little gel grow into a fine, moral young lady, although more's the pity I haven't seen her in a Heidi dress for years . . ." more sniggers and Laura remembered her mother's Austro-Swiss phase when even poor Ferdy, aged eight, had been forced into lëderhosen and Rosalind had made them sing "Edelweiss" to her dinner-party guests.

"Well, ladies and gentlemen, I'm sure you've heard enough from me." "Hear, hear," shouted James and Laura saw Oriana edging her way through the crowds towards him, "but I'd just like to add that in all the time I've known little Laura I've never known her say an untrue, unkind or unfair word. There are not many people one can say that about. Added to that, she's a beautiful woman, a successful publisher . . ." Why didn't he shut up? After over ten years in the business she was only a junior editor, for God's sake. Her boss would think she'd been lying to them all – "and a warm, caring person. Robert is a very lucky man. And if I may say so, Richard and Helen are very lucky children."

Laura clenched her fists in embarrassment and willed him to stop. "Ladies and gentlemen, I propose a toast to the bride – and to all her future little Heidis."

"The bride. Laura." Glasses were raised and lowered to slack mouths. A brief silence was followed by half-hearted applause and a jerk of conversation. A minute later the level of noise was back to normal. Laura's father led the Colonel to where she was standing, watching her friends and relations drink her father's champagne in her honour.

"A lovely day, Laura. Here's a little something to help you on your way. Not very imaginative but . . ." he passed her an envelope.

"Thank you, Christopher," she said, not opening it. "And thank you for the speech." The poor old duffer had not meant to be tactless. "It was lovely."

She turned to Robert. "I think I'm going upstairs to change."

*   *   *

Laura folded the wedding suit neatly in polythene and put it into her suitcase. She checked her room and the bathroom one last time and closed the lid of the case. The sight of her left hand lying on the dark canvas surprised her. She had never worn rings until she was engaged, and the solitaire emerald and fine gold band beneath it made her hand look like a stranger's. She liked the sight, and smiled, wondering when she would be used to it.

There was a knock at the door. "It's all right – come in."

The door opened to Julia Sinclair who looked in with a worried face. "I'm so sorry. But I missed you in the line 'cause I got here late, and didn't see you downstairs and just wanted to tell you I love you."

Julia was truly her closest friend. Less gamesy and horsy than Charlotte, less complicated and dangerous than Melanie, Julia was funny, wise, mad, bad, but at bottom completely good. She would try anything "to see" but was hooked by nothing. After a long career of not quite promiscuity, she had settled down to live with a man she mothered and tormented. Laura could not understand their love but respected its truth. She knew that though Julia had chosen domesticity of a sort, she had to have an element of doubt even in her security.

"I love you too and I missed you downstairs. I thought you hadn't made it."

"Laura! This is not a dinner party. I do have some sense of occasion." Julia laughed and crumpled on to the bed with a fine disregard for her six-hundred-pound suit. "Well that's the last time you'll be sleeping in your virgin bed. How do you feel?" She looked at Laura curiously. She was never at all sure how she felt about weddings, was incapable of arriving at them on time, wanted almost to pretend that no such thing existed.

Laura sat down at the dressing table. "Nothing really – although do look at my hand," she waved it about with a laugh. "You should be telling me, you're more married than I am in a way."

"Almost married and young married are two very different things. We could leave each other at any moment." Julia said this all the time, ignoring the fact that Viv's and her lives were as tied up together emotionally and financially as if they had been married for years.

"Less of the young, please. Robert's done that bit already and I'm far too old to play the blushing bride."

"You did pretty well during the speech."

"Oh, the *speech*, my God!"

"Pretty good hell. I did feel sorry for you. Tell me more about the Heidi dress."

Laura explained the edelweiss phase and they giggled.

"Ferdy in lëderhosen – you've got to find a picture. Will he blush if I sing to him? I've always wanted to make Ferdy blush."

"Laura, darling." Mrs Sawyer appeared at the door and gave Julia, of whom she disapproved, her "charming" smile. "Oh, Julia, hello. Laura, I think you ought to think about going soon, darling. Today you're like the queen. Nobody can leave before you."

Julia remembered her manners and unfolded herself from the bed. "Hello, Mrs Sawyer. It's been a wonderful party, thank you. I'll leave you to it. Good luck, Laura. Give me a ring when you get home." She left the room singing "Small and white, clean and bright," ignored by Mrs Sawyer.

"Are you ready then? Ferdy said he'd bring your luggage down." She walked round Laura, tugging at her collar and brushing the hair from her face. "Congratulations, my love. We've done it. Now, have you got your money, your traveller's cheques, your ticket, your passport . . ."

Listening to her mother running through the familiar list, Laura felt wildly happy for the first time that day. "Robert's got them. He's got everything," she said calmly, although inside she was singing "Robert's got everything. Always will have. Everything." She hugged her mother warmly, surprising them both. "Robert's got everything," she repeated, embarrassed.

"Good. Well, see you downstairs."

Once again, for the very last time, Laura looked round the room. She sentimentally touched her teddy bear, her glass swan from Venice, the dried seahorse she had found on the beach with her grandfather the week before he died. It was years since this room had been her refuge, her one place of privacy in the noisy family home. But still it represented her past. Her childhood was here, but also her youth. This was where she came when her affairs ended, when she felt ill, when she needed to escape from London life. This was her place of security – her own room in her father's house. It was a long time since she had left home for the first time, a naive virgin, but Laura realised with a shock that it was not until now that she was truly relinquishing her place under the paternal roof. She would no longer sleep here on visits. Now she would be upgraded to the sprigged green guest room at the end of the passage. This room would be gradually cleaned out until it became just another spare room, one with a cot for the grandchildren, perhaps. Oriana was always complaining about how ill-equipped their mother was for the next generation.

Laura did not dare go downstairs in case the laughing, semidrunk crowd of her nearest and dearest broke her mood. She looked out of the window at the view of the Devon hills she knew so well and with a sigh picked up the hat her mother insisted she wore. The cotton dress and matching jacket were simple in an expensive way. "Not too *jeune fille*," her mother had said, "but very becoming." She knew she looked her best – prettier than in the silk suit she had worn to the registry office. She had been so frightened of trying to look like a bride that she had gone too far in the other direction and looked almost severe.

Hat in hand, she checked everything was in her bag – passport, ticket – all with Robert – and, knowing she could not put the moment off any longer, left her room. She stood at the top of the stairs looking down for a moment before anyone saw her.

"There she is," shouted Oriana, and all the faces swung up towards her.

Robert was waiting at the bottom of the stairs and she met his eyes and smiled as she began to walk down. Someone began to clap and others joined in. She heard James cheer and Melanie's enviable wolf whistle. She saw Julia's eyes fill with happy tears and her father reach out and hug his wife. But mostly she saw Robert as, with one hand on the banister, she walked on down to him.

It was as though she were walking down the aisle.

They sat in the back of the car, silent at first, embarrassed to talk in front of the driver and embarrassed to say nothing. Neither of them realised he was listening to Belinda Carlisle through tiny headphones. Then Robert reached for her hand.

"Thank you, darling."

"Thank *you*. And I'm sorry about Poppy." Poppy, instructed to kiss "Uncle Robert" goodbye had been violently sick onto his shoes. "Or, I should say, sorry for James. He's such a fool sometimes – he should know not to give children champagne by now."

"Don't worry. You forget I've been through all that." Laura smiled. Well at least her new stepchildren had got past the being-sick-on-people stage.

"Do you want to sleep? We won't be at Heathrow until seven." They talked for a while about the party, who had been there, who had failed to turn up, who had behaved badly, who had looked pretty, until Laura, exhausted, fell asleep in her lawful husband's arms.

At Heathrow, they checked in and stood at the bar waiting for a drink. "A large gin and tonic and a large whisky and soda please. Sandwiches?"

Laura nodded. She had eaten none of the lunch Oriana and her mother had spent weeks preparing and was ravenous.

"And two rounds of smoked salmon sandwiches, please." He paid, and turned to Laura hesitantly. "Darling, do you mind if . . . ?"

She did, intensely, but shook her head. "Of course not. And say hello to them from me." As he turned away she added hastily, "Give them my love," and Robert came back, his face alight, and kissed her.

2

Robert put the key in the lock and turned it twice. The door clicked and he pushed it open, flicking a switch inside the hall. The passage filled with a harsh light and Laura, standing a little behind, blinked. Robert turned to put an arm round her shoulders and lead her in, but the corridor was too narrow for them to stand comfortably side by side and Robert hung back, feeling faintly foolish. Laura kissed his cheek, and he said, "Welcome home, darling. Here we are."

She nodded and laughed. "Shall we go in?"

Laura knew the house of old, but it felt strange to be coming "home" to Robert's. It was a Fulham house like many others, with double rooms made into one on the ground floor and a kitchen partly reclaimed from the garden built on to the back. It was furnished well but unimaginatively, and Laura could imagine how Robert had just walked into Peter Jones and ordered what was necessary without really thinking too hard or wasting too much time. The result was more masculine than most of the house's counterparts in the area, and the more pleasant for it. The colours were plain and simple, the rooms uncluttered. Laura had always supposed that Robert's wife had kept nearly everything from their shared house, but had never liked to ask too closely. The sitting room could perhaps do with a few more pictures, a few more cushions, a rich-coloured rug over the neutral-coloured carpet, but it was certainly not stark. There were well-read books on the shelves and an air of masculine self-sufficiency which she supposed she would inevitably change.

Laura walked uneasily around the sitting room, touching a

chair, fiddling with a pen lying in the middle of the small reproduction desk. Robert watched her from the doorway. At last he said, "Have a drink?" and, relieved, she nodded. He disappeared and came back a moment later with a bottle of champagne and a grin. "She remembered," he said, taking two glasses from the drinks tray and putting them on the coffee table. Laura felt a sick lurch in her stomach until, unscrewing the wire round the cork, he added, "Molly, the cleaner. You'll meet her tomorrow – pity I won't be here. I asked her to be sure and remember to put a bottle in the fridge when she came in this morning. She can't always be relied on."

He popped the cork and filled the two glasses. "Here you are. Welcome and God bless." He raised his glass in a toast and Laura copied him.

Their honeymoon had been a minor success: bad weather had at first depressed them, but they had enjoyed their shared interest in good food and Robert was a better sightseer than Laura had expected. They had stayed in a small hotel on Lake Garda, and had taken day trips around the shoreline, or into Verona. By the end of the week the sun was beginning to shine and Laura felt relaxed and content. Occasionally, she thought ahead to the first weekend at home, but on the whole she put it out of her mind and enjoyed a more carefree Robert than she had yet seen. He made many jokes, and some of them were very funny. He was also very sexy in holiday mood.

Now they were back, though, Laura knew she was going to have to face up to the realities of her new life. She had no illusions: at her age she knew it would be hard to adapt to someone else's routine. She had never lived with a man before – of course, she had stayed nights and weekends with her boyfriends, but she had never kept more than could be carried away in a plastic shopping bag in any man's house, nor had she allowed them to clutter her drawers with their socks or her bathroom shelves with their shaving tackle. Living with Charlotte, or any of the girls who had preceded her, was one thing – they had been tenants in her house and had always kept almost totally separate existences. But she realised that she barely knew what time Robert left for the City, whether he had cooked breakfast, whether he'd want to use the bathroom first or second. It was ridiculous. A girl of her age marrying in the 1990s with almost as little idea of what to expect as a nineteenth-century virgin.

They sat at opposite sides of the room, sipping the champagne, Laura avoiding Robert's eye and wishing it were the morning.

"Laura."

She looked up.

"You know, I don't mind about this house, I really don't. If there's anything you want to do to it – you know, curtains or whatever ..." She smiled at him and crossed the room to sit close to him on the sofa.

"Thank you. I don't know now – but maybe." She was truly grateful to him for his awareness of her feelings, and tucked herself into the crook of his arm. "It would be nice to make it a bit more my own, and we will need more shelves when I move my books in."

"Oh, I know how women love changing things. Camilla was never happy with a room for more than a year." Once again Laura told herself that she must learn not to mind how often he mentioned his ex-wife. After all, they had years spent together in common, and the children ... Thank God this house had never been theirs, only his, bought after the separation when Robert realised divorce was inevitable and he must have a base for the children's second home.

Laura felt Robert shift as he squinted over her head at his watch. "Seven o'clock. I might have a shower, if you don't mind, and then where shall we go to dinner?"

Laura thought a moment. "Why don't I cook here?"

"Absolutely not, my darling. Until tomorrow we're still on honeymoon and you shan't lift a finger."

"I'd rather."

Robert started to protest until he saw her face. "All right, if you really mean it. I'll run you down to the supermarket."

"No, you have your shower. I'll take myself. Can I have your keys?" Laura had no keys yet to the house she must call home. She took the Banham from him with a quick kiss and left the room. Closing the front door behind her, she paused for a moment, breathing in the sweet smell of jasmine from a neighbour's garden. She loved Robert, she really did, but she wished he would realise her position. Her new stepchildren were coming for the weekend in two days' time and she desperately wanted to know her way around the kitchen by then. To have to ask a six-year-old where the wooden spoon was kept would mark her for ever as an interloper.

She unlocked her Fiat Uno and drove off to the late-night supermarket. She would cook Robert something spectacular, and the rhythm of cooking would lead her into the rhythm of her new life.

Robert was back at work the next day, but Laura had decided to stay away from her office until the following Monday. She wanted to play at being a married woman, go to the butcher during the day, pick up her two cats from Oriana and settle them into her new home. She wanted to be there when Robert came home in the evening and have a house full of flowers and smelling of good cooking. She supposed she wanted to consolidate her position.

Oriana was as friendly and irritating as ever. She wanted to hear about the honeymoon, but did not listen to the answers. She told Laura about how the wedding party had finished, about James's disgraceful behaviour but how good he had been since, about the photographs that were waiting at their mother's. Laura drank the cup of weak percolated coffee and wished she were not returning to work on Monday. They took Poppy for a walk in the park and Oriana told Laura that they were buying a puppy, a black pug, "so good with children", Oriana said, although Laura was not so sure about that.

Then with Whiskas and Choosy in their baskets, she drove back to Fulham and introduced them to the house, to the tiny garden, and realised that she must have a cat-flap put into the back door. She hoped Robert would not mind.

By four o'clock she was longing for Robert to come home and resisting the temptation to ring her office. So she shut the cats in the kitchen and drove to Sainsbury's.

Walking around the supermarket, looking at the smart women with wedding rings and headscarves and trolleys piled high with fruit juice and baked beans and Shreddies and minced meat, Laura almost laughed aloud. She had rarely been food-shopping during the day, and this was a bit of middle-class London life that was new to her. Who were all these women and was she really one of them? No, she would be back at Howard and Neville on Monday soothing authors and turning down manuscripts. She would be shopping with hoi polloi on Thursday evenings when these women were safely in their cosy middle-class houses, headscarves folded away and children put to bed. Although when she had children . . .

What did children eat? Richard and Helen were too old for nothing but fish fingers, too young for the chicken and apricot fricassee she had planned to cook on Friday. God in Heaven, did they all eat together? She should have asked Robert, but was glad she had not. What would they talk about? Perhaps she should buy them a present, but she dismissed that idea immediately. *Don't suck up, Laura,* she told herself.

So she bought fruit juice and Shreddies and minced meat. Lasagne must be all right, and roast chicken for Sunday lunch. And cottage pie? Or stew? She could not face the idea of stew in June and stood at a loss.

"Macaroni cheese." Laura jumped. A kind-faced man in tortoiseshell spectacles and a polo neck was looking at her. "They love macaroni cheese. Children," he explained.

Laura blushed. "How . . . ?"

"I remember feeling just the same when my wife left me," he said. "Stepchildren?" Laura nodded. "She used to cook them fish fingers and I couldn't bear the smell," he went on. "But when it came to it I couldn't think of a single other thing they liked. I saw you looking at the frozen hamburgers and thought I'd bet you'd never thought of buying them before. Don't worry. It only took me two meals to realise they'd eat anything."

"Well – thank you."

"Don't mention it." And, throwing some tomato ketchup into his trolley he moved away. "Good luck."

He had cheered Laura up immeasurably and she whisked around the store in ten minutes. He was right. She was the grown-up and the children could eat what she cooked. And why should she be so nervous? She was used to children, and had often entertained her nephews and nieces.

When Robert came home, the shopping was unpacked, the

table laid and the chicken and apricot in the oven. His wife was cheerful, warm and at home. Their marriage had begun.

Robert went to pick up the children on his own. Laura said she wanted to have their supper ready for them, and she did not want to confuse them by appearing at their mother's house. Robert had come home early from work and changed out of his suit. Until his marriage to Laura, the children had always come on Saturday morning as his office hours were too irregular for him ever to know until the last minute at what time he would be home on Friday. Things could change now, and after this first week Laura could pick them up, or Camilla drop them, at six thirty in the evening. Laura would want to know the children properly, he said, and she knew he desperately wanted them to think of his house as their home.

It had been decided that they should eat together this evening, although normally they would feed the children earlier.

Laura waited for them to arrive, fidgeting unnecessarily in the kitchen. The lasagne was baking, the salad-dressing mixed, the Mars bars melted for the ice cream. She felt sick at the thought of eating (normally she was just back from work at this time, not even ready for her first gin and tonic), but at least it meant she would not have to sit staring at the children with nothing to do.

At last she heard Robert's key, and went to the front passage.

"We're back, darling." He was smiling broadly, Richard in his arms and Helen standing in front of him holding a large rag doll.

He loves his children so much more than he does me, Laura thought. *So I must love them too.*

"Hello, children," she said, kissing them both quickly on the cheek. "What a lovely doll, Helen. Shall we take your things upstairs?"

Helen stared for a moment. "No."

Laura looked desperately at Robert, who put Richard down on the floor. "We'll do it after supper, shall we? Come on."

They trooped into the kitchen and stood looking at each other. This was silly. Laura decided to take the brisk approach.

"Let's sit down then. Helen, let Richard sit next to your

father and you sit next to me. Robert, would you turn the salad?"

She took the lasagne from the oven and served it out, cutting up Richard's helping. Helen announced she did not like it but ate it quite happily when nothing else was offered.

By the end of the meal Richard had lost any shyness that might have temporarily overcome him and was banging his spoon on the table and talking about pigs. Helen chattered away about her school, addressing all her remarks to her father but thawing slightly towards Laura when she was given the ice cream with melted Mars bar sauce.

Laura took Helen upstairs and put her things away, but it was Robert who put the two children to bed. It was better that way.

They spent a long, long evening watching television and not talking very much. When they finally went to bed, Laura's head was slightly fuddled with wine and the effort of living through the day. It was the first night since their wedding that they did not make love.

Laura insisted that they take the children on an outing the next afternoon. Robert did not want to leave the house, saying that he had traipsed around the zoo quite often enough in the past and they should spend time together at home. In the end they compromised with a walk in Regent's Park which no one enjoyed. They arrived home cross and damp, but at least the ice had been broken. Helen even helped Laura lay the table for tea, making Laura glad she had done the groundwork and learned where everything was kept.

Helen was a pretty child, with eyes almost as green as her father's and shoulder-length dark hair. She obviously loved her school, talking about it and her best friend, Sarah, almost non-stop.

"Why don't you ask Sarah to come for the day next weekend?" Laura suggested. "I'll write to her mother if you like."

"No. She comes to Mummy's, thank you," Helen said, and did not mention her friend again that day.

Laura found Helen easy to talk to, which was a relief, but she remained on guard with the child. There was something very adult, almost knowing, about the way she watched Laura. It was as though she were summing her up, or learning her by heart.

After their high tea the children were put in front of the television for half-an-hour to watch a cartoon Helen had chosen from the video shop that morning. Laura sat in an armchair with a cat on her knee and read *The Mayor of Casterbridge*. She looked up once to find Helen staring at her. Laura smiled, but with no change of expression Helen just turned her gaze back to the screen.

Richard was, on the other hand, a pure delight. He was easy, affectionate and rumbustious. His hair was dark like his sister's, but curly, and his eyes were blue. He shouted very loudly, banging things together and roaring with laughter. His legs were chubby and he stomped. He wanted to be a farmer with ten thousand pigs and one chicken, but Robert hoped that his endless questions meant he had a lawyer's mind. Helen wanted to be the woman on the television who advertised Fairy Liquid. Laura knew that meant Helen saw herself as the little girl in the advertisement, but was not prepared to worry about that. Laura knew that little girls simpered, and knew that one day they grew out of coyness.

After the cartoon was over, Robert gave the children their baths and put them to bed. Laura did not offer to read Helen her story, but when Robert called down the stairs saying Richard wanted her to come and kiss him good night, she felt a leap of joy.

He was lying under the duvet, warm and sweet from his bath. The ends of his hair were damp and sticking to his face. Laura sat on the bed beside him, thinking that she must give the hideous Superman duvet cover to Oxfam and buy something nicer. Richard was already sleepy, but he took his thumb out of his mouth and smiled. He put up his arms and Laura leant down into his bear hug. "I like you," he said when he let her go. "I'm going to tell Mummy you're nice," and he put his thumb back into his mouth, his eyelids drooping.

Laura looked at him for a moment and then bent again to kiss him. It was not going to be hard to love this little boy.

Laura went to church the next morning without the children. Robert said they had never been before and it would confuse them. Laura was not really sure why she still went herself. She did not know if she was a Christian, but she liked being near people who were. She had gone through a religious phase in her early teens, and had somehow never lost the habit of churchgoing. It was something she kept quiet about, more because she thought people would think she was showing off than because she was ashamed. Although she was not sure she believed in God or His Son, she believed in the moral values taught and thought the Christian story was as pretty a way of dressing them up as any other. Sometimes she went to the Oratory with Aimée and the children but she secretly thought the Catholic Church a little vulgar.

She went back to the church near her old house in Battersea. It was not that far from Fulham and she knew what to expect. As usual the congregation was tiny – fifteen or so – and dominated by elderly women whose wedding rings were loose on their fingers and whose high, quavering voices were loose in their throats. They sang "He Who Would Valiant Be", one of the hymns which made Laura wish she were a more committed Christian. She had read John Bunyan at school and, in spite of Melanie's jeers, thought him a Good Thing.

As she left, she slid the copy of *Hymns Ancient and Modern* on to the pile beside the door and tried to avoid Mrs Ince who was lying in wait for her.

"Hello, dear. How nice to see you back. And how was the wedding?"

"Lovely, thank you." Laura nodded and tried to step by the stout figure in the powder-blue coat. "No children with you?" Mrs Ince asked, skilfully blocking the doorway. How *did* the woman know?

"No, they're with their father."

"Oh, he prefers the local church, does he?" Mrs Ince was understanding. "Well, it's very nice for us that you're loyal to St Peter's, isn't it, Reverend?"

"Indeed so." Reverend Fraser had broken veins on his fleshy nose and the faintly musty smell of the old. If he had not stuck to the King James Version Laura would not have stuck to him. His housekeepers never did. "I hear we're to congratulate you." Laura was embarrassed. He should not be praising her for a marriage that, according to his beliefs, was no marriage.

"Thank you, Reverend. I'll see you soon." She fished the keys out of her bag and nodded to Mrs Ince, but the old lady was eager for more and trotted out beside her, eyes greedy under the shiny straw hat.

"Maybe you'll bring your husband another time. We should so like to meet him. And the children. A lawyer, didn't I hear? How nice. Very secure, lawyers, aren't they? Very comfortable. So you'll be selling your house. House prices these days, I don't know – I suppose you will get . . . ?"

To Laura's relief they reached the Fiat before Mrs Ince had drawn breath.

"Well, very nice to see you, Mrs Ince. Yes, it's on the market. Goodbye." She put the car in gear and drove off chuckling at her escape.

"That was Camilla. She said she'd be here at five." Robert put the telephone down with a clunk and reached into his pocket for a cigarette. Laura met his eyes, but could not say anything as Helen was sitting beside her with wide-open ears.

"Lovely," she said after a moment. "I'll get the children's things together after lunch. More pudding, Helen?"

Robert looked at her gratefully and passed his plate. "Yes, for me. Delicious."

"Thanks."

"I don't like it," Helen pushed the food around her plate.

"Oh dear. Well, finish it up and I'll try and remember next time."

Helen stuck out her lip. "Mummy doesn't make me finish things."

"Yes, she does, Helen," Robert said mildly. "Come on."

"Well, she doesn't make things I don't like."

"Helen." The child looked at her father, then took the wisest course and ate her summer pudding.

The doorbell rang at five to five. Robert opened it and Camilla swept past him. "Hello, darling. Have they been good?"

She strode into the sitting room. The two women had not met

before, and Laura had been dreading this almost since she first knew Robert.

Laura put out her hand. "Hello." There was no need to say who she was.

"Hello." Camilla's handshake was brief but firm. She was undeniably pretty with expensively streaked ash blonde hair swinging in a shiny bob around a small, neat head. Her eyes were big and grey, fringed with naturally dark lashes. Her nose was small and straight and probably not the one she was born with. The only fault in her face lay in her too thin mouth. She smiled, but her expression remained cool. Laura looked her in the eye and smiled back. She was determined to hold her own. She was the wife now, this was her home, Robert loved her.

"Well, it's nice to meet you at last," Camilla said graciously. "I hope the children were good."

"Yes." *And they are beginning to like me, a little*, Laura thought. *You won't be able to stop that happening.*

"Of course, they're used to strangers – since our separation, you know." Laura felt a flicker at the implication, but knew that Robert would not have lied to her. There had been various babysitters, of course, but no stream of women. Only one other girlfriend had ever been introduced to the children.

"Yes."

"And, of course, they know the house. Still, they'll be glad to be home."

Laura would not fight back. Manners, not cattiness, were to be her weapon. "Would you like a cup of tea?"

"Thank you, I must rush. I don't like the children to get back too late." She ran her eye up and down Laura, assessing her. Suddenly she looked genuinely amused. "Well, I must say you're not what I expected." She touched her blonde hair and looked at her long, beautifully painted nails. Laura's nails were trimmed short, her hair an indifferent light brown. Laura knew that she would lose any beauty contest between them, but knew too she had won the man fairly and completely.

"The children are playing upstairs. I'll call them."

"Don't move a finger. I'll get them." Camilla was out of the room before Laura could move, hair and short skirt swinging around her.

Robert came down the stairs with the children who kissed their mother, shrieking about the cats and couldn't they have one at home, Mummy, *please*. Richard ran in and flung his arms round Laura's legs. Helen followed more quietly. Both kissed her goodbye and as Laura straightened from their embrace, she met Camilla's eye and allowed herself a smile. Robert saw them all out.

"Robert, darling, I must congratulate you. Your new wife is really very sweet," Camilla said loudly as the door closed behind her.

3

Laura went back to work the next day. She had almost been looking forward to it, but on Monday felt curiously flat. People asked
how the wedding had gone and were briefly interested. The girls
in her department had a present waiting for her: some tumblers
and a jug from Habitat. She looked at the Children's Biographical
Dictionary she was editing and realised how shoddily the job had
been done: author in a hurry to earn the delivery advance and
get on with his novel, picture department uninspired, margins
narrow and print too small for any child. Neither she nor anyone
else could be proud of the job. For the last few months she had
thought of little else but her wedding and her future and now she
was cross with herself for letting her own concerns come in the
way of her work. Ah, well. She flicked through the camera-ready
copy, not caring if there were mistakes and then pulled herself
together and turned back to the beginning.

She had lunch in the local pizzeria with some of the girls. The
jokes were the same, the gossip the same, the hate figures the
same. Louise in the publicity department was having great fun
touring with a famous tennis player whose autobiography they
had just published, but was frankly ready to shoot a mid-list
novelist who was never off the telephone. "I mean she *really*
honestly thinks it's a work of art. And I have to keep agreeing.
If I get the review space, she complains because everyone's rude.
If I don't, I'm not doing my job properly and she's going to write
to everyone from Rupert down. She wants a party for three
hundred people and I've been told I can have £25 to spend on
taking her out for a drink. What do I do?"

Sarah, the novel's editor, giggled. "Tell her."

"For God's sake, you lot have it easy. You commission the books, put in a couple of commas and leave us with the dirty work."

"Not again, Louise. Go and work in the City if you don't like it."

Laura, bored, spat out an olive stone. They had all had the same conversation so often. They fantasised about leaving publishing, complained about the bad pay and the authors, fell out about proof dates. But no one ever left. The hours were good, the company on the whole convivial and occasionally someone famous came into the office and cheered everyone up.

"What about you, Laura?" Louise passed her glass for a refill. "If I were you I'd be out of here like a shot."

Well, maybe, Laura thought, but said, "I like it well enough. Why leave?" *On the other hand* ... For some time now Laura had felt more than just fed up with her work. But what was the alternative?

"I suppose there's no point until you have children," Sarah agreed. "Any plans?"

"I have stepchildren – and we've only just come back from honeymoon after all." *But it would be nice.*

"I would, straight off. I might anyway. I mean, I'm twenty-nine and Geoff's never going to make a move." Louise was gloomy and the others looked at her sympathetically. They had heard her story often enough, but agreed that after three years Geoff should make up his mind one way or the other. If he was not going to marry her he should stop wasting her time. In their late twenties and early thirties, all the girls were beginning to feel the years rushing by.

"Well, tell me if you do and I'll join in," Laura said lightly, and pushed back her chair. "We'd better get the bill. I'm only on Louis XIV and I've got to check the whole book by tomorrow morning."

Back at her desk, she worked for only half-an-hour before flagging. Louise was twenty-nine and worried: she was thirty-four. Perhaps they were right. She wanted children – maybe she could not afford to wait. Aimée was her age with four children, Oriana two years younger and pregnant with her second child. But then women had children in their late thirties now, and safely. Why rush? She was barely married, they had time.

She looked back at the simplification of Mary Queen of Scots's life and her gaze wandered back to the window. Richard was a darling. Wouldn't it be all the better to have a Richard of her own? One she did not have to share with Camilla. A full cousin for Poppy and the others. Robert was a good father, she had seen that. Most women did not have that assurance when they married. *What shall I cook for dinner?* she wondered. *Maybe some pork chops with prunes? I must talk to Robert – soon. Why shouldn't we have a baby now? Why not?*

"How are you getting on?" Keith from the production department asked, his head poking through the door, and she jumped.

"Halfway. It'll be with you on time." It was this that she resented, the constant questioning and interference. If only she could work alone, she would enjoy it more and be more efficient. Laura sighed and put her mind back to her work.

"So, how's it so far?" Julia poured two glasses of wine and lit a cigarette. "I want all the details."

"Great. The children were fine after the first hour. I met Camilla."

"And?"

"She seemed nice."

"Which means she was poisonous. Come *on*."

Laura told Julia everything: the blonde bob, the amused stare. Richard's goodbye hug. "But the children are the main thing. Robert minds so much."

"Will Camilla start the wicked stepmother bit?"

"I hope not. I'm sure she won't on purpose; it's just that . . ."

Julia nodded and angrily stubbed out her cigarette, reaching for the packet immediately.

"I know. My mother did it for years after Daddy remarried and I'm sure she didn't meant to. Although I don't know – what's the access?"

"Access? Oh, three weekends a month and half of holidays."

"Then you'll be OK. Just don't rush things. Shall we have another bottle?"

Laura was tempted, but wanted to be home before Robert.

• Sophia Watson

"I've got to get supper on the way home. Perhaps another glass."

Julia waved at the waiter who paid no attention, so she went to the bar with a sigh. Laura fiddled with the stem of her wine glass, relieved to have a friend she could really talk to, a friend who could be wise and truthful. *Don't rush*. Well, no one could say she had rushed much in her life so far. A small house, bought at the time when the market was low, so safe and sensible its value seemed barely affected by the recession. A respectable but hardly high-flying profession. A – late – ? marriage to a successful man. And next. Children, of course. Sainsbury's on weekdays and a cottage in the country.

Julia came back to the table, giggling, on the tail end of a flirtation with the barman. *Don't rush*, indeed. Julia had rushed from man to man, with an occassional stop off at the Praed Street clinic for sexually transmitted diseases. Until she had rushed herself into love with Viv and was now rushing round and round the decision to marry.

"Are you and Viv going to have children?" Laura asked.

Julia took off her jacket and crumpled it onto the chair beside her. "I hate this place. They think if it's dark and hot, a place has got *ambience*. Yes I suppose we are. Well, of course, we are."

"Will you get married then?"

"Laura, not that again. I don't know. Viv says we'd have to. He's so old-fashioned sometimes. But then he's a bastard himself so he minds about that kind of thing. And you?"

"I don't think nowadays . . ."

"I meant children."

"Oh, yes. I hope so. Robert loves his children."

"Yours would be his too." Julia's voice was gentle.

"Of course." Laura gulped at the acidic white wine. "You're right. This place is awful. Let's do it together."

"What?"

"Have children. At the same time."

"*Now*?" Julia sounded horrified and Laura laughed, backing down.

"No. One day."

*　　*　　*

• 32

Laura gave her first dinner party as a married woman the next week. Avocado soup, leg of lamb and cheese and grapes. Robert went to Oddbins and came back with some medium-priced Beaujolais. "The man tried to flog me some Australian muck, but as long as I can afford to pay the difference for French, I will. Who knows what the convicts put with the grapes?" he joked as he put the box on the kitchen table and looked around for the corkscrew. "Do you want a glass now?"

Laura asked for a gin and tonic and debated whether to steam or boil the carrots.

The dinner went quite well, but could have been more jokey. Adam Tucker, a colleague of Robert's, and his wife Emma were interested to meet the new Mrs Bedford, but Emma at least seemed too reserved to make much effort. Adam was small and jumpy, with a big nose and a nervous wink. He took a great liking to Aimée, who was recovering from summer flu, and talked earnestly about Europe with Ferdy. Melanie, the wild card, arrived late and antagonised Emma by trying to flirt with Adam who either did not notice or was too frightened to respond.

When Laura stood to clear the plates and make the coffee, she was surprised at Melanie's offer of help, but nodded thanks. Melanie, carrying one dirty knife, followed her into the kitchen.

"Well, you *are* grown up," she said, leaning against the fridge and watching Laura scrape the muck from the plates. "I mean you've always been one for dinner parties but this is different, isn't it?"

Laura paused before agreeing. She was never completely sure how Melanie would use her words.

"Yes, it's different," she said finally. "And better."

"How?"

"Oh, I don't know. I suppose I'm just not . . ."

"Scared?"

Laura looked up, surprised at her friend. Melanie could be untrustworthy, dangerous – but she could be perceptive. She had never followed her thoughts through to their obvious conclusion before, but in one word Melanie had found the answer. She was no longer frightened.

Already she had learned some of the disadvantages of marriage, hers in particular. Camilla would remain an ogre to her, she knew that and could bear it. The children were a mixed blessing – a joy in themselves, but an extra burden in a new marriage. She would not compete for Robert's love, but would have to accept that much of Robert's heart was theirs alone. And there were the petty things – Robert's refusal to let her sleep late at weekends, his occasional insensitivity, the way he kept putting sugar in her tea . . .

But he was there. She loved him and he was there. She had a home now, not just a house, and a husband to sit at the head of her table. She no longer had to go to dreary parties feeling urgent, feeling sick, just in case . . . she no longer had to lie awake at night worrying about a lonely old age, wondering how much of the year Ferdy's and Oriana's children would put up with her. She was safe and she was no longer scared.

"I suppose you're right," she said. "Although I hadn't thought of it. How silly."

"Not at all." Melanie picked up the kettle and filled it, her back to Laura. "We've always been different, I know. But don't imagine we're that different."

"How's the coffee coming along, darling?" Robert appeared in the doorway and they both jumped.

"Not too quickly. Come on, Melanie, we've deserted them for too long." Laura squeezed her friend's hand as she took the kettle from her and motioned her back to the dining room. Well, well.

Adam and Emma were the first to leave – the baby-sitter had to be driven home, they explained, as they thanked Laura. Adam kissed Melanie goodbye, infuriating Emma who felt she had to follow suit. After noisy farewells on the doorstep they left, Emma taking the driver's seat.

Back in the sitting room Laura refused offers of help and they all slumped back and dissected the evening.

"You can't help it, can you?" Laura asked Melanie, who was helping herself to more whisky.

"What?"

"You know as well as I do. Flirting."

"Come on, Laura, you're not to start getting po-faced now you're a matron."

Laura chuckled. "I never came out of the starting gate alongside you, and don't forget it."

"I don't know," Robert said, and Laura blushed.

"Did you flirt with Ferdy like that when you first knew him?" Aimée asked.

"Yes, but he didn't notice. I gave him up as a lost cause years ago." Ferdy was proud, Aimée almost offended until she decided that Melanie was after all almost one of the family by now.

"Do you have the children this weekend?" she asked Robert, who she was finding easy to like but hard to talk to naturally. He was so quintessentially *English*, she reflected. Ferdy, hardly the Italian-waiter type, was a fireball of passion compared to this well-turned-out new brother-in-law.

"Yes, from Friday night," he answered and she saw how his green eyes lightened at the thought.

"Why don't you come over for lunch on Sunday? They've barely met ours so far."

Laura met Robert's eyes and he nodded. "We'd love to. Let's hope they'll be friends."

"Can I ring for a taxi?" Melanie reached for the telephone. "You can't make children like each other just because you want them to . . . yes, I'll hold. When I think of the whining drips that Dad forced on us in the holidays. Mind you, his friends were mostly hell so what can you expect."

"Thank you, Doctor Spock." Laura wondered if Melanie was turning into one of those spinsters who knows best about other people's children, and was immediately horrified at the thought. Heavens, she had been married less than a month and was already behaving like all those women she'd resented and feared at dinner parties through the years.

Melanie slumped in the back of the taxi and considered the evening. She'd had mixed feelings when Laura had told her she was to marry Robert; the most powerful was one of extreme irritation. Irritation with Robert, who she found dull, and with Laura for being taken in by him. Although Laura and she had always had very diverse social lives, she had also felt a tinge of jealousy — would Laura remain her friend once she was happily established in her marriage?

Melanie was honest enough to be sure that Laura would be happy. She knew Laura wanted to Be Married, and knew too that Having Children was an important element in Laura's picture of her future life. And although Melanie found Robert dull, she was sure he and Laura were well suited.

Melanie, when not led astray by the weaker side of her nature, was intrinsically fair-minded. She knew part of the reason she found Robert boring was that she had never really tried to know him. Perhaps she should, she thought idly as she lit another cigarette. He was all the things she instinctively despised: conventional, unspontaneous, ambitious. But she had seen him and Laura together enough to realise the relationship worked. He was always relaxed near Laura, more likely to speak out, to enter an argument for argument's sake. Laura needed a steady man, someone on whom she could rely, and Robert needed someone with whom he was at ease. Melanie wondered what his first wife had been like to him to leave him so permanently challenged by women.

Once Melanie had overheard Robert and Laura when they thought they were alone together. They had been out in the garden on a summer's day not long before their wedding. They were all at a barbecue at someone's house, rock and roll blaring through open drawing-room windows. Melanie suddenly heard them laugh together, a laugh of such intimacy and warmth and genuine enjoyment that she had felt stricken by jealousy. Then, coming out into the garden, she saw them dancing together with a fluid grace not usually seen in the English and wholly unexpected in this couple.

"I didn't know you could rock and roll," she said sourly as she poured herself a Pimms.

And it turned out that neither had known the other could until then, and they laughed again and stopped dancing and looked faintly embarrassed and very *happy*.

Remembering this, Melanie knew that her friend was lucky in her marriage, and thought that if Laura could surprise her oldest friend after so many years, Robert was lucky too.

This dinner party proved that. Laura was obviously in her element. Their conversation in the kitchen had surprised Melanie as much as it had Laura, and she felt angry that she had given herself away. For the thousandth time she wondered what she really wanted of life and for the thousandth time she answered herself. *I don't know, but something different. Not this, not any more.*

"This" was a two-bedroomed Notting Hill flat, it was a succession of short love affairs and a continuing relationship with a married man whom she supposed she loved – if not, why did the other affairs never give her the strength to leave him? If ever she came close to admitting to herself that there was no love in that affair, she would put a brake on her thoughts – if there was no love, there was certainly none elsewhere, and she was not ready to concede that she lived a loveless life. She had friends – good friends she could trust. As well as Laura, there was Lucy Jones, a mucker from her junkie days who trod roughly the same path as Melanie through life. And Jonathan Cooper, a gay man from her art student days, who was always good for a drink or as a holiday companion.

Perhaps that was why she mocked cosy domesticity: she did not want it for herself, but seeing it work for other people made her feel uncomfortable.

She paid the taxi and fumbled with the door key. The last whisky had been a mistake, but what the hell. She had not felt like going home early. In fact she had been the last to leave. She often was.

Back in her flat, she flicked the answering machine on and poured herself some whisky. There was a message from Nicholas, the married man, cancelling their date for the next night, and another muffled voice which could have been her brother.

Melanie turned on the television and put her feet up on the sofa. A black and white film flickered a background to her thoughts and she was suddenly angry. Angry with her brother for never ringing and then ringing indistinctly, angry with her father for never being there, angry with Laura for having a neat husband and a large family, angry with herself for being drunk and flirting with all the wrong people.

Maybe it was time to give up drink again, but even as the thought crossed her mind one hand was topping up the whisky in her glass. Why should she? She knew all the arguments for being sober, and none seemed half as attractive as the undoubted benefit of the odd drink. She drank because she enjoyed it, and she only needed it because she enjoyed it. She did not need it as a substitute for anything else – she had a full social life and plenty of friends. And if she was dependent – and she was honest enough to know she was – it was a dependency that could be broken any time. She had done it before and it would be no trouble to do it again.

The thoughts whirled through her tired brain. With an effort Melanie sat up straight. Drink aside, she knew she had to make some decisions about her life, but perhaps now was not the moment.

The Melanie Freeway she presented to the world was raffish, hopeless and cheerful. More often than not the inner Melanie and the outer were much the same. But whatever her faults, Melanie was neither stupid nor insensitive. She clung desperately to the few people she counted as true friends, although they themselves were very rarely made aware of her need for them. Laura meant the most to her: Melanie would never forget how Laura had stood beside her throughout her drug-taking days. Sometimes, when Laura's calmness seemed more like smugness than a virtue, she could not resist wounding her friend, but when she did she felt guilty and hurt herself. Laura was an easy target, and it was unfair to take advantage of her.

Melanie hauled herself from the sofa and went to look at the bath in the hope that being in the bathroom would help her decide whether to bathe now or in the morning. Looking at herself in the mirror she forced herself to take stock.

She had put on weight, her hair was too long and not quite clean enough, make-up was smudged under one eye. Even given that it was late at night she was not an encouraging sight. Small wonder that she was in the flat alone. She wondered whether Laura and Robert had felt sorry for her as they watched her into the taxi, and the idea made her flush darkly. Why should they? Many people would be envious of her freewheeling lifestyle, the parties and the men. And even if she did occasionally want something different, that something was not a house in Fulham and another woman's children. She had her own relations, after all. Maybe it was time to see them again.

Her brother Adam had not played a very honourable part

in her life: kept away from her in her schooldays, he had reappeared as she arrived in London and had certainly not dissuaded her from the drug world. At the time she had been delighted with this darkly handsome stranger – he was an ideal companion, but because of their relationship was entirely safe. Later, when she was first cured, she had resented him and seen him as almost evil.

When Adam stopped taking drugs, he stopped dramatically. Unlike Melanie, he left Farm Place and never touched another drink. He married Kim, a quiet and understanding girl some years younger than himself and trained as an accountant. He wore suits and changed his children's nappies. His hair was short and he had put on weight, which did not suit him. His face was round and pasty and he looked vaguely North African. His relationship with Melanie was more complicated than ever: his guilt at the part he had played in her downfall made him swing from overzealous attention to long gaps of silence. When they did meet they had very little to say to each other. All they had in common were an out-of-date list of dealers and hazy memories of holidays in Spain when the moon turned pink and statues wept real blood. They were not conversations Adam enjoyed but there was nothing else. Adam resented the fact that their father did not conceal his dislike of him, and Kim, trying desperately to be a good sister-in-law, only made matters worse. She and Adam were vegetarian but she always cooked a steak for Melanie and Melanie always baited her by encouraging the children to try it.

Nevertheless, Adam was her brother, and with her mother dead and her father so rarely in England, he was all she had. If it had been him on the telephone – and even if it had not been – Melanie decided she would ring him and ask him and Kim and the three children to dinner. Or lunch, maybe. Or an outing – that was it – an outing of such magnificence the children would never forget it.

Grand gestures came easily to Melanie. It was the day-to-day ordinariness of human contact she sometimes found so hard. And, just for a moment, as she stood looking at her blurred reflection, she saw that a day at the fair, or a circus, or a trip to the moon, was not the answer. If she really wanted to heal the rifts and know Adam and Kim properly, she was going to have to step towards them.

With a sigh, she turned from the mirror and began pulling off her clothes. It would have to be a vegetable pilaff Sunday lunch. If she could face it.

And then the other problem – Nicholas. It had gone on long enough. Some day soon she must get rid of him. She fell into bed and switched off the light. Adam – Nicholas – it was too late at night to make decisions. She would think about it all in the morning.

By the time Laura had washed up, she was tired but on the whole pleased at how the evening had gone. The food had been good, she had not disgraced Robert and even Melanie had, if you excepted the flirting and the occasional tactless comment, behaved well.

She plumped up the sofa cushions and locked the front door. When she went upstairs Robert was already in bed reading and Laura moved quietly around the room, taking off her make-up and folding her clothes precisely. When she lay down she found her head was spinning slightly. Only a little, but that last glass of wine had been unnecessary. She looked up at the ceiling, almost enjoying watching it swing around above her, and waiting for Robert to put down his book. She must not doze off. She had something important to discuss with him. Seconds later she was asleep.

Suddenly everybody was pregnant. Not only Oriana, but the copy-editor at work and two of the literary agents with whom Laura had worked closely announced their pregnancies. Laura queued in Boots behind a woman buying a Clear Blue predictor test. She went to Laura Ashley to buy a new nightdress and saw they had developed a whole range of baby clothes – or had she just not noticed them before? A huge new Mothercare opened across the road from her office and Laura was horrified to catch herself eyeing the doorway. Sock Shop had a whole corner full of divinely tiny socks and bootees. Women in flowery smocks stood on every corner. Even smarter chains suddenly seemed to be taking an interest in maternity wear and Laura realised she was making mental notes to remember this against the day . . .

Why the sudden rush? Laura gazed out of her third-floor office window and tried to rationalise her feelings. Of course, she wanted a baby – she had always planned children, always loved her nieces and nephews and looked forward to having her own. But why this overwhelming urge which was fast becoming an obsession? She now turned to the *Independent's* health page first and pored over arguments for and against natural childbirth and birthing pools in the Sunday papers.

Laura would sit on the tube, counting the pregnant women she saw on her daily journey, guessing at their ages, working out an average for the day, the week. She read the birth column in *The Times* and *Telegraph*, half-appalled at how many children were born each day, and none of them hers.

She remembered the days, three or four years earlier, when everyone seemed to be wearing a wedding ring and she had sat on the bus or train, mesmerised by some plain woman and wondering how anyone with such a nose, such eyes, could have found herself a husband, while she, whole in limb and mind, clear-skinned, regular-featured, perfectly "nice-looking" as her mother would say, was still ringless.

That was all right now. She had her emerald and, more importantly, her gold band. She had Robert, she added quickly to herself, pushing away the thought that tickled away at the edge of her mind for the first time. Dear, reliable, dependable Robert.

Yes, she had Robert. But, she realised, it was already not enough.

4

Laura and Robert had not, when they first met, fallen into each other's arms in recognition of twin souls. That was not the way either of them would behave. Laura was thirty-three, and schooling herself for a life of spinsterhood. With a sigh she would admit that she had not been lucky with men: the puzzle was whether she was too cautious or not cautious enough.

She had arrived in London aged nineteen and not only a virgin but unused to men. She had an older brother, of course, but that was not the advantage some of her schoolmates supposed. It was not until she was eighteen that she had been included in any of Ferdy's plans and even then it was an exception, not a rule. Ferdy and his friends were serious public schoolboys, as shy with girls as she was with them, and totally incapable of anything but awkwardness when faced with Ferdy's quiet younger sister. Rosalind was another disadvantage. She would urge Ferdy to have friends to stay for the weekend as it would be nice for Laura, and then monopolise them with conversations about Maupassant and Gide.

So when Laura moved into the small shared house in Battersea that Rosalind had discovered through friends of friends she was shy, diffident and curious.

The two girls Laura was to live with were the owner of the house, Sarah Hardy, a trainee at Christies and Julia Sinclair who had arrived there by much the same route as Laura. Sarah welcomed her, told her the bathroom and kitchen rules, asked whether she would rather join the kitty system or buy her own break and milk, assured her that as long as fair notice was given, no one minded leaving the house free while another girl gave a dinner party and poured Laura her first gin and tonic. Realising that Laura had very few friends in London she invited her along everywhere for the first fortnight until she tired of her role and left her protégée to fend for herself.

Julia was, at first, rather less forthcoming. She and Laura edged round each other, both polite but unsure. Julia, who found Sarah's ebullience exhausting, presumed Laura would be the same eager type while Laura was daunted by Julia's flip cleverness and bright blonde hair. Both girls were older than Laura and seemed to her infinitely more sophisticated.

Within a month they were all used to each other and, apart from the occasional early morning grumble, getting along well. Laura had begun her six-month secretarial course and had been promised a job as an editorial assistant at Bergman and Lessing when she had finished. The course bored her but there was an end in view and she worked conscientiously. By coincidence, Julia was already in publishing, working as a reader at The Bodley Head, and she went off every morning in the expectation that today would be the day she would discover the new Graham Greene. And Sarah was fronting the Christie's desk, assured that by doing so she was picking up a great deal about the art world and would soon move on to greater things.

Laura loved London. She would walk home along the autumn streets, clutching her *Evening Standard* (bought because it made her feel a Londoner – read only for the television page) and glory in her freedom. For the first time in her life she could disappear for hours on end and no one need know where she was. Julia had been to university and Sarah had had a year abroad as a chalet girl and with a friend in Kenya, so both were mildly amused at Laura's excitement. It made no difference. To prove her point, she spent an evening alone at the cinema. She did not much enjoy the experience (and never repeated it) but it was made worthwhile when she walked into the sitting room and Julia looked up and only said, "Hi. Had fun?"

Sarah's boyfriend, Edward, worked in the City and spent a great deal of time in the Battersea house. With him acting as host, Sarah gave endless dinner parties. The food was vile, the wine (bring a bottle) usually worse, but everyone made a great deal of noise and had a lovely time. Sometimes Julia or Laura were asked (Julia usually made her excuses), sometimes not.

But Laura was asked on the night, just after she had started her job, when Christopher Brown was there. He was very proper, slightly less rowdy than some of Sarah's other friends, and best friends with Sarah's Edward. He looked a tiny bit like Tom Cruise. He was also the first man to ask Laura out more than once.

The first time, after a lot of giggling, Sarah said she and Edward were going out to dinner with Christopher and why didn't Laura come to balance numbers. The second time Christopher plucked up the nerve to ask her himself and a sticky evening was spent in the local trattoria, followed by coffee at Laura's and silence all round. After a while Julia went to bed but her tact made Laura more nervous. The third time Christopher took Laura to the new Alan Ayckbourn and then out to a Chinese restaurant and, although he talked a lot about his job in financial futures, a subject about which Laura knew nothing, she enjoyed herself thoroughly.

Christopher was in many ways ideal for Laura. It turned out that they knew people in common – friends of Ferdy's mostly – and that they had been to many of the same teenage parties without ever having met. Christopher's aunt lived half-an-hour away from the Sawyers and his cousins were old friends of Laura's. They could laugh at his uncle's eccentricities, which led to discussion about their parents. Here, too, they had much in common. Like Rosalind, Serena Brown was fey and had taken up European literature late in life. Like Laura, Christopher was often embarrassed by his mother's flirting and extravagant scenes. They tried to cap each other's tales of maternal bad behaviour, laughing and exaggerating wildly. It turned out that Christopher's father was a melancholic drunk and their mood changed as Christopher told her of this unhappiness. Laura was a good listener, but she was also clever at turning the conversation before Christopher could say more, that he might later regret. By the end of the evening they were laughing again over memories of holiday disasters and Laura knew that she and Christopher were bound to become close friends if nothing more.

So she rang Rosalind and asked if she could bring a couple of friends down for a weekend. Rosalind, who had been intensely curious about her daughter's new life, agreed at once and urged her to bring as many people as the house could hold. Which threw Laura into a panic as she suddenly realised she did not really know very many people that well.

In the end, Julia and her current boyfriend, John, Sarah and Edward and Christopher all took the train to Devon. Moving the Dulka Road set to Devon was not very adventurous but she did not really want Melanie charming Christopher (Rosalind would do enough of that given the chance) and she was not yet sure enough of any other of her new friends to mix her social circles. At the last minute she rang Ferdy and begged him to come too.

Which was her mistake. The weekend was a failure in a totally frantic way. Michael Sawyer spent most of his time in the garden, joined occasionally by Sarah who claimed to know all about potentillas and roses and went on to tell him about them, and Julia who made no claim to know but asked questions and forgot to listen to the answers.

Rosalind tried out all her new Mediterranean dishes, so Laura's first kiss (which took place in the car park of the local pub) was garlic-ridden and punctuated with tomato pips coming loose from between clenched teeth. Christopher was polite to Rosalind, but knew no French literature and failed to be overcome by her charm. On Saturday evening, John went to bed totally drunk and on Sunday morning, Rosalind was horrified to see Edward coming out of Sarah's bedroom. "But he was meant to be sharing with *John*," she told Michael, who could not see why she minded.

And, worst of all, it was clear by Sunday afternoon that John was on the way out of Julia's life and that before too long Ferdy would have taken his place.

All part of growing up and being British, Laura told herself as she sat on the train home to London, and at least she had got to know Christopher better.

Christopher was part of Laura's life for the next four years. It was a relationship – rather than a romance – built on trust, companionship and lack of curiosity. They came from the same sort of background, had gone to the same sort of schools, were basically the same type. It was easy for each to slot into the other's life, although Laura joined Christopher's world rather then he hers. But although there was no great passion in their love, there was a staid affection, a non-demanding love that seemed to Laura, who knew no better, enough. Hers was not a demonstrative family and she had been brought up to believe that signs of affection were vulgar. It had been dinned into her head to such an extent that she almost thought strong feelings themselves were vulgar.

And then there was sex, to which Christopher introduced her a month or two after the Devon weekend. Well, that was all right, and after a while she really could see the point, but it was the same as everything else with Christopher: easy, comfortable, sometimes even quite fun, but never really exciting. Laura supposed that the raunchy novelists just made it all up and that Melanie enjoyed it so much because she was always on some other kind of high at the time.

After the affair was over Laura was careful not to undermine Christopher or the time she spent with him. When she had become a little more experienced she recognised that some of the blame for their relationship's lack of excitement lay with her. She, after all, accepted what he did give her and did not ask for more. She had not been brought up to expect more. They did things together and enjoyed each other's company in a way that many of Laura's peers did not with their lovers. He was more than someone to eat, drink, dance and screw with. Although he did not offer or inspire grand passion, he did free Laura from her limited world of family and girls' boarding school. He was a totally respectable boyfriend, but sometimes he said things that would have horrified Rosalind. He never fell for Rosalind's brand of charm, and that was a blessing. Unfailingly polite to her, he remained puzzled and unimpressed by her half-baked literary allusions. By implication rather than confrontation he made Laura realise that her mother was not particularly clever or beautiful. The breakthrough was not so much Laura's being able to leave her mother's shadow as realising that her mother cast no shadow. "Well, isn't she a bit – pretentious?" Christopher once said, and in a moment Laura grew up.

It was not until the end of their third year together that Laura admitted to herself quite how dull Christopher really was, and it took another year for her to summon up the strength to finish with him. After all, life with him was easy. He was generous and good-natured; they never fought and barely even quarrelled. He had no irritating characteristics, and in the end even this was an irritant in itself.

She would not admit it at the time, as she shied away from the fear that she might have used him, but Christopher had served his purpose. His stability had given her confidence. As he and his friends laughed at her jokes she was made to realise that she could be funny. She also began to notice that she was the joker, the leader. Christopher was a strong rock behind her but gradually Laura knew she needed a man who would take her hand and lead her forward, not just be there to catch her when she fell back. She began to yearn for an adventure. She had loved him at first, but one morning she woke up and realised this just could not go on. A life with Christopher would not end in poverty or disgrace, she would not become a battered wife nor he a drunk. She would just die of boredom, which would not be fair on either of them.

It took all her nerve to tell him, and even more strength to resist his miserable incomprehension, his late-night telephone calls, the bunches of roses. Why did he wait till now to tell her how much he loved her? It was far too late.

So Laura began to enjoy being on her own. Parties unnerved her at first, she was so used to being accompanied, but not for long. She missed Christopher, but got along without him very well. She listened to a great deal of old music, indulging her Radio 2 sentimental streak with ballads and moony country-and-western tales of lost love and betrayal.

Meanwhile work was progressing well. After two years at Bergman and Lessing, she was promoted away from her sec-retarial work and became a reader. Three years later she was beginning to work on some of the less important books and a year after that she changed jobs and worked, briefly and unhappily, for a feminist publishing company. That year was a mistake, but at least by changing companies she had speeded up her promotion.

Laura knew she would never be a great publisher. She doubted if her name would ever be well known in the trade, let alone outside it. She had application, but no gambling streak. She recognised that it did take a certain flair to be a successful publisher, and became gradually aware that she did not have that flair.

She minded at first, but not for long. Not as much as she had minded about Christopher, and that had been of her own doing. After all, she was not that ambitious. She would like to be allowed to take on slightly more demanding books, but would never want to run a company herself. The only threat was that of boredom, so she took to changing her job every eighteen months or so, until she finally changed tack entirely and, tired of novels about middle-class people living middle-class lives, moved first to a company for which she ran a list of spy thrillers and then to the children's department of Howard and Neville.

There was no real boyfriend for years after Christopher. Men took her out – she was never lonely or at a loss – but while she enjoyed the odd affair she never approached either Melanie's or Julia's cavalier attitude to sex, even before herpes and Aids began to haunt the single. For Laura, sex was never just something to do, it was always part of a bigger package. She wondered if she were priggish, although after a spontaneously taken week's holiday in Portugal with a man she barely knew, she realised there was nothing wrong with her sexual appetite. She had begun to discover how to have fun. A man could be entirely suitable (and all her lovers were) but that did not mean that away from his City desk or court of law he could not be foolish and young and free.

But then came Frankie. Frankie Lyndon was a softly spoken blue-eyed Irishman. "Every girl's fantasy," Julia murmured when she met him. "Well done!" Laura herself was amazed that he had taken up with her, even more so when his interest did not flag. At first glance Frankie was almost ugly. At second glance he was clearly the most attractive man any girl could meet. Sitting opposite him on a bus would brighten a girl's day. But to be his lover . . .

He was, officially at least, a marketing man for a major car production company. But the ordinariness of his job was made up for by the fact that he was also a poet – not just a scribbler, but published.

Laura met him through Charlotte, who had become her friend during her work with the feminist publishing house. Charlotte now worked in the publicity department of Faber and Faber and had been in charge of promoting *Apple Pips and UFOs*. It had not been an easy job. "I get on with him very well, but the truth is he's bloody arrogant," Charlotte told Laura. "He's not just a male chauvinist, he's an everything-that-he-is-and-I'm-not chauvinst. He can't see that cars and books – especially arty-tarty poetry books – have to be promoted in completely different ways. But he's so charming I give in to him every time. He's dangerous."

Charlotte and Frankie stayed in touch after the publication of the book, and finally Laura met him. All Charlotte's words of warning were immediately forgotten. Laura had not been so badly in love since she had had a twelve-year-old's crush on Ferdy's best friend, Tom. He was never out of her thoughts, her heart jumped each time the telephone rang and sank each time it was not Frankie. She was constantly afraid that he would never call again, that he would see through her for the boring mouse she really was and would leave her. She never, ever took for granted when she left him that she would see him again.

And the truth was that she did not really even mind his chauvinism. She too had been brought up in the school that said women cooked dinner and men went to offices and bled radiators. Frankie took her out to dinner, the theatre, the cinema. He courted her as old-fashioned, or chauvinist, men do and he seduced her in record time. Before too long the dinners and theatres happened less often and Laura was cooking for them at his flat more often, but that seemed natural. She sewed buttons on his shirts, she even occasionally ironed them. Nothing could damp Laura's passion which for the first time in her life was as physical as it was emotional. Frankie completed Laura's education, was tender and funny and wild and untrustworthy and very, very sexual. Laura, despite her never-ending fear that she would lose him, relaxed and was truly happy.

Charlotte had been right, of course. Frankie was arrogant. But in Laura's eyes even his arrogance had a certain manly charm.

She wondered sometimes how he kept his job and supposed that underneath everything he was a middle-class boy with a sense of responsibility, something at least in common with her other boyfriends.

Julia teased her about her new domesticity and asked when Laura was going to move into Frankie's Notting Hill flat. But he didn't ask her and Laura was not sure it would be a good idea. At the back of her mind she knew she was after more than the squalor of a shared life without promises.

Sarah Hardy then became engaged and Julia and Laura were given notice to leave the house they had shared for so long. Julia suggested she just move in with Frankie before he noticed, but Laura, hoping her future homelessness would prompt him into thinking about their future, waited.

Frankie remained silent. And Laura remained in love.

With some help from her father, Laura bought a small house in Battersea and Julia and she moved in just before Sarah's wedding. Julia did not stay for long. The time had come for her to settle down, she announced. She had been going out with Viv for eight whole months now, and knew he was the man for her, so with nods and becks and wreathed smiles, she set off to begin to live happily ever after.

Laura asked Charlotte to move in with her and then began to panic. Perhaps Frankie would never ask her – she was not like Julia, they all knew that. She wanted to be married.

With the admission came fear. She told herself not to be hysterical. She was only twenty-eight and it was not as if all, or indeed many, of her friends were married. Ferdy had married a French girl, Aimée Martin, who was Laura's age, but then the French were different. Sarah was married and Julia as good as. But she only had to look around her to see that people were marrying later. Only a few months before, the production manager at work had married – for the first time – at forty.

Finally she decided that she had to talk about it. It took her two months to face Frankie with what she knew would be a row, but she seemed to see less of him these days. He was always busy with the damn cars and his poetry.

She tried to approach the subject lightly, but in a way that would leave the question in his mind. "What do you think you'll be doing in ten years' time?" she asked him as they lay in bed with the newspapers one Sunday morning.

"Ten years? God knows what I'll be doing next week," he answered, reaching for *The Sunday Times* Book Supplement.

"No, I mean, really. You must have some idea. I thought marketing men spent their whole lives predicting the future."

"All these years and you still don't really know what I do in the day," he said, putting the paper down to think. "I thought people stopped this game when they left school. But OK – I'll have left cars and will be famous for my poetry throughout the land. Even the tabloids will be tipping me for the next Poet Laureate. I might be living in Dublin again. I'll probably have an arts show on television – that's how I'll get famous – and I'll have brought poetry to the people almost single-handedly. With the help of Shakespeare and Donne and all that gang."

There was a pause. Laura wondered whether it was worth going on, but knew she had to. She had to know.

"Don't you ever think about being married?" And immediately wished she had not.

"Yes. Every time I go to a wedding and see another one fall. You know me, Laura. I'm not the marrying kind. If I were, I'd probably be married to Celeste by now with three children screaming every time I'm trying to find a rhyme for cat." He turned to look at her and added, gently, "I won't ever marry, Laura. I'm too selfish. I just don't want to be tied down. Maybe in my sixties I'll marry for company, but I can't even see that, can you?"

Laura got up and went to the kitchen to make breakfast and think. Maybe she would be the one to change his mind. Maybe. He had lived with Celeste for three years before she gave up hope of his marrying her, but then Celeste was different. Much younger than him for one thing, uninterested in his poetry for another.

Frankie was older now, and Laura, seeing him with his nephews and nieces, knew that he was fond of children. She was sure he would want one of his own one day soon. The other point about Frankie was that even as a poet he was returning more and more to his conventional upbringing. Poet Laureate – media personality – this was not a man who yearned to roam the freedom of the open hills with a knapsack on his back and a volume of Yeats ever to hand. Laura knew Frankie by now, saw beyond the irresponsible charm that was so attractive. She was sure that he would marry, settle down. He would not give up his poetry, she would not want him to, but he was already letting go of his stubborn independence.

Laura wasted another year before she admitted that she had lost. There was only one more card to play, and using it was an enormous gamble.

She left him. Sadly, warmly, she left him. And waited. But Frankie knew himself better than she did. He was sorry, he missed her, but he would not marry. They saw each other occasionally, had dinner together, flirted in a painful, pointless way.

Six months later he had a new girlfriend, and within a year was married. Laura had known him after all: but she had not been the right girl.

And so she worked, and waited, acted as agony aunt to her friends and as the years ticked by quietly began to despair.

By the time she was thirty-three Laura was reconciled to the fact that all the men she met seemed to be married or fixed up with long-term girlfriends. Robert, when Laura first met him, seemed another one of these. At a Sunday lunch party with his two small children, Laura said hello and noticed his eyes. She wondered in passing where his wife was, but her interest was not quickened even when Charlotte explained that his wife had left him.

"No one knows what it's really about and he won't say. She doesn't seem to have another man and he certainly doesn't have a girlfriend. Johnny claims she told him that she couldn't go on living with a man who hated parties, but then Johnny would."

"What's she like?"

"Camilla? Pretty in an expensive way. Lots of blonde hair and droopy designer clothes. Quite rich – her father's in beer and won't let poor Camilla suffer for not having married a peer with land. Spoilt as hell, but quite fun. She always looks *amused* and you never know whether it's at you or with you."

"Sounds a bit of a bitch."

"A bit. But in the end you can't help liking her. She *is* more

Sophia Watson

fun than Robert, I suppose. He's somehow frightfully *worthy*, the way he looks after the children and being potty about her after so long. He won't look at another girl."

Charlotte's information was not entirely correct. As far as Robert was concerned, he looked at Laura and saw something in her during that first lunch party, although they barely talked. She was quite pretty with a wonderful laugh, but did not say much. There was a calmness about her which he liked immediately, but watching her during the course of lunch he felt there was more to her than she presented. She seemed like every other nice middle-class girl but Robert sensed a vulnerability, maybe even a sadness, which appealed to him.

Robert had heard of Laura before – they had friends in common – and it was just chance that they had never met. He knew of her as a girl whose friendship was very much valued: one of his school friends was married to one of hers and when the marriage had broken up Laura's had been a name that both parties spoke with affection and gratitude. That was partly why he had noticed her gentleness with some surprise: in as much as he had thought of her he had imagined her to be someone assertive. Now he had met her he saw a need for strength as much as strength itself. He also saw a humorous glint in her eye as she silently watched an almost acrimonious discussion between Charlotte and her current boyfriend. He liked that very much.

Robert accepted a glass of cognac which he neither needed nor really wanted and looked across the table at Laura again. He still could not help but compare women with his wife. Camilla was more obviously attractive than this girl, always the centre of attention, making the quick joke for the easy laugh, but despite what Charlotte had told Laura, he was no longer "potty about" her. He never spoke out against her but her selfishness and egocentricity had finally eaten away at his love, even his affection, for her. His sorrow at their final break-up came from losing the children, not from losing her. He felt guilty to admit it even to himself, but when she had finally packed his bags and said he must leave, it had been an enormous relief to him.

He had taken out an enormous mortgage to buy himself a house in Parson's Green Lane, in Fulham. He had done his

• 54

best to make it into a home for the children. He worked tremendously hard: he had to, to pay for Camilla and the children and the mortgages. He also needed to, because there was nothing else apart from his mostly absent children to keep him going. The thought of another wife had not occurred to him, although he had dated a few girls, mostly to see if he could. But that evening, after the children had been picked up by Camilla and he sat alone in front of the news with a glass of whisky, he decided he should ring Charlotte and ask for Laura's number. He would like to see her again, just to see if he had been right about her.

Laura and Robert met again, at dinner this time so the children weren't there as a distraction. And before very long Robert began taking Laura out regularly.

At first Laura thought he was just lonely, unused to spending his evenings in an empty house. But she soon realised there was more to it than that, and when she did she jumped back. The man was married, after all. "Potty about" his wife. She was not going to involve herself with other people's complications. No way, José.

And yet, at the same time, she knew that if he tried hard enough, Robert would win. She had in a short time come to depend on him, on his quiet humour, his doggedness, his companionship. There was more than that, too: he put the lie to the cliché that men in suits are no good at lovemaking. Frankie had reinforced that belief for Laura: her only real lover had been an Irishman and a poet and there was no hope of such love again. Or so she had thought. Before long Laura realised that if Robert tried, he could make her love him. She wanted to love someone: but she was thirty-three. She could not afford to love another Frankie. She was ashamed of her thoughts, but they were there.

So, not for the first time in her life, Laura stood back and waited. Robert waited too. He loved her first, and he knew that her standing back was to do with the vulnerability which had first attracted him to her. He would not, though, make the next move until she relented just a little; until she admitted to herself that she loved him.

It was not, after all, very long before their waiting was

rewarded. Within a year of their first meeting *The Times* bore the announcement that Robert Bedford of Fulham was to marry Laura, daughter of Mr and Mrs Michael Sawyer of Devon.

5

Turkey, of course, with chestnut stuffing and maybe one other. The pudding was obligatory but she would cheat and buy a couple of ready-made. Brandy butter for sure – it was the only reason for the pudding. Laura shifted her briefcase to make room for someone to sit beside her and closed her eyes, trying to concentrate. What could she produce to make the lunch memorably different?

The jolting of the bus made her drowsy, and the lunch began to seem less important. It didn't really matter. The children would only be interested in their presents, and Robert would only be interested in the children.

But if she let her mind wander it would go back to the same old thoughts which had been increasingly obsessing her.

"Children?" Robert had said. "A baby? But darling, I thought . . . Well, we've got Helen and Richard."

He had recovered, of course. Robert was not unreasonable. It was just, as he had explained to her so often since, that he had not thought. And of course he loved his children and understood that she loved them too, but that it was not, in the end, quite the same. Laura remembered how she had been worried at not knowing which brand of toothpaste Robert preferred and was horrified that she had married a man without discussing the question of children. She, too, had just taken the subject for granted. Discovering this total misunderstanding that had been allowed to grow between them made her fear for others that must be lurking around the edge of her marriage.

In the end, Robert, sensing her urgency if not believing that it was necessary, agreed that if she really wanted children there was no good reason for her not to "go straight ahead". So at the end of July, Laura, feeling surprisingly nervous, threw away a half packet of contraceptive pills that she would not take. She was surprised that there was no immediate difference. She had expected to feel younger, to look changed in some way. For years of her life she had relied on the security of the pill: in an odd way she mourned its passing. It had served her well.

Or had it? "Fifteen years? Well, you look healthy enough," her gynaecologist said as Laura struggled back into her pants and tights after her smear test. "The results will be back in a few days, but everything seems fine. So you don't want a new prescription?"

"No, I thought . . ." Laura was unexpectedly embarrassed.

"Yes, it's probably wise. What had you thought of using instead?"

"Nothing."

Doctor Evans looked up with the briefest smile. "Trying to get pregnant?" What a stupid question. Laura nodded.

"Um. Well I suggest you take some mineral and vitamin supplements. Helps get the system going. But don't expect anything to happen for a while. The pill often renders women temporarily infertile. And after fifteen years . . ."

"For how long?" Laura tried hard to pretend the subject was anything but her own body. For years she had loathed these visits and dreaded their indignity. This time, she needed to participate beyond offering up her body to Doctor Evans's bored scrutiny. She had to overcome her distaste in order to ask questions. It was bound to be worse when she was pregnant.

"Were your periods regular before you went on the pill?"

So many years ago. She could barely remember. "Not entirely."

"Then don't expect your first period after you stop taking the pill for some time – it could be as long as six months. If you have any worries, call me. If you think you could be pregnant, come and see me. Good luck."

He scribbled the bill as he talked and pushed it across the table to her with another tight smile.

Laura felt let down as she paid the receptionist and turned her collar against the drizzling rain. But she did not see what else he could have said, so she hailed a passing taxi and directed it to Howard and Neville.

That was only four months ago, and Laura knew there was no reason to hope to be pregnant yet. But that did not stop her thinking. She had told herself that she was not to worry until a year had passed. She was not worrying. She was just thinking.

The conductor rang the bell and Laura gathered herself together in readiness for her stop. It was time she started Christmas shopping, and she had no idea what to buy the two children.

She opened the front door to hear the telephone ringing and, tripping over the cats, she reached it just in time.

"Laura, it's Camilla. Is Robert there?"

"He won't be back for an hour yet." Laura tried not to sound cross.

"Of course, how silly. Well you'll do. It's about Christmas. You see, I've been thinking about it and I really think it would be better if the children came to me after all."

"Camilla, Robert—"

"I know I had them last time but what with all the – excitement – this year . . ."

"It's not for me to decide or discuss. I'll tell Robert you've called and he'll ring you when he gets home."

"I'm out tonight. And there's nothing to discuss. Nice to talk to you."

"Camilla—" but she had rung up.

Laura put the telephone down and looked at it thoughtfully. Camilla was normally more polite to her, to the point of saccharine. Perhaps it was because she was expecting an argument that she had been so brusque. But Laura was sure there was more to it than that – there had been something about Camilla's voice . .

Robert was, of course, furious when he came home and Laura told him about Camilla's call. He had been looking forward to Christmas with Laura and the children and had been talking about it even more than Richard and Helen.

"She's usually perfectly reasonable – about things like this," he said, dialling Camilla's number for the third time although Laura had told him she wouldn't be there. "And apart from anything else, she hates Christmas, always says there's too much sentiment and pine needles everywhere. I suppose her parents could be putting on the pressure, but the children are going to them at New Year anyway. Oh *hell*. I wonder what's going on." And he hung up with a bang.

Laura brought him a whisky and soda.

"Robert, she sounded odd to me."

"Camilla? What do you mean, odd?"

"I don't know – odd."

"Probably embarrassed, expecting you to fight back. You should have, you know. You must fight for them too."

Laura pushed down a wave of anger at his unfairness. She was deliberately careful not to enter into the arrangements precisely so that she would not be accused of interfering. Now she was being told she should enter the lists, but she was not yet prepared to do so.

She spoke calmly, "Look, there's nothing we can do now. Tomorrow's Friday and you'll see Camilla when you pick up the children. You know I couldn't argue with her, it would only have made things worse. So let's forget about it for now. Unless there's a very good reason, I'm sure she'll come round."

Camilla did not change her mind, and although she came up with no very good reason, Robert, always ready to avoid a confrontation, sadly agreed to change their arrangements. "I can't make it out," he told Laura. "She says a lot of stuff about all the changes this year."

"I.e., me."

"Yes – so the children have to be with her and her parents. Then she implied she's got someone she wants them to meet. I think she's up to something."

"I told you she was odd."

"That's not what I said." Laura could only go so far in her criticism of Camilla and she knew when to stop.

"So who's the new man?"

"I don't know – I'm not even sure there is one. I think the children would have said something if there were someone new on the scene. Apart from anything else, I'm sure she'd tell me if there were someone."

Laura, suspicious of Camilla's ability to play games, said

nothing. But she began to think that it might be a good thing if Camilla were to remarry. It would leave the Bedfords much better off, for one thing. And would perhaps divert Camilla's energies away from troublemaking. Laura was somehow uneasy at the idea of a Camilla for ever on the loose.

"So what do you want to do at Christmas? Stay in London anyway?"

"I don't mind. It just won't be the same."

"Well, we can think about it. Although, if we want to go to Devon, we'd better tell Mummy soon. You know what she's like."

Camilla had already found a reason for keeping the children that weekend, and Robert and Laura were going to stay with a colleague of Robert's in Sussex. Country girl though she officially was, Laura packed her case wearily.

Timmy and Miranda Reed were typical nouveau-country-dwellers. As soon as they left London they adopted an extra-ordinary wardrobe of browns and muted greens, flat caps and newly pressed tweeds that immediately marked them for what they were. They called publicans "Landlord" and once, to Laura's horror, Timmy had tried to tip one. Although the house was comfortable, everything about it was wrong: the chintzes matched too precisely, the Floris essence in the bathroom was always a brand-new bottle, the field in front of the house was somehow too neat. Laura suspected that the cut flowers came from an Arundel florist, not the garden or surrounding woods.

This year, Timmy had taken a day at a neighbouring shoot and had asked Robert and Laura to join the house party. Robert, a gentleman farmer's son from Yorkshire, was delighted. He had been brought up shooting and missed the occasional smell of cordite and the heavy feel of a wet bird hanging from his shoulder. Laura was pleased for him, but dreaded the prospect of a day lolling by the fire with moleskin-clad wives, or standing freezing by Robert as he missed birds and felt a fool. She found herself wishing the children were coming too.

They arrived just before nine, to be greeted by an over-enthusiastic red setter and a spaniel puppy. The other guests – a young banker and his shapely girlfriend, an accountant with a wife who ran her own knitwear company and their two small children, another lawyer with his pregnant bride – had already arrived and were changing for dinner. Timmy, genial in a velvet smoking jacket and brand-new embroidered slippers from Tricker, poured them drinks and showed them upstairs to their room.

"Don't hurry, there's time for baths," he assured them. "There's plenty of hot water," he added, leaving the room.

"There would be," Laura muttered as she began to unpack. "And we all know there's time for a bath means do wash the London grime off you and slip into something slightly more glamorous before we see you next."

"What's the matter with you?" Robert asked, coming out of the bathroom.

"Well, *glamour* in the country!" Laura said, gesturing to the thick corded tassels around the chintz pelmet, the neatly made twin beds, corners turned with a chocolate on the pillow, the chintz-covered dressing table, the towelling robes laid out by the bathroom door. "It's like a hotel."

"I don't mind it for a change," Robert said mildly. "And I wish you'd stop being so ratty. Perhaps you're pregnant."

The thought made Laura sit down on a bed. She ran her mind through her feelings over the past few days, wondering if he were right.

"Or premenstrual," he added, sipping his whisky. "Come on, you have first bath."

Dinner was delicious, but no fun. The three lawyers talked shop while Timmy's wife, Miranda, discussed knitwear and babies with Tanya and Frances. Laura, cross and tired, could not bring herself to make enough effort to join in and sat longing for bed. She ignored Robert's warning looks, knowing she was letting herself in for a curtain lecture. If she were quick enough she would stall him by being asleep before he came up. And she would try harder the next day. She began to dislike the outgoing, pregnant Tanya. For her confidence. And the fact she did not go to work. She knew she was being unpleasant and unreasonable and escaped to bed as soon as possible, resolving to wake more cheerful.

*   *   *

The day dawned bright and brisk and Laura, looking out of her window as she dressed, decided to go out with the guns. Her nose was slightly stuffy and her head gave warning of aching soon with the close heat of the house, besides which, accompanying a gun was a good way of cornering his attention as they waited for birds. She felt as though she had not had a real conversation with Robert for weeks.

The other women were not going to come out until after lunch and Laura piled into the truck with the men feeling relaxed and looking forward to the morning.

It was ideal. The sun shone in the cold blue sky, the air was crisp with the faintest hint of wind, dead leaves lay thick on the ground, coated with enough of the night's frost to crunch underfoot. They jolted across a field, men checking their gunbelts and whisky flasks, dogs whining eagerly, tails thumping against knees.

Robert squeezed her hand briefly. "Thanks for coming out."

She smiled and waved at the window. "That drew me as much as you," she teased. "Just make sure you get something for the pot." She thought for a moment about the social ritualisation of the hunter, but knew that despite any pheasant lovers' society or anti-blood-sport brigade, something in her would always love the idea of her man killing food. Even if Sainsbury's was only a five-minute drive from home.

The guns and dogs were decanted from the truck and given their instructions. Robert and Laura walked in silence across the ploughed field to their peg, mud clogging their every pace.

"I was very tired last night," Laura said as Robert filled his belt with cartridges and loaded his gun.

"Is that by way of an apology?" he asked, Laura's plan of avoidance having worked the night before.

"Well, yes. Mummy always says if you're going to do something you don't want to do, do it with good grace. And I must admit, I didn't."

"You were bloody rude," he said calmly, and Laura bit back the answer that would only lead to an argument.

"I know. And Timmy and Miranda are really very nice. I was mean and foul and I'm sorry. But I still don't like Tanya."

"What's wrong with her? She seemed sweet."

Exactly. "Oh, I don't know – there is just something about her."

The sound of beaters tapping the wood ahead of them rang out hollowly. The accountant's dog whined and sat on his cartridge bag to get a better view. Jo saw Laura looking at his dog and waved his flask. "It's the damn waiting that gets to your nerves," he yelled cheerfully.

"We've only been married a few months, Laura," Robert said, looking straight ahead at the wood. "You mustn't start getting worried about – anything."

Laura was startled; with the wind taken out of her sails so abruptly she had no choice but to change tack.

"I'm not – honestly. It's just that I know how you hate not having the children with us all the time, and it would be so lovely to have our own family. It would be nice for the children too, you know. Settle them more – children like order. And if Camilla's going to start being difficult—"

"It's a one-off," he said. "She promised."

"Darling, this weekend and Christmas make two already, and as you say, we've only been married a few months. But that's not the point – it's just – well, I wish I could feel you were more enthusiastic about the whole idea. It would make so much difference."

"Darling Laura, I can assure you that my attitude of mind makes absolutely no difference to the chances of conception. Biology is biology, and it's nothing to do with mind over matter."

"That's not what I mean."

With squawks from the birds and hollers from the beaters, six pheasant broke from the wood and headed into the open air. Robert fired and missed, fired again and a bird fell with a satisfying thud just behind them.

He reloaded happily. "It cheers up the whole day if you shoot a bird cleanly on the first drive," he said. And added. "Laura, my own fool, I may have been slow on the uptake, but if it does make any difference you should realise that I should like nothing in the world so much as your children."

It did make a difference but it did not make her pregnant.

*　　*　　*

Melanie hung up the telephone and stared at it crossly. It was unreasonable to expect her friends to be on call when she wanted them, but there was something about the satisfaction in a recorded voice announcing its owner was somewhere else having fun that was almost offensive. Already feeling low when she had dialled Laura for the fourth time that weekend, she was now in a mood which could only end in a quarrel or tears.

Weekends are the gloomiest time for the unmarried half of an adulterous affair, and usually Melanie was careful to arrange some social life for herself. But somehow, this weekend had arrived unannounced, and now Laura was out of London, Jonathan was on holiday in Africa, Lucy was off on a dirty weekend with her new man and she was cross and alone in her flat.

She considered the television and a drink, but decided she needed to get out of the house, so she wrapped herself in her coat and wandered on to the street, walking aimlessly until she saw a taxi. It was not until she was in its back seat that she decided where to go. "The zoo, please," she said, and sat back to think.

There was no question but that Laura's wedding had brought Melanie to some sort of crisis. She could not think why – other friends were married and Laura was so obvious a candidate it should not have been a shock. Yet, somehow, Melanie was aware that the discontent that had been brewing inside her for months stemmed from Laura's engagement.

Now, in the taxi, sober, on the way to what remained of London Zoo, she decided she could no longer run away from her discontent. If she did not face up to it soon – and do something about it – it threatened to take her over.

Narcotics Anonymous gives a good grounding to anyone ready for some introspection. Once Melanie had admitted to herself that there was a problem, it was an easy step to begin considering where the problem lay. And it did not take too long before the question had turned about on itself, and she was asking herself if there was any area of her life that was at all satisfactory.

Her love life, if she was completely frank, was a disaster. She had had more than her share of lovers, even if her junkie years were left out of the picture. Of those tens – not to mention scores – only two had ever really mattered, and only two (not the same two) had lasted beyond a few months. One was the improbably named Stanley, Lucy Jones's brother, who was the only "decent", as Laura would say, lover she had ever had, and the other was Nicholas. The affair with Stanley had finished eight years earlier in a Niagara of tears – his – and recriminations – hers. Stanley made the mistake of asking to marry her. For Melanie, who had never quite trusted Stanley (how could she trust a man who was foolish enough to love her?) this was the final straw. She not only refused to marry him, she accused him of trying to take over her life, to control her, to stop her being herself. She tried very hard never to think of Stanley. The split with him was the nearest she ever came to going back to drugs, and the only thing she sometimes regretted. The truth was, Melanie thought, as she watched the dirty grey streets through the taxi window, she could not really have loved him. Even she was not so self-destructive . . . was she?

Nicholas was another story. He had started off as another dinner-party flirtation, but it had run away with her and she had ended the evening in bed with him. If anyone had told her he was married she had not taken it in, although if she were honest it might not have made much difference. It was not until much later that she learned that the night they met his wife was in hospital, having just been delivered of their first child. By then it was too late to go back – the affair was of too long standing and the wrong had been done – but she did feel her first hint of distaste for him when she found out.

Nicholas was not good-looking but there was an understated sexiness to him that was very attractive. He was a city slicker, clever, funny, as unscrupulous in his career as he was in his personal life. His charm – and his success – lay in his eloquent eyes which could send messages of desire, humour and a sureness of his conquest that very rarely failed him.

It was something else which Melanie had grown to dislike in him.

Yet after two years she could not shake herself free of him. She had been continuously unfaithful and was sure he had as well. She was certainly not waiting for him to leave his wife: one of the things she thought she still liked about him was the way he had never even pretended that he was going to, had never for a moment claimed that he loved her. Perhaps this honesty was why his wife stayed with him. Perhaps she just did not know what he was like.

And yet Melanie was beginning to think she deserved better. It was perhaps just the tiniest bit insulting that he did not even bother to pretend. The other men were never more than pastimes – and why did Nicholas deserve so much of her attention? Other men were almost as good in bed.

The taxi arrived at Regent's Park and Melanie, wondering why she had come, paid it off and waited behind a man and a child at the ticket booth. It was cloudless and sunny, and the cold had not kept many people away. Melanie wandered through the crowds of children and, leaning against a fence, watched an elephant scratching against its pen.

So men were a disaster.

Friends were all right. Weren't they? Granted, she was on her own at London Zoo surrounded by men with their children and the odd teenage couple, but that was more to do with being single than friendless. She thought for a moment. No, she knew she could always count on Laura and Lucy. She could always get drunk and weep with Jonathan, or ring him up and suggest a spur-of-the-moment outing such as this. There was a lot of flotsam and jetsam in her life, but that was bound to be the case with someone of her age and with her past. No, she need not worry about friends.

Bored with elephants, she decided that as she had not seen a tiger for a long time this would be a good moment. And it was then, looking at the beasts pacing back and forth, that she forced herself to face the truth.

She was very like the tigers, after all. She had enormous amounts of energy which she dissipated in useless nervous activity. Because the truth was, she had nothing to do. Where, to her, lay the difference between a weekday and a weekend? Only in the fact that she expected all her friends to be available at the weekend, and only some of them during the week. Her income was large enough for her to survive without working, but not large enough for her to pursue the time-killing pleasures of the really rich. So she had fallen into the drug scene and now passed her hours in drinking and watching television.

She was not stupid, not old, but not qualified and very lazy. She did not want to be lazy any more. She wanted to get up in the morning with something to do.

But what? An office job was out of the question. She was too old and too proud to start at the bottom and besides she could not think of anything any of her friends did in offices that sounded at all like fun. She wanted a job that would stop her boredom, not compound it. There was very little choice. She could not write, she could not sing, she could not really paint, although she had a good eye—

Melanie stopped in her tracks. Of course, that was it. Why had she not thought of it years ago? There was the ideal job. She would be her own mistress, she would answer to nobody and work the hours she chose. All she needed was a small amount of capital, good contacts and a good eye. And as that was more or less what she could offer the world, it seemed as if she had found her ideal métier.

Melanie was so excited she almost ran out of the zoo, hailing a taxi at once. Melanie Freeway – art dealer to the as yet undiscovered artist. It had a certain ring.

So who should she ring up to celebrate with?

Laura's months passed in the same pattern. A week of gloom, a week of hope, a week of "it will never happen", days of "will it, won't it?" and then the darkest depths of despair. Laura had never had an obsession that compared. Not Ferdy's friend Tom, not Frankie, certainly not Christopher or Robert – no man had ever occupied her brain as exclusively as this hunger for a child.

Oriana's baby was born in mid-December, a boy named Alexis, and Laura was pleased, visited mother and child, brought appropriate presents, said the right things. But her heart was not in it as it had been when Poppy, or Ferdy's children were born. There was an edge there. She despised herself for it, resumed her churchgoing in an effort to purge it, even confessed it to Charlotte who sighed and said she felt the same way about other people's engagements, but she could not drive the demon out.

Oddly enough it was her father who noticed the sadness in her and who, in his quiet way, offered the most comfort. They met at Oriana's one Sunday teatime. Helen was organising Poppy and Richard into some game of her own devising, Robert and Ferdy were discussing the state of the Princess of Wales's heart with eager ignorance, and Oriana was telling her mother about the new baby's wondrous delights. Laura and her father talked easily about nothing, Laura wishing he were in London more often and resolving to ask herself down to Devon for a weekend soon, when suddenly he reached across the table and on the pretext of taking a biscuit squeezed her hand for a moment.

"Cheer up, chicken," he said. "There's always Aunt Mary," and he went calmly on with telling her about the delights of his new part-time gardener.

Aunt Mary was an example so extreme as to be almost ridiculous. She was Michael Sawyer's sister, the elder by five years, who had married and moved to Scotland when she was only twenty. There were no children, for reasons that the family (always eager to speculate on such matters) could not fathom. Her husband was well off, she did not have a career "and there's nothing else to do in Scotland". But although everyone wondered, no one dared ask.

Mary came south twice a year, but after Michael married, the visits became less frequent and although he was too loyal to say so he knew that his wife was at least partly the reason. The sisters-in-law were unlikely ever to become bosom friends, but Rosalind's delight in her three "perfect" children drove her most fecund friends to despairing boredom and was unlikely to appeal to a childless wife of fifteen years.

Mary and Ian tried to adopt, but by then it was too late. "They say we are too old," Mary wrote in an unusually frank letter to her brother, "so the dogs and sheep will have to go on being my family. The pity of it is that we kept telling each other not to lose hope, that there was plenty of time. We should have lost hope years ago. Then, at least, we could have adopted children. I am so afraid of being alone when Ian dies."

Mary was forty-three when she was told she was four months pregnant. She was nursing her father-in-law through a long-drawn-out dying and by then hope had long since disappeared.

The baby was born whole in body and mind. The day Fiona was born was the only day Laura had ever seen her father cry and the only day she had ever seen him really lose his temper with Rosalind. "You'd have thought that after twenty-four years of thinking about it she could have come up with a better name than that," Rosalind had said, rubbing a clove of garlic round a salad bowl.

Thinking of Aunt Mary not only reminded Laura how many years there were to go before she need despair, it also made her feel ashamed. She had not been waiting long and she was overreacting. She not only had Richard, whom she now adored, and Helen, who became weekly easier and more tractable, but she also had years of research and technology on her side. Although, of course, it was too soon to be thinking along those lines, wasn't it?

"Test tube, Mrs Bedford?" her doctor said, peeling off the thin plastic gloves. "I think we are jumping the gun a bit there."

"I don't want it to be too late,' Laura muttered, determined to see this through.

"I wouldn't even consider it for at least a year. You are under thirty-five, you have been off the pill for less than a year, we know there is no problem on your husband's side and can see no reason to suspect any on yours. Mrs Bedford, no doctor would even consider putting you forward for in vitro fertilisation, fertility pills or anything of that sort at the moment."

"There must be something . . ."

"Yes there is." He looked at her not unkindly. "You should take a holiday, change your job, move house. Whatever it takes to make you relax. If that doesn't work, we'll think again."

One evening, Robert came home from work with a big smile and an envelope which he slammed down on the kitchen table. "Surprise change of plan," he said.

Laura looked up from her chopping board. "What?"

"Look interested. We're off to Venice for Christmas."

"But . . ."

"But nothing. You've been looking too forlorn recently. Your parents will understand. Let's make the best of not having the children. We're going to have a really luxurious time. It's all booked. We're flying on the 23rd and are staying four nights. The Danieli, my darling."

"The Danieli?"

"Why not? You need a holiday, so let's do it in style."

Laura thought of endless reasons why they could not go, but Robert was determined to take her – and determined that she should look forward to it first. By the next evening Laura had talked to her mother, who had been briefed by Robert and was understanding to a fault, arranged for the cats to be looked after by a neighbour, imagined herself drinking Americanos in Harry's Bar and was more relaxed than she had been for a long time.

The holiday was a perfect success. Robert and Laura felt carefree, young and curiously unattached. They enjoyed old-fashioned luxury and a first view of Venice which was almost tourist-free and gleaming with a fine rain. They ate gluttonously and joyously, they bought leather in the markets and glass animals for the children at Murano, they sent postcards and drank cocktails.

On Christmas Eve they both went to Midnight Mass at St Mark's. The huge church was full to overflowing. Old ladies, heads covered with black lace, knelt and told their beads between smart Venetians and scruffy students. The Cardinal took Mass, processing down the aisle attended by an army of priests. The air was heavy with the smell of incense and the intoned prayers of hundreds of worshippers.

Although Laura did not speak Italian, she had been to Mass often enough with Aimée to know roughly what was happening. For the first time she found the Catholic service deeply moving. Her uptight English view of the vulgarity of the Roman Church was swept away by a sudden understanding. The monumental beauty of the building, the simple faith of the congregation, the thick smell of incense almost overwhelmed her, and she had to put her hand on the chair in front to steady herself. Perhaps, after all, this was the truth. Perhaps Reverend Fraser's wheezed mutterings were but a poor shadow of religious feeling.

The next morning Laura woke wondering what had overcome her the night before. But although she tried to dismiss her feelings, (even almost persuading herself that she had felt faint because she was pregnant) the emotion she had genuinely felt left a lingering sensation behind. She shelved it: it was something to be brought out and considered in private. Now was not the time.

Away from home, Laura felt more clear-headed than she had for weeks. Robert saw the change in her and was relieved. The holiday was after all quite expensive. He remained convinced that Laura's infertility was due to nothing more than tension.

Unlike most holidays, the Bedfords' short stay in Venice did them both lasting good. Six months into the marriage, with the children a perpetual emotional presence, they had not yet had a chance to consolidate. Both returned to London feeling stronger separately and together than they had yet.

6

Laura and Robert celebrated their wedding anniversary two days early – the real day was Sunday and the children would have been there. It was one of those evenings which, looked forward to too much, is an inevitable disappointment. Robert had decided dinner out at the Ritz was the right thing, Laura had hoped to be taken to the latest Andrew Lloyd-Webber with dinner afterwards. However, she could not but feel looked after as they sat sipping cocktails and looking at the menu.

She had promised herself not to mention babies or the children, resolving to make it an evening entirely theirs, so was the more surprised when Robert, taking a nut, said,

"Have you talked to Camilla recently?"

"No, not particularly. Well, nothing more than arrangement talk anyway. Why?"

Robert hesitated. "I saw Simon at lunch today. Haven't seen him for a bit – began to wonder if I'd done something to offend him. So I rang him up, fixed lunch, and after a bit of shilly-shallying we made a date."

"So what was it all about?"

"It wasn't anything I'd done; it turned out it was something he'd been doing."

"And?" Laura began to suspect the truth.

"Well, it came out – he's been having an affair with Camilla, was worried how I'd feel."

"Why did he tell you?"

"He thought the children would have, or dropped hints at least. Poor chap, he was in a fearful state."

The waiter came and took their orders. Laura, feeling they needed them, ordered another screwdriver and whisky sour.

"Do you mind?"

"I've been wondering about that all day. Yes and no, I suppose. I know I shouldn't – it wasn't until well after we divorced – not until you and I were married even, but . . ."

"Chaps don't sleep with other chaps' girls even if the other chaps don't want them any more."

"Something like that." Robert smiled. "I want her to find someone new, of course I do."

"But not someone who's just slipped out of your own front door."

"Exactly."

"Is it still going on?" Laura accepted her second drink with relief and took a long sip. She had skipped lunch and the alcohol was beginning to go to her head.

"No, and in a way this is even worse. She left Simon for another man she'd only just met. A wild card apparently, not anyone anyone knows and a painter to boot."

Laura, conscious after her affair with Frankie of how very unbohemian half the art world was, smiled. "Robert, don't be stuffy. How do you know he's not painting comissioned water-colours of village houses for old dears and retired majors?"

"Simon told me. It's orange daubs with bits of wire stuck on. And it's not the art that bothers me anyway."

"What then?"

Robert leaned forward with a very serious face. "Parties," he almost whispered. Laura could not help but laugh.

"*Parties*? Come on, Robert."

"No, listen. All night, any night, last minute. Let's drive to Dorset, I hear there's a party on. That sort of thing. I mean – she's thirty-five, not seventeen."

"Look, Robert, aren't you overreacting? The children haven't complained about anything being odd. And we have them at weekends so what does it matter if she does spend the night on the tiles? Why shouldn't she take advantage of being single?"

"These are the kinds of parties that happen midweek."

"Well, as long as there's a baby-sitter. Look, do you want me to sound out the children?"

"*No*. They're not to be used as spies. It just worries me."

"Your table is ready, sir."

Robert looked up, and forced himself back into the evening. "Thank you." He stood and looked at Laura. "I just wondered if she's mentioned anything. But come on, darling, this is our evening. Let's enjoy it."

They arrived back, both a little tipsy. It made Laura tearfully giggly, Robert steady and stolid. The answer-phone light was flashing.

"Leave it till morning," Robert suggested, but Laura was already pushing the playback button. There were two messages.

"Robert, it's Camilla. I've made a muddle. Can you ring me? Bye."

"Laura, Julia here. You'll never guess what I've gone and done. Oh, hell – I'm pregnant. Isn't it wonderful?"

A clunk and silence.

Julia's problem had always been her charm. She was not particularly pretty – anyone who bothered to analyse her face would decide that her looks would not last into old age – but she was so enormously attractive that very few found time to wonder about her charm before it seduced them. Her power lay not so much in her undeniably straight nose, good teeth or wide blue eyes as in her infectious giggle and boundless enthusiasm for life. It found her jobs, it made her friends and it bowled men over.

From an early age, she had delighted in her attraction for men, reckoning it lucky that they liked her as much as she did them. She thanked her stars that she had been born in an age when it was not only accepted that a pretty girl had plenty of lovers, but possible to have the lovers without fear of children.

She was not really promiscuous, she thought, and her friends agreed. She just took full advantage of the time and body she lived in. She believed that she would probably marry one day, and when she did no dowager duchess would be freer from scandal than she. Until then she experimented with men and drugs much as others of her circle did with ethnic cooking. And rather more successfully. She tried all kinds of men and drugs, liked some more than others, but was addicted to nothing more dangerous than tobacco.

She received more proposals of marriage than a modern girl has a right to expect, perhaps because she so clearly did not suffer from the fear of being left behind or alone. She was more like a man than a woman in her outlook, and if ever a swain so much as hinted at stability, a future, plans, she would conjure up the picture of a Volvo estate on the school run and move on. Yes, she would probably marry, but not yet.

Her mother, not knowing quite how close to the wind her daughter sailed, nevertheless despaired, and by the time Julia was thirty there were no more dinner parties arranged around local (Wiltshire) young men who might one day become JPs and who would definitely inherit a medium-sized farm near enough for Mrs Sinclair to baby-sit.

Julia reached thirty – and thirty-one and thirty-two – with no qualms and no plans to change her life. She had modified her behaviour a little, sticking to occasional lines of cocaine and giving up one-night stands, but she was happy to go on as she did. She saw friends become engaged without a twinge of envy, and listened to their tales of pregnancy with an open heart.

And then she met Viv.

Viv was ugly-attractive, with a big nose and a squishy face. He was a Great Dane of a person, with the same controlled strength and soppy eyes as the dogs. He was brought to dinner with Julia's mother by some neighbours, and even Mrs Sinclair did not give him a second glance as possible son-in-law material. It was not just his ugliness, his very goodness set him apart, and Mrs Sinclair thought she knew enough about her daughter to know how far she would run from that.

She could not have been more wrong. Julia flirted with Viv through habit, because he was the only man there within forty years of her age, and was piqued at his lack of response. By the end of the evening she was sure he liked her, but could not understand why there had been no flicker of sexual interest from him. She had already seen beyond the ugly face and was beginning to find him attractive, although he was very different from the well-suited men who usually took her out.

She helped her mother dry up the plates in silence. Mrs Sinclair did not comment until Julia had put the glasses in the wrong cupboard twice.

"Are you all right, darling? You're very quiet. Do go to bed if you want. I'll finish on my own."

"Of course not. Why don't we have a nightcap before we go to bed? I'm not very tired."

Mrs Sinclair was surprised: Julia looked exhausted and they very rarely sat up together, but she agreed and poured two small glasses of whisky.

"So why was Viv staying with the Robertses?" Julia asked, curling her legs under her and staring at the fireplace.

"He's Jim's godson and Sarah was telling me everyone's rather worried about him."

"Why? He doesn't seem the sort to cause a moment's worry to a saint."

"That's exactly it. His parents were worried he was going to enter the priesthood, but now it looks even worse – he's thinking of going off to Africa."

The logic baffled Julia for a moment. "Is he a Catholic?"

"No, C of E. So at least he could have married if he'd been a priest."

Julia knew better than to bother to point out how many single women lived in Africa. "I don't get it."

"Well, the mother's not very well, but she's been saying that for years. He's an only child, illegitimate, and she's always been very protective of him – bad chest when he was little – that sort of thing. So now he's decided that he must go off and teach in Africa. As if a London comprehensive wasn't bad enough."

Julia's opinion of Viv began to waver. He sounded terribly dreary, put like that. Where could the jokes be in someone with such an earnest view of life? Julia thought jokes were very important.

"Could he be gay?"

"Julia!" Mrs Sinclair started to look shocked, but thought better of it. After all, she had been married and divorced by the time she was Julia's age and heaven knew young people were more sophisticated now. "No. At least, if he is, either Jim and Sarah don't know or are being very cagey about it. Actually, now I think of it, last time he was down here he brought a girl with him. Jim and Sarah assumed he must be going to marry her but when nothing was said realised he was just being modern."

"Perhaps he has a broken heart," Julia suggested, and her mother laughed.

"You're being very romantically minded. Don't tell me you took to him?"

"Mummy, honestly, do you think he's my type?" Julia drained her drink and stood up. "The whisky's done for me, I'm off to bed. Goodnight." Her mother returned the kiss, but as she turned out the lights and followed her daughter upstairs, she realised the question had been left unanswered.

Viv rang Julia a week later and took her to the theatre. Although the play was a farce, the evening was a sedate affair. The comedy was bad, dinner was in a not very expensive or particularly good fish restaurant in Covent Garden. Viv was not at all like most of the men who took Julia out. He was dressed as casually as though it were a weekday supper in the country, he made no effort to keep up a flow of jokes and stories, his charm was too subtle to be at all intentional. They talked calmly and *quietly* and as though they were very old friends. As Julia let herself into the house she wondered why she had not been bored.

Within a month, Viv had silently shelved plans to go to Africa and was applying for teaching jobs in north London. Julia was uncharacteristically shy about introducing him to her friends – she was convinced by now that she liked him, but was still trying to work out why. If she had any inkling as to what was going on inside her, she did not want well-meaning friends to notice or explain.

After eight months, Viv asked Julia to marry him. She refused, saying she would move into his flat but could or would make no promises. He refused to let her change her address without marrying him until he decided that it might be the only way in which she could be made to realise – or admit to herself – that he was the man for her. He never discussed how or why he had changed his plans to travel, but Julia was aware of what he had done and was frightened by it. She would not go to church with him, but she stopped mocking religion and even tried not to use "Christ" as an expletive.

No sooner had Julia moved in with Viv than he began making whimsical speeches about children. Julia was adamantly against the idea, but vaguely promised to think about it when she was thirty-five. After all, that seemed so far ahead it would almost certainly never happen. And if it did, who was to say she would even be with Viv?

He, having planted the idea, said nothing more. Julia being Julia began to wonder if maybe the idea was such a bad one. She said nothing to Viv but sometimes she forgot to take the pill. Often she forgot. She only occasionally remembered. Somehow, the bigger the chance of something going wrong, the more exciting sex became. And the knowledge that the danger was a secret from Viv (which it was not at all) made it all the more delightful.

She was not worried when her period was late. It had happened before. She was not even especially worried when she realised that she must be pregnant. (If she were honest with herself she was by now pleased.) The sight of Viv's face when she told him (in an aside from discussing summer holiday plans) was what put the fear of God into her. The pure delight which flooded his face the second after she told him she had half-expected: the moment of triumph that he could not at first disguise from her gave her pause. So was Viv, good, kind, Christian Viv, really just like all the other men who sought to control women by one means or another? How could he triumph at such a moment? And was the triumph over her, or at his virility?

"Of course, I won't have it," she said, deliberately using the first person singular. His look of horror was revenge enough, if revenge were all she was after.

"But it's ours – it's not even an accident, Julia." Viv took a breath to control himself. He knew better than to play into Julia's hands by overreacting. "You said you'd become sloppy with the pill. You must have wanted it – or half of you must have."

"Oh, Viv, you know me. I didn't want the baby. I just liked the danger, I liked the feeling that I was dicing with death. I'm sorry, Viv, it went too far."

"You were dicing with *life*, Julia, not death. For once in your life you should have thought. It's not a game. I'm not a game – neither is the baby."

"For God's sake, don't go all Christian on me. Viv. I'm sorry if it's upset you but in the end it's not up to you."

She trotted out the tired old arguments. My body – my right to choose – my life – not able to survive on its own – man's culpability. She looked at Viv's face and heard the noises coming out of her mouth. And even as she spoke she was frightened. Frightened that this time she had gone too far, that she might be losing Viv as she spoke. She wished he knew she herself barely believed what she was saying, hoping he would be able to give her the time to apologise, to admit at last that she loved him, that maybe this baby was more than a possibility. But she could not stop the cruel, pointless words pouring from her mouth. It was as though she were in a play, as though she, along with thousands of other modern young women, had been predestined to spout this tripe because they had won the right to spout it. And it was not until she had taken her place on the stage and begun saying the set piece that she had ever considered the meaning of the words.

Viv sat silent under the onslaught. When Julia had finished, he hugged her and she cried. And he knew he had won.

Laura and Julia met in the wine bar that was their usual haunt. Both were subdued, Julia toying with a cigarette packet in an attempt not to smoke and with rings under her eyes, Laura feeling that champagne was the last thing she wanted but that it would be unfriendly not to order it.

"Well, it's all pretty complicated. I've never believed that people *could* get pregnant by mistake in this day and age, but there you go."

"But you're both pleased?"

"I was horrified at first." Julia could not bring herself to be entirely truthful. "In fact, I was determined not to go through with it. Why should I? It didn't seem right that our whole lives should be disrupted by one night's carelessness. And we could always have another one later. But when I realised that one of the reasons I was anti it was because I was so cross about the summer – I mean beach holidays with a belly really aren't on, are they? I began to think again. And then one morning I woke up and suddenly thought *I'm pregnant. I'm going to have a baby* and I was so ridiculously happy about it I knew I had no choice."

"And Viv?"

"It's what he wanted, you know that." Julia did not elaborate.

"So what next?"

"What do you mean? Bloated bosoms and huge stomach followed by sleepless nights and school fees, I suppose. We're going to be dead broke of course – we've decided to have three in a row now we're having one."

Laura laughed. "You're not exactly consistent, Julia. Less than a year ago you were looking horrified at the idea of having a baby, now you're halfway to being the ideal Weetabix family. No, I meant is Viv going to make an honest woman of you?"

Julia chewed an olive before answering. "I really don't know. He wants to. The minute we decided to keep the baby he said we should get married, but I'm not so sure. Apart from anything else, don't you think we'd look rather silly?"

"Not at all. It's sillier *not* to if that's your only reason."

"I suppose so. Of course, Mummy would love it, but that's not really a reason either."

They sat in silence for a while, thinking. Laura was sure that her friend would end up by conforming to her conventional middle-class background; Julia was wishing she could find a way to give in gracefully.

"Anyway, what's your news? I haven't seen you for ages. How are the children?"

"They're fine. Their mother's been making life a bit difficult for us, but that's only to be expected. She was furious when Robert found out that she'd been having an affair with Simon Eustace – remember him? The handsome, dopey one – and has been taking revenge on him ever since."

"How is it Robert's fault?"

"God knows. And he took the whole thing very well and didn't even bring it up. He's much more worried about her new boyfriend who does sound a bit wild. Sasha Limpnakoff, a painter."

"I've heard of him. He's nearly famous, if you know what I mean. But exhibits in Portobello Road rather than Cork Street.

I met him once too. From what you say about Camilla I'm very surprised he's her type – he's incredibly handsome, drooping eyelids, even a scar. But his life is as far from Camilla's as the moon from the sun. He locks himself away to work all day, then parties all night – and he barely opens his mouth except to mutter something which from anyone else would sound hopelessly banal but from his glorious mouth sounds deeply profound. You said Camilla shops all day and spends her evenings at Chelsea dinner parties. How on earth did they meet?"

"At a private view, apparently. Friends of friends kind of thing. Robert's worried because they go to too many parties."

Both girls laughed, but Laura went on. "Mind you, it does sound more serious than I thought at first. Richard's taken to talking a great deal about someone called Flap. It turns out Flap is Sasha's thirteen-year-old daughter and that she often baby-sits for them. Well, you know how Robert fusses about the children at the best of times – he nearly had a fit about a painter's thirteen-year-old baby-sitting his ducklings. I calmed him down and made him promise not to make a scene with Camilla, but then Richard said how nice it was that Flap reads them a story when they get up as well as when they go to bed."

"Implying?"

"I thought that it meant Flap stayed there at weekends sometimes and enjoyed mummying them. It does, but sometimes Camilla and Sasha go out and don't come back, leaving Flap in charge overnight."

"Oh dear."

"Oh dear exactly. So that did it. Robert lost his temper, Camilla lost hers. She rang and accused me of trying to alienate the children from her, which is totally unfair, so I lost my temper too. That made Robert lose his again. All this in endless telephone calls. The children turned up last weekend in a dreadful state. God knows what she'd been saying, we didn't try to find out. Now the summer holidays are coming up and she's threatening not to let us have them for our half. She says it's bad enough my poisoning them against her three in four weekends, but I could do irreparable harm in three weeks and she won't have it. It's been a nightmare. I don't know what this Sasha does to her, but she's turned totally paranoid."

"Or guilty. Do you want another drink? I'm going to get some orange juice," Julia interrupted.

"I'll have the same." Julia waved to the waiter and ordered the juices. When she looked back at Laura, her face was worried.

"Can she do that – stop you having the children?"

"I don't think so. But the trouble is that Robert's given way to her too often. Weekends here and there, last Christmas. We had them at Easter but she whittled down the days till there was almost nothing left. It's odd really. You'd have thought all this partygoing would make her want to keep her weekends free rather than the other way round. I think she does it more to get at us than because she wants to see the children."

"What does Robert say?"

"Even he is getting fed up. The thing is that although they have joint custody, she has care and control and therefore ultimately has the say. He's meant to have three in four weekends and half the holidays, which is pretty good compared to some people's access, but if she could prove we were unfit . . ."

"Don't be silly, Laura, how can she? All that's changed is that Robert's married you, and you don't have a stain on your character. Or not that I know of – and I've tried to lead you into sinful ways often enough."

"Well, we'll see. I think what she'd really like to succeed in doing is to change the holidays around – we've rented a cottage in France for three weeks and she'd love to sabotage that plan. We tried to keep the cottage secret from her for as long as possible, but you can't tell the children not to say things to their mother, so that was that. By the way, I wanted to ask if you and Viv would like to come and stay with us there at the beginning of August. Would you?"

Laura had indeed been planning to ask Julia to stay with them, until she heard her plans to go to Kenya. When she learned of Julia's pregnancy one of her first thoughts – after the wave of jealousy that left her feeling physically sick – was that now perhaps Julia and Viv would come with them to France. Then she was unsure whether she actually wanted them to come: she felt almost betrayed by Julia's pregnancy, and it had taken an enormous effort to rise above her feelings and carry her original, kinder, impulse through.

"I think that would be lovely. We were thinking of going on safari and beach-bumming in Kenya, but now that doesn't seem such a good idea. Can I talk it over with Viv?"

"Of course," said Laura, signalling for the bill and taking her chequebook from her bag. Although you may be honeymooning by then – who can tell?"

One of Robert's yearly treats was Henley Regetta. He had rowed for Oxford and his win of the Diamond Sculls over twenty years earlier was still talked about – and not only by him. So every July out came the pink ("cerise, Laura, not pink") socks and the boater and the bottles of champagne and off he went.

The year before had been Laura's first. Bluff chaps in multi-coloured blazers had clapped Robert on the back, congratulating him on his new wife. Older men, shoulders stooped and withered in blazers that had proclaimed their manly strength fifty years earlier, bought Laura Pimms and told her old racing yarns.

Surprisingly enough she had enjoyed it, and was looking forward to this year's Regatta. Robert would go every day, but Laura would only join him at the weekend. She knew the form now, which always made things easier, and with a light heart had bought a new dress and hat for Ladies' Day. Robert had suggested she ask a friend to come too, hinting that he did not think Melanie would really enjoy the day, so Laura had invited Charlotte for the Saturday and Ferdy and Aimée for the Sunday.

Charlotte had been overjoyed. "Husband-hunting ground," she said simply. "Honestly, I don't know what's wrong with me. I can't even get a boyfriend these days. Two dates and it's either bed or goodbye. They don't even give me a chance any more. Is there anything you should tell me? Personal problems?"

"You should relax," said Laura, wondering who had told her the same, then remembering with a rush. "Well, it should be fun. Although when you see the oarsmen you'll have no eyes for anyone old enough for good husband material."

Robert and Laura set off early on Saturday morning. The boot was filled with icebags and bottles of champagne, smoked salmon and heavy fruit cake. The picnic hamper was on the back seat, the hats were on the picnic hamper, the sun was shining. Robert looked very fetching in his blazer, pressed white trousers and faintly spivish co-respondents, Laura was in a pale green fitted linen suit and looked her summery best. They were in high spirits which even the traffic could not dampen. Laura played spot the Henley-bound and pointed out silly hats, Robert checked his watch, swearing the journey was taking even longer than usual and debating whether they would have time to stop off for a drink at the Flowerpot. "Which I swear is your favourite pub in England," Laura teased. Robert smiled, pleased Laura was in such a good mood. They arrived in plenty of time and Robert was greeted by the car-park attendant, Barney, like an old friend.

Charlotte had spent the night before with a friend who lived nearby and arrived at their parking space as they were unpacking the boot.

"What fun," she said, handing Robert a bottle of champagne and kissing Laura. "And what a lovely day. Do you think we'll be allowed to swim in the river between races?" Robert was in too good a humour to rise and kissed her in welcome.

"Do you know Timmy and Miranda Reed? They're coming too today – they're good fun, know the form, been coming for years. And Simon Eustace – used to row with me at Oxford."

Charlotte shook her head. "I think I met Simon at your wedding but the Reeds not, and new friends are just what I need. The sun comes out to shine more clearly on the rut I'm in. I've got to do something different – any ideas send me a postcard."

"And meanwhile you're starting with Henley."

"That's it."

"What could be better?" Robert handed Laura and Charlotte their Stewards' Enclosure tickets, looking dubiously at Charlotte's skirt.

"*On* the knee," the girls chorused. "But only just," Charlotte admitted. "Still I'm sure you'll agree I'm looking perfectly proper."

"You are. The Reeds won't be here for a half-hour or so – they know the parking number and I'll leave the keys and guest badges for the Enclosure with Barney in case they want anything out of the car. Eustace will have his own badge, of course. Ready for a Pimms?"

"Yes, please." Neither girl drank much in the day as a rule, but Henley was different. So with the car locked up, chairs and table set out on the grass, champagne left in the icebox in the shade, they strolled off towards the Enclosure.

Robert pointed out the regulars as they went, nodding to the old major sitting covered by a rug and nursing a gin and tonic, gently poking fun at the owners of a huge Rolls-Royce whose table was laid with a white cloth and silver, greeting a liver-and-white spaniel tied to a car fender, ("he comes every year but I've never learned his owner's name"), touching his boater to a group of women being given champagne beside an open Saab. "Now there's a chap that takes it seriously," he approved. "Same space every year, proper form." His soul mate, a character straight from Dornford Yates, waved. "Come over for a drink sometime." "Love to," and on they went.

Although the first race had yet to begin, the Enclosure was already filling up, at this stage mostly with men. They walked through the Enclosure to the boat tents where muscled youths hung around chatting. A few nodded at Robert, presumably in recognition of his blazer, and he wished them luck. Oarsmen in tracksuits queued for a cooked breakfast outside the boatmen's tent. "Care for a sausage?" Robert asked, but the girls, slightly to Robert's disappointment, preferred to return to the Bridge Bar for their promised Pimms.

They waited for Robert by the river, under the trees, feeling faintly guilty at the prospect of drinking before eleven, but knowing it was all part of "the form". Robert arrived from the bar, carrying a pint and two halves of brimming Pimms. "Happy Henley," he said, lifting his glass. "It looks like being a lovely day."

They drank thirstily. "The joy of Pimms," said Laura, "is that at first it doesn't taste like a drink."

"Thanks so much for asking me," said Charlotte. "I've always wondered what went on here." She watched the crowd for a minute. "What's so nice about it is how everyone is gathered together determined to have fun. No bad temper or grouches allowed. Like a really good wedding, I suppose, although without all that danger of ex-girlfriends and broken hearts."

"Maybe no broken hearts, but I bet you any money you like that at least one of us bumps into an old flame during the course of the day."

"A fiver," said Robert promptly. "But you must both play fair and admit if you do meet an old boyfriend."

"You're on." Laura and Robert shook hands, sloshing Pimms onto the rail.

"So – sorry for asking – but what actually happens?" Charlotte asked. "Apart from anything else, if we're drinking already I can see I'm going to have to pace myself."

Robert looked a little dumbfounded at the question and Laura came to his rescue.

"Well, you have a drink, and bump into your old boyfriend, and go back to the car and have a drink there—"

"Help yourself anytime," Robert interrupted.

"—then maybe watch a race or two. There are deck chairs by the river."

"And I forgot to give you the tickets but I've booked seats in the stand for you."

"Robert and Simon can go in the floating stand by the finish because they're members of Stewards', but we mere mortals are not so privileged. If we're really lucky Robert'll buy us a drink in Leander – the clubhouse for the grand and glorious in rowing. They'll disappear occasionally and leave us to our own devices."

"Which are?"

"Oh, eyeing up fit young men in Lycra and drinking."

Charlotte looked a little bemused, but politely said, "I see."

"Then there's a picnic at the car at lunchtime when we all meet up and then the afternoon when it all happens again."

"I see," Charlotte repeated.

Laura laughed. "Don't look so panicky. It's actually great fun. The other game is counting Laura Ashley dresses. They really come out at Henley."

The announcer started talking over the PA system, and Robert said excitedly, "The first race has begun. Stay there, I forgot to get programmes," and rushed off.

• Sophia Watson

"I don't want to be rude, but nothing much seems to happen," muttered Charlotte.

"It doesn't, but does that really matter? Honestly, I felt like you last year but you'd be surprised how fast the time goes – unless it's raining."

Robert reappeared clutching programmes. "I know what you forgot to mention – we can walk up to Temple Island and watch the *start* of a race," he said triumphantly.

Lunch was a genial affair, Timmy as expansive as ever, Simon so relieved he had not forfeited his friendship with Robert that he tried really hard and even made a few good jokes. By then, everyone was drunk enough to be feeling on a high without danger of feeling ill later.

"No more drinking after lunch," Laura declared, accepting a glass of champagne. "Anyway, I've some races to watch."

"Do you know," Miranda Reed said, taking a slice from the Paxton and Whitfield pork and apple pie, "this is I suppose the ninth year I've been to Henley and I've never yet seen a race."

Laura looked at Robert, who seemed unfazed by the announcement. "But what do you do?" she asked.

"Oh, I don't know, have a drink, meet friends, sit in the sun." Laura looked at Charlotte and quickly away for fear of catching a fit of the teenage giggles. They had early decided that the way to enjoy the day was arbitrarily to choose a team and then cheer them on to glory. "It's like watching the racing on the television except we're outside," Charlotte had said earlier. "No betting, but you can still convince yourself you are."

The six of them sat happily in the sunshine, eating and drinking and filled with wellbeing. They were joined briefly by acquaintances of Robert's who came to say hello, stopped for a drink and wandered off again. A man who had once coxed for Eton, Robert's accountant whose company took a hospitality tent every year ("Not the same thing at all, but it wouldn't be polite to tell him," said Robert as he left), and Louise from Laura's office – they all passed by, took a drink and left.

Finally, feeling full and dozy, Laura decided to make a move. "I'm off to listen to the band," she announced, picking up her hat. "Anyone interested?" Charlotte and Simon said they would go and buy coffee and brandy, the Reeds wanted to stay where they were. So Robert and Laura strolled off arm-in-arm together.

"Is Charlotte enjoying herself?" asked Robert.

"Yes, I'm sure she is. I don't know what she was expecting, but she's thrown herself into it. And of course the sunshine helps."

"Oh, heavens, it looks like I owe you a fiver," Robert muttered, stopping in his tracks.

"Aha. Who is she, which one?" Laura asked, looking around. She didn't have to look far. Sitting with their backs against the bandstand, ignoring both the loud oompah of the band and the feet of passers-by, were Camilla and a man. Their heads were close together and whatever they were saying totally absorbed them.

"What *are* they doing?" Robert was horror-struck. Camilla had been to Henley with him for years. She must know by now it was not good form to sit on the grass. On the riverbank, maybe, but only just, only if you were still young and thin and pretty *and* watching a race.

"Oughtn't we to go and say hello?" Laura wondered.

"What has she done with the children?" Laura remembered the conversation she had heard between Robert and Camilla on that subject. She had agreed to have the children for Henley weekend, adding how relieved she was when July came without her having to "doll up, lengthen my hemline and drink warm champagne". "In fact she loved it," Robert had told Laura. "Or if not she's a much better actress than anyone would have suspected."

He tightened his grip on Laura's arm. "I'll talk to her later," he said, turning away.

But he was too late. Camilla stood, caught sight of Robert and – there was no other word for it – yelled, "Robert! What a surprise!"

If Charlotte's skirt was just on the knee, Camilla's touched hers only by a fraction. She looked creased and messy, with chipped nail varnish and unbrushed hair. For the first time since they had met, Laura felt she looked the better and was almost glad of the meeting.

"Robert, I'm glad to have bumped into you. This is Sasha Limpnakoff, a dear friend of mine. Sasha, this is my ex-husband Robert Bedford and his wife Laura."

Neither Robert nor Laura could find anything to say. Faced with the much-discussed Sasha they could only stare.

He was undoubtedly the best-looking man Laura had ever seen, and the least conventional. His hair was almost black, long, thick and tied into a neat ponytail with a patterned chiffon scarf. His eyes, dark brown and long-lashed, would not meet Laura's but flitted busily around taking in nothing. The scar Julia had mentioned was a thin deep curve from temple to chin, but managed to enhance rather than mar his looks. A hooked nose and square chin gave him the appearance of a matinée idol.

While Laura was taking in his face, Robert was staring at his clothes. Over massive white bell-bottoms he wore a knee-length multicoloured tapestry coat and immaculate white blouse. A piece of chiffon matching the one in his hair was wrapped around his waist. A cross between a stage pirate and a designer hippie, he was as unexpected as he was beautiful. There was really very little to say.

Robert said it. "Is this your first visit to the Regatta?" he asked, grittily polite.

"Absolutely not. I rowed for School and have come every year since I left." Sasha's voice had an upper-class drawl which neither Robert nor Laura was expecting. Robert was totally taken aback; Laura, entranced despite herself by this vision, could still not help but laugh at Robert's discomfiture.

Robert looked at Laura crossly and turned to Camilla. "Where are the children?"

"Oh, I left them next door with Mrs Bartholomew. You know how she's always got on with them." Camilla's tone was flip, her eyes shifted past Robert as she spoke. Robert opened his mouth, looked at Sasha again and changed his mind.

"Actually, I was hoping we'd bump into you," Camilla went on. "I've been meaning to talk to you about the summer. Do you mind if I change the arrangements?"

Laura's heart sank. What were they to do with a cottage in France for three weeks with no children? The children's friends would have to be put off and it would be too late to ask more of their own: it was the first week of July and holidays were booked, plans made.

"Camilla, don't you think . . ." she started, but stopped at a look from Robert.

"I don't think we'd better talk about this now, Camilla," he said. "I'm not in the mood for an argument."

"I thought you'd be pleased." Camilla was huffy. "I couldn't have been sweeter when *you* went and got married. The least you could do—"

"Married?" Robert and Laura spoke together, Robert looking at Camilla, Laura at Sasha, identical expressions on their faces.

"Sasha and I are getting married at the end of the month. We're planning a long honeymoon – Kathmandu, actually – and I wanted to talk to you about arrangements for the children."

Laura could not take it in at first; she looked at Robert who was beaming, but her own immediate reaction was more selfish. Camilla – married – Kathmandu – Sasha . . . Where did that leave Robert and her? What about the children? Oh *please* let France still be on. She had not realised until then quite how much she had been looking forward to the holiday.

"How long will you be away?" asked Robert.

"About three months. It'll mean you keeping them all the summer. You may think it's a lot to ask but quite honestly they're your children too. Of course, Mummy says she'll have them as much as she can, but I do want to avoid leaving them with an au pair. If you refuse to have them I can get one, I suppose, but it'll be difficult so late and you know these foreign girls . . ."

Laura looked from Camilla to Robert. With everything his ex-wife said his smile widened, and Laura felt a corresponding relief. France would still happen, and more than France. They were to have the children with them for weeks, perhaps months. Oh, help, how would it be organised? Richard was only part time at nursery school, Helen came out of school at three fifteen, she herself did not leave work until at the very earliest five thirty . . .

Robert was only delighted, with no thought at all for practicalities. "An au pair? Don't be ridiculous. Of course we'll have them for the whole time." In his excitement Robert hugged both his wives and almost kissed Sasha. "Congratulations. Many congratulations. Camilla, I've got to get back to my guests. But come round for a drink next week and we'll sort everything out. How wonderful."

The two couples separated, Camilla and Sasha in search of a drink, Robert and Camilla to walk back to the car. Robert was overwhelmed with happiness at the prospect of having the children to himself for three whole months, and Laura too found herself delighted.

It was only as they arrived back at the car that Robert's delight turned to the worry Laura had been expecting.

"Laura, darling – what do you think about Sasha?"

7 $\int$

Robert's worries about the suitability of Sasha as a stepfather to his children did not diminish but in the end there was nothing he could do. The children seemed to like him in an apathetic way, and they adored his daughter Flap. Laura reasoned that just because his clothes were eccentric and his profession unconventional he could not automatically be labelled immoral. She pointed out that a happy Camilla should mean a reasonable Camilla, an argument that did not convince Robert, and that above all there would be three months of having the children to himself.

He was by nature a silent man, but Robert brooded a great deal during the weeks following the news of Camilla's remarriage. At times he told himself that he was being overprotective of both the children and indeed Camilla, that Sasha was, of course, not his type but that did not mean he would not be kind to his family. He thought not only about Sasha but about himself, amazed at how little he must know about the woman with whom he had lived for so long. It baffled him entirely that she should find Sasha more than passingly attractive, that she could really be considering spending the rest of her life with this fop. Their last years together had been for the most part bitter and tormented, but there had been happy times: at the beginning when he had just been setting out and she had encouraged him ever onwards, always waiting for him with a smile and an idea for fun. She had been a refreshing change at the end of a hard day's work, a light touch in an otherwise unremittingly hard grind. Perhaps, he now thought sadly, her encouragement had only been for material gain and social status, perhaps the ideas for outings and jaunts had just been the thin end of her new party-crazed wedge.

Camilla and Laura were two very different women: at least on the surface. Robert wondered a little unhappily about Laura. For the first time he asked himself whether the vulnerability that had at first attracted him to her might not turn into something more pernicious. Pray God she was not as neurotic as Camilla, pray God that the longing for a child, which he could see was overtaking her, would not obsess her entirely. Robert thought too about his children. Like a child himself, he counted the days until they were coming to Parson's Green, but at the back of his mind was always the fear that their living full time with him and Laura would make her own childlessness the harder to bear, and might even turn her against them.

More than any single thing, he wanted Laura to be happy. Happy with him, happy with his children, happy with or without her own. His years with Camilla had been tempestuous from the start, even the early, loving days had been punctuated with tremendous rows and (on her part) saucepan throwing. His love for Laura was much calmer but ran much deeper. Perhaps he should say so more often, he thought, but then, being an Englishman, did not.

Instead, he occasionally voiced his worries about Sasha and let Laura calm them as best she could. Camilla finally came down to earth for long enough to have a serious conversation with Robert about her future. She told him that Sasha earned enough to support them all if need be, although, of course, Robert would continue to pay child support. Sasha was as well known in his world as Robert was in his, and that even if the worse came to the worst and fickle fashion in art changed, he also had a not insubstantial private income. "So Camilla's not exactly fallen for rough trade after all," Laura said, then wished she had not.

Sasha was to sell his flat and he would move in with her, so that the children's routine would not even be disrupted. Flap was coming too, of course: her mother was a subject never mentioned.

"And as for the parties that worry you so much – well,

before too long we'll just be another staid married couple," Camilla reassured Robert. She even went so far as to move her wedding forward to fit in with the children's holiday plans.

"So you see, it'll be all right," Laura promised after Camilla had gone and the children were safely in bed.

Camilla wanted the children at her wedding, and invited Robert and Laura too. Laura took the children shopping for presents, but talked Robert out of accepting their own invitation. It was not just that she would feel uncomfortable, she also had a feeling that all Robert's worries would resurface if he met Camilla's new friends.

The children came back glum. "It wasn't *proper*," Helen said sadly, sitting in her bath and staring at the taps. "There weren't any bridesmaids."

"Does that mean they're not really married?" Richard looked up from his plastic scuba diver.

"No, they're definitely married," Laura said firmly. "You only have bridesmaids when you get married in a church."

"And a white dress?"

"Yes, usually."

"And bells?"

"Yes."

"Why didn't they go to church then? *I'll* be married in a church."

Laura wished Robert were there to help her out. What would he want her to say? There was no choice but to plough on with the truth. She thought of the Children's Problems series of books Howard and Neville published and tried to remember *Mummy and Daddy Get a Divorce*.

"If you've been married before, you don't get married in a church. Your Mummy and Daddy were married in a church, with white dresses and everything. I expect Mummy's got some photographs she could show you. But then because they weren't as happy as they thought they'd be, they separated. Then when you find someone else you get married in a different way, that's all. But you're still married."

Helen thought about this for a moment. "So you didn't have a white dress when you married Daddy?"

Laura was glad her mother was not hearing this conversation. "No."

Helen's face lit up with relief. "Well, that's all right then. *You're* properly married."

As Robert had been due to have the children for only the first half of their summer holidays, they had left only a few days between the schools breaking up and their setting off for France. Laura spent those days making lists and shopping. She brought back from work six new books each for the children, bought two packs of cards, a games compendium and took them to choose their new bathing suits. She bought sun hats and Ambre Solaire and guidebooks and mosquito repellent. She bought Weetabix and baked beans and tomato ketchup "just in case". She bought herself two new bathing suits and four new cotton dresses and one rather grander dress in case they ever found a baby-sitter. She bought Robert and Richard matching Bermuda shorts and Helen a divine sundress. She spent an absolute fortune. Robert smiled and gave her a cheque.

Finally, with the cats safely at Oriana's, the note out for the milkman and all the plugs pulled out of their sockets, the car was loaded up and they were on their way.

The children sang "She'll be coming round the mountain" for half-an-hour and then began bickering.

The holiday had begun.

Laura and Robert had been married for over a year, but for one reason and another had never before been away on holiday with the children. Now this summer holiday was to extend into three months of day-to-day living and Laura was in two minds about what lay ahead.

In one sense she was glad. She knew how happy it would make Robert and by now she too was genuinely fond of her stepchildren. A part of her also thought that being part of a real family would unlock whatever it was that was blocking her fertility, although the more logical Laura denied this.

On the other hand, she was frankly afraid of what lay ahead. Weekends and even holidays were one thing, but would she really be able to cope with work sandwiched between school runs, supper every night on time, no more spontaneous drinks after work or cinema outings, the search for baby-sitters. (Sasha had left Flap's number at her grandmother's, but Laura doubted that Robert would approve of that.) This was being a stepmother in earnest.

Before all that were these looked-forward-to holidays, and the whole family was resolved on enjoying the three weeks ahead. Laura occasionally worried that the children would miss Camilla and play up, but she put such thoughts behind her.

The children ran wild on the ferry, totally disappearing for long enough to throw Robert into a panic, but returning triumphant just as he was threatening to have the boat turned back. At last they were put into the cabin Robert had booked, and Richard sobbed himself to sleep after being refused permission to sleep in the top bunk.

Robert locked the door on them and joined Laura in the Monet bar, a dark room furnished with plastic bamboo chairs, plastic plants and plastic trelliswork. They sat sipping whisky and watching the other travellers.

"You get a real cross section here," Robert said, spilling peanuts onto the green plastic floor.

"Only the middle classes down. Some people fly first class." Laura was tired and thinking about bed, but they had agreed to give the children a chance to fall asleep first.

A man who looked like a teacher was playing cards with his pregnant wife; two teenagers held hands and drank beer; two girls giggled over their rum and cokes as they eyed up a gang of young men with T-shirts cut low over their pectorals and under their arms. "If this is a cross section of English society I'm moving to Australia," Laura said.

"You might have a point." Robert looked gloomily at the T-shirts. "Still, at least we've got a cabin. Let's take a walk outside and visit the duty free: then we can get some sleep. We've a long drive tomorrow."

By the time they had arrived at their cottage late the following night, Laura was beginning to wish they had stuck to Brittany, or better still, Gloucestershire. But the cottage looked clean and comfortable, and the caretaker who handed over the keys was friendly and had gone so far as to make the beds. The children were too tired and cross even to think of exploring: Helen expressed mild fears about spiders, Richard hoped for snakes and they were both asleep.

"And tomorrow it really starts," Robert said, hugging Laura at the bottom of the narrow wooden stairs. "Do you know this is the first time we've taken the children somewhere entirely new where they haven't been with Camilla. Darling, I do hope you enjoy it."

"I will," she promised. "Tomorrow. But till then I can't even think. God bless," and leaving Robert to turn out the lights she almost crawled up to bed.

The next day they woke early. Laura threw back the shutters to see miles and miles of nothing but countryside. The cottage was on the crest of a hill, surrounded by fields full of searing yellow sunflowers. Far away a range of almost black hills met the brilliant blue sky. There was no smudge of white cloud, no breath of a breeze. The air was clear and sweet, somewhere nearby a lonely bird warbled its foolish song. It was going to be a very hot day and their holiday was going to be a success.

Robert turned over in bed and grunted. "Turn out the light."

"It's the sun. Come and look." A thumping came through the wall. "Come on, the children are awake."

They burst into the bedroom. "Laura, we can't open our window things. We can't see."

"Shutters. I'll help you. Get Daddy out of bed then we'll all get dressed and look around the house and see what we need."

That week, which had been set aside for the four of them, passed in hours. None of Laura's fears became reality and the family settled into a happy and relaxed *modus vivendi*. No one was sunburned or sick, the children spent their days in the pool and their evenings bicycling along the cart tracks that surrounded the house. The board games stayed untouched in their cellophane wrappers and the books were only read for ten minutes at bedtime before the children fell into a deep sleep. Laura and Robert had the evenings to themselves, and sat out in the dusk drinking long cool drinks and wishing they had booked the house for longer. One evening, the caretaker agreed to baby-sit and they went out to dinner in the local town where they ate cassoulet, the local speciality, and returned home slightly drunk on Armagnac.

The night before their first guests were due to arrive, Laura and Robert sat by the swimming pool looking out over the valley drinking gin and bitter lemon and relishing their last evening of privacy.

"The children are enjoying this holiday more than any other we've ever been on," Robert said. "And that's thanks to you. It's been wonderful, Laura."

"And will continue to be I hope," she answered. "Although it's been so perfect so far that something's bound to go wrong."

"Don't say that." Robert touched the arm of his deck chair.

"No. Well, I've loved it too. I must admit I was worried, but it couldn't have been better. You know, when we're together like this it really feels like a family. I'm not saying the children think I'm their mother, but somehow it feels as though they've forgotten that I'm not."

"I know what you mean. I don't know why we didn't all go away together before."

"It wouldn't have been right last year. The children – Helen anyway – were too wary and I'd have tried too hard. That's what I mean about being a family at last." She took a sip and paused. Robert's mood was calm, the atmosphere was perfect. Tomorrow it could all change. She took a breath. "You know, I've been thinking."

She waited for a response, but Robert said nothing. She saw him tense up and knew he was expecting her to talk about babies again. But although her plan was connected with babies, she had sworn to herself that she would not trouble Robert with her fears on that score during the holiday. With no lead from him, she had no choice but to jump straight in.

"I've been thinking of giving up work. Or at any rate working from home. I wouldn't earn as much – for a while at least – but I'm sure I could manage to pick up quite a lot of work in time. I've been in the business for years, after all."

Robert had relaxed but still said nothing. He stirred his ice with his finger, giving nothing away.

"Could we afford it?" Laura asked.

At last he looked at her. "Why?"

"You know how fed up I've been there recently. I was thinking of applying to move somewhere else, but the jobs in the *Bookseller* all look the same. I'd earn maybe a couple of thousand more a year, see some new faces, then just get embroiled with another set of office politics. I don't ever want to be a managing editor or director anywhere – what I like is editing. So, as I don't want to be on the hierarchy ladder, why not get out altogether? Neville would certainly employ me and I met someone from Walker Books the other day who said he was sure I'd get work from them. A couple of my books have done very well recently, and I know at least four of my authors who would want me to go on editing them and would put pressure on Neville's to use me."

"How long have you been thinking of this?"

The desire had been there since even before her marriage, although Laura had not thought seriously about the possibility until the gynaecologist had told her to make some change in her life. She was not going to mention that conversation though.

"Vaguely for a long time, but only seriously during the last few months. But you know how being on holiday puts things in perspective, so I thought I wouldn't say anything until I'd thought about it away from home and the office. And then I had to admit the children came into it." This was her trump card and she was careful not to overplay it.

"How?"

"These three months ahead. It seemed to me that if I was going to take the plunge and work from home this would be the ideal moment. I'd be there when they get home from school – could pick them up even. If money does come into it, which I don't think it really does, it would mean a positive saving on taxis and child minders. And I'd like it, I really would like it." A year ago, even six months ago, Laura would never have believed it of herself. But it was absolutely true. Somehow the children had stopped being a duty – pleasant often, but still a duty – and had become something more to her. She really did want to be home for them, to be an active and loving part of their lives. The feeling had crept up on her by stealth, but the truth was it had rooted. She loved Richard and Helen. They were her family.

Robert did not react as she had expected. There was no ecstatic embrace, no "Now you are in truth the mother of my children." Instead, there was quiet consideration and the look in Robert's eye judged rather than approved. She could not bear the silence for long and broke it: better to hear the verdict against her than sit like a child outside the headmistress's study.

"Well?"

"We can certainly afford it; so as far as that goes I don't see why you shouldn't do what you want. From that point of view you could give up work entirely. But are you sure you've really thought it through?"

She flushed angrily. "Of course. Don't be silly, Robert. You should know me well enough by now."

"I do. I'm wondering about any other motive. Be honest, Laura. Has your having children anything to do with this?"

In a split second she decided she had to come clean but tread warily. "Yes. But it's not the main motivation. I was told that if I changed my life it might help me to relax about babies and that might make the difference. That's what made me start thinking about it seriously, I admit. But you have to believe me that the more I thought the more sense it made in every bit of my life."

"I can't see that sitting at home brooding will make matters any better."

"I won't be brooding. Don't you see, Robert, I've always wanted to be a real wife. Since I was a child. I bypassed tomboyishness, I never took to casual affairs. I've always wanted to be there for the man I loved. I wouldn't dare say so to half my friends, and I know it's old-fashioned and probably ludicrous, but to me there would be no shame in being a housewife. If I can't be a mother, I can be a good stepmother and justice as well as affection say I should be for Richard and Helen what I would hope to be for my own children. On the other hand, I'm used to working and like what I do, so my working freelance would be a self-indulgence rather than a nod towards feminism. I know I'm lucky – you can afford to keep me. But that's an extra that makes my wishes possible – it hasn't fostered the wish. Don't make your mind up now. I know that if I'm asking you to support me – which is what it comes to, at least until I've established myself as a freelance – I can't expect you to agree straight out, or even at all. But please, don't insult me by thinking this is just a whim. I'll go and get supper." She stood and strode away towards the house.

"Laura." She turned. "Have you ever thought of being a lawyer?" Robert was smiling now. "I take it that the case for the defence is completed? Well, you've swayed the jury. I didn't know I had such an old-fashioned wife."

"Did you ever read *Good Wives*? I suppose not." Laura was back by Robert's side. "I'm afraid I cried when Meg couldn't get her jam to set and the awful thing is, I probably would again. You can't get less feminist than that."

"Don't worry about feminism. If you'd be happier working from home – or not at all – then hand in your notice when you get home. Send them a telegram tonight. I honestly don't mind. Meanwhile let's go and get supper together. You may be old-fashioned, but who's to say I can't be a New Man?"

The whole tenor of their holiday changed the next day with the arrival of the first of the guests that would crowd out the house, Julia and Viv with Helen's school friend Susie. For the rest of the holiday the house would be full. Julia was healthily pregnant, Viv cautious and nervous but very proud. Laura found herself relaxed enough to feel no resentment: her own life was about to change for the better, everything would be fine. So she joined in naming baby conversations, reassured Julia that she looked pregnant but not fat, agonised with Julia through her to-marry-or-not-to-marry dilemma, and even hinted that she was beginning to think that now was the time to have a baby herself.

Susie was not an enjoyable child to entertain: for the first day or so she was homesick and difficult, then the two little girls went into corners, excluding an increasingly morose Richard.

After Julia and Viv left, the arrival of Ferdy and Aimée with all four children broke up the children's squabbles. Then games were invented, rivalries begun and as quickly forgotten, secret clubs started and an endless trail of soggy towels led from the swimming pool up the stairs to the bedrooms and back. The sun shone strong and hot, the air smelt of rosemary, thyme and Ambre Solaire. The children turned brown without thinking about it; the women turned brown by dint of perseverance; the men turned brown and pink in stripes.

When Laura waved Aimée and the children off three days

before the end of the holiday, it was with a sense of sadness: the holiday had been such a success that for once she really did not want it to end.

Melanie arrived that evening and so the grown-ups, now down to the Bedfords and Ferdy who was to join Aimée at her parents' later in the week, decided to call in the baby-sitter and go out for dinner.

Melanie was totally unsuitably dressed for the South of France on a warm evening. She arrived off the aeroplane dressed in high heels, shiny silver lycra tights and a short black tulle confection. "I guessed we would be going out to dinner," was her defence as she kissed Robert. "Maybe it is a little hot. You do all look healthy, I should have come out earlier."

By the time the luggage appeared on the carousel they were all hungry and making small talk to take their minds off their stomachs. So it was not until they were at last sitting around a table, with the question of ordering fully discussed and settled and bread and wine in front of them, that they really relaxed into the evening.

Melanie greeted the news that Laura was to give up work with cries of approval. "At last. No one can say you haven't given it a fair shot, but that's that. So what will you do instead?" The idea of freelance editing did not interest her, but the thought of Laura becoming a full-time mother – and to someone else's children at that, as she was at least tactful enough not to say, although her face clearly expressed the thought – frankly horrified her.

"It's your decision, but honestly, I reckon you'd be bored out of your skull by the end of the first tin of baked beans."

"You're thinking of yourself, not me," Laura said mildly.

"Do you think she will?" Robert made a soggy pellet of bread and rolled it between his fingers. "I must admit I'm worried about that."

"She won't," Ferdy said. "I know Laura – maybe better than either of you. You're both imagining yourselves in that position, not Laura. You two are total opposites – Robert would go mad without a structured working life, Melanie with anything faintly resembling structure. And both of you would hate living entirely around children. You would, Robert, think about it. If Laura can get the balance right, I really think she will be happy."

Laura looked affectionately at her brother. "Thanks."

"I've always known you were an old-fashioned girl," he said, pouring more wine.

The hors d'oeuvres arrived, but as soon as the waiter had gone, Melanie returned to the attack. "If Ferdy's right it'll be all very well while the children are around – but what happens when Camilla comes back from her honeymoon and whisks the children back to Stoke Newington or wherever she's going to live? What then?"

"By then my freelance work should be under way, and if I want to, I'll just take more on. And the weekends will be the same."

Melanie made a face at a piece of beetroot. "From what you say about Camilla, she won't like it."

"It has nothing to do with her. And I can't see why she should mind anyway," said Robert.

"For one thing, she won't be able to complain that the children aren't being looked after properly. No, I won't shut up, Laura, you know it's true. From everything I've heard it's obvious that underneath all the civility she's boiling with rage at how well the children get on with Laura. And you know damned well that if it hadn't suited her to leave the children with you all summer she'd have done everything possible to stymie this holiday."

Laura looked at Melanie amazed. She was always a straight talker, but this was sheer provocation. And she seemed entirely sober.

"Melanie."

"Melanie nothing, Robert. Why do you always pussyfoot around it? It doesn't make life any easier, especially for Laura. Why always be so *polite?*"

"It's loyalty, not politeness," Ferdy suggested.

"Well, he should be being loyal to Laura, not Camilla."

"You're probably right." Robert's reply shut Melanie up more effectively than any line of self-defence. "I suppose the truth is that I had got into the habit of defending Camilla by the end of our marriage, and it was a habit that turned out to be difficult to drop. But I still think you're wrong about Laura, Melanie. I really do think she'll be happy. And in an odd way you've finally convinced me of it. Even more than she did, or Ferdy."

Melanie shrugged and made way for the waiter. A plate of pigeon and *cèpes* was put in front of her and she eyed it greedily, then inspected the others' plates. "Looks like I made the right decision," she said. Then added "I'm sorry if it's a case of Too-Far Freeway again, I must have drunk too much on the aeroplane."

They all laughed – Melanie was for once so obviously sober that the apology must be meant. "Anyway, I'm very glad to be here, wish I'd come for longer and here's to you." She raised her glass. "Thanks for having me and good luck, Laura."

Laura was grateful to Melanie for her outburst. It had settled Robert's mind and she would now go straight back to London and hand in her notice without qualms. But she did hope that Melanie would not cause any further traumas during the last few days left of the holiday. Robert only half-liked her and had had to be persuaded into agreeing to Laura's inviting her. He was worried that she would drink too much in front of the children or say anything she shouldn't. On Melanie's first morning the two women had gone food shopping together and then stopped at a café for a drink. Laura, as light-heartedly as she knew how, passed this message on.

Melanie thought about being indignant, but decided she could not find the energy. The sun was hot, the melons smelt delicious and after all she was on holiday. Also in her heart she could see Robert's point. "He's not to know that where children are concerned I'm as restrained and pure as the Pope's mother," she said. "I can see what you're getting at and don't worry. No swearing, no drinking – or not much – and no anti-Camilla references. Ludo and swimming-pool games will be my prime preoccupations from dawn till dusk. And if I do anything I shouldn't after dusk, I'll do it quietly. How are you getting on with them anyway? This must be the longest stretch you've ever lived with them."

"It is, but it seems to be working. As far as I can see they're not even unsettled by Camilla's marriage."

"Who is this Sasha? He sounds very un-Camilla."

"Sasha Limpnakoff. Apparently he's quite well known."

Laura was surprised at Melanie's reaction. After a moment of blank astonishment, she burst into shrieks of laughter.

"Don't be *ridiculous*! You must be joking."

"Of course not. Why?"

"Darling, he's not just quite well known – he's infamous. For God's sake, he's been around for ages. Sash and Camilla! I should have guessed – but how on earth could I?"

"So you know him?"

"I had an affair with him years ago, but you must remember – I told you about him – not that I was making much sense then."

"Sash," Laura said slowly.

"*Yes*. Sash. You always refused to meet him 'cos you knew you disapproved."

"He was your dealer."

"Mine and most of West London's. You could always reach him and his stuff was always good. And he ends up marrying Camilla."

Laura stirred her *citron pressé*, her mind blank in shock. What on earth would Robert do when he found out? What was she to do? Thank God the children were with them, that she had time to think . . .

Melanie patted her hand. "Don't look so horrified. He's not dealing any more as far as I know. And he's certainly not taking smack any more. I heard he'd been in Broadway – it took months but he came out clean."

"He drank vodka when they came around."

"Did he?" Melanie was interested. "But I drink again and don't take drugs – you know I don't. Some of us manage it."

"Yes, but . . ."

"But you wouldn't put me top of any ideal step-parent list. You've got a point."

"You see, Robert's been so worried. I thought he was fussing, but now . . . You know, there are nights when they don't come back till morning, they take off across England at the mention of a party – I thought she was just being rather aggressively single or just loopy in love. Do you think they are taking anything?"

"Oh, I'm sure they smoke dope – maybe coke at parties. I'm sure they don't take smack."

Melanie thought she was being comforting, but Laura thought of Robert who believed marijuana was the devil's nuclear weapon and her heart sank.

"Ecstasy?" she said forlornly. "Ice?"

Melanie laughed. "You've been reading too many tabloids. I'm sure that if he were taking ecstasy he'd be back on heroin. But I can find out what the score is when we get back to London if you want."

"I wish you would." Laura paused, her mind groping towards an idea that remained obstinately just out of reach. "Melanie, will you do me a favour?"

"Of course. Name that tune."

"Don't tell Robert any of this."

"Shouldn't he know?"

"Well, yes, but not yet. There's no point his getting in a frenzy if it turns out that Sasha's been clean for years and is totally respectable." She knew it sounded lame, and she was not yet sure herself why she was keen to keep Robert in ignorance. "Well, anyway, I'd just rather he didn't know – until you've done your detective work at home. Please?"

Melanie grinned broadly. "You're up to something, Laura Sawyer. But I love an intrigue. You're on, on condition I'm kept informed of developments. Secrecy is the order of the day. And now let's have another drink. And whatever you do, don't worry."

Melanie waved for the waiter, and Laura sat back, not listening to Melanie's surprisingly good French. She needed time to know what she thought, but while a part of her was sure that it was wise not to worry Robert unnecessarily, another part of her, the straightforward element which so disliked secrecy and intrigue, felt ashamed. Robert was not very fond of Melanie, and she knew how angry he would be if he thought she was colluding with her friend behind his back. Especially on the subject of his children.

She nodded thanks to the waiter and sipped her drink. She would wait and see, and decide later. She was on holiday now and there was nothing anyone could do.

* * *

Melanie had not seen Sasha recently, but she was now confident enough of her new position in the world of modern art to be sure she would be able to carry out her promise to help Laura. Being a woman of impulse, she had begun work towards her new career as soon as she arrived home from the zoo. Being a woman of impulse, she did not have a great deal of follow-through. So having made a few telephone calls to friends who all thought Melanie's idea was good – or at any rate amusing enough to encourage – she found herself agreeing to go out for a drink to discuss plans and ended up doing more drinking than discussing and going to bed too late to be able to do anything useful the next day.

But Melanie's crisis of the soul had been real, and although she was easily diverted, her decision had been taken seriously. In between drinks and parties and television watching she began to make plans. She rang up all the itinerant artists she had taken up with at one time or another and went to see their latest work. She started going to art galleries and put herself onto the mailing lists of all the dealers in modern art. She became a familiar face in Portobello Road and Cork Street. Before too long she was fitting the drinks and parties and television around the art. She did not give up drinking, but her friends noticed that apart from the occasional binge she drank a great deal less. Some of her friends were disappointed.

So far Melanie had neither a place nor any painters to exhibit, but by the time she set off for her stay with the Bedfords in France she was more cheerful than she had been for years. Yet for some reason, despite all the tête à têtes the two women shared in France, she never even hinted to Laura that she was making plans to change her life. She knew who she wanted to represent, and knew to within three galleries where she wanted to show them, but until she had gathered together the last bit of self-confidence she would need to make her approaches, she wanted to keep her plans to herself. She preferred the big surprise to endless discussions. She felt much the same about her information gathering on Laura's behalf. She would wait until she knew enough to end Laura's doubts – or verify them.

8 ∫

Laura spent a great deal of time over the next few weeks worrying about Robert. Was she interfering too much or not enough? Were the children Robert's business or were they hers as well? She wanted above all to protect Robert: she felt that she had brought extra troubles to his door already and did not want to make more difficulties. There was after all nothing he could do about the Sasha gossip, and after all Laura had heard nothing about his present, only old news about his past. At the same time, though, she felt that her knowledge was a very powerful weapon, even though she did not yet know what war she was fighting.

Melanie had kept her promise and said nothing to Robert either. Nor did she mention the subject to Laura, knowing that Laura was relying on her for more information.

The Bedfords arrived back in London a contented family, and the children settled immediately into the new routine at Parson's Green Lane. The holiday had been an ideal bridge between living at Camilla's and Robert's so, apart from the odd emergency run to Chelsea for a favourite toy or essential piece of clothing there were no traumas. An expensive but trustworthy Australian girl was hired to pick the children up from school and look after them until Laura came home and the whole family immediately took to her.

Laura's resignation did not go so smoothly. On her first day back at work she announced that she was leaving and asked if it were not possible to stop immediately rather than work out her month's notice. Andrew Howard, the managing director, believing that she was leaving for another job, was at first resentful. When he heard her plans he was horrified.

"It has nothing to do with me, of course, but are you sure you've thought about this seriously enough? Not working isn't like being on holiday, you know. And your stepchildren will be at school all day . . ."

"I know all that."

"Apart from anything else you're very good at your job. You know that Henry Palmer won't work with anyone but you, neither will Joanna James—"

"I hope I will still be able to edit them – freelance."

This disgruntled Andrew. "You know our policy on using freelance editors. It's just too expensive. And unless we need someone with specialist knowledge or the author insists . . ." he stopped, seeing the trap he had built for her snap down on himself.

Laura smiled sweetly. "Look, Andrew, you know that since I've been married there's been no other reason for me to work than the fact that I like my job. I'd willingly work out the month, but as the children are at home now, it seems silly. Why don't we call the next month's work working from home rather than freelance work. Financially that will work out in Howard and Neville's favour. You know I've three major books that must be in production soon – the James by the end of the month and the Lancaster and Brewer titles by halfway through October. The four 'How to' books can be passed on to Sarah if you want, or I can finish them myself. You know you can trust me to be honest with my time – if I get through them this month I'll say so. After that it's up to you whether you employ me again or not. I hope you will, but I'll also look elsewhere."

Andrew looked more friendly. "I can see you have thought it through. And of course it's none of my business, but still—"

"Exactly. Thank you. I'll come in until the end of the week to sort out my desk and let everyone know what's happening."

"We must have a drink one evening. We'll miss you – I hope you miss us."

Laura, always brutally honest, hesitated. "I don't know, I'm sure I will in some ways. At the moment, I'm just excited – it feels like leaving school."

Andrew laughed. "Well don't get into trouble in the big wide world. And don't forget that drink."

In fact, Laura felt more apprehensive than liberated as she left the building that Friday for the last time. It was not until she closed the door behind her that she felt a burden not so much lifting as being placed plum in the middle of her back. The feeling shocked and frightened her. Had she, despite all her protestations to the contrary, rushed blindly into a new way of life that would bring her nothing but increased duties with no satisfaction? She turned back towards the door. Perhaps she should ask Andrew to reconsider her resignation, or at least allow her to work part time.

She dithered on the pavement, knowing that she was too stubborn to admit to a change of mind, almost sure that she had made the right decision, still fearful of an unstructured future. But of course there was to be structure. She held a briefcase full of manuscripts, she had two small children to look after and a house to run. She did not need to go back into that building at all. She did, on the other hand, need a drink, even though she had had a long and mostly liquid goodbye lunch with her workmates.

The pub on the corner was quiet, with only a few labourers from a nearby building site propping up the bar and ignoring the sign which read "No work clothing" in an attempt to lure those who worked in suits rather than hard hats on to the premises. Within half-an-hour it would be packed with short-skirted secretaries and ambitious junior executives drinking rum and coke and dry white wine.

Laura ordered a glass of wine then changed her mind. A large gin and tonic would help steady her better. She took the drink to a corner table and sat, her mind a blank, her eyes on the flesh showing between a workman's T-shirt and his drooping trousers. So this was it. Freedom.

The gin and tonic turned sour in her mouth. She never could appreciate alcohol on her own. Far from enjoying an illicit pleasure, she felt only guilt with no accompanying thrill. She had often wished Melanie were more like her in that respect.

Melanie. The thought of her friend cheered her. This was a moment when only Melanie would do. She needed mocking, chivvying, and generally shaking up. Melanie would make drinking fun and, after an hour or so with her she would return home cheered but reminded why she preferred a life of responsibility to one of hard-working dilettantism.

The publican nodded her towards the pay phone at the back of the public bar. Laura dialled, holding her breath against a lingering smell of lavatory freshener and chips, and prayed her friend was in. She was in luck.

"Melanie? It's Laura. I need a companion. Could you bear to drop everything and meet me for a drink?"

"Sounds like the invitation I've been waiting for all day. What's the matter? Robert done a bunk?"

"No, I've left work. The children have gone to their grandmother's for the weekend so this is my last fling." They quickly arranged to meet in a wine bar halfway between them and Laura rang the home answering machine to tell Robert she would be back late.

Melanie was already waiting with a bottle of champagne when Laura arrived at their meeting place.

"Congratulations. So you're out of the harness at last. You don't look too excited about it, though. What's the trouble?"

"Oh, I don't know," said Laura, watching as Melanie poured her a glass of champagne with long-practised ease. "Life's crossroads sort of thing. It's odd; you spend years fantasising about being able to give up office life and when you can, you find yourself almost frightened of it."

"All those fish fingers and children's parties stretching ahead of you," Melanie suggested.

"No, not that. That would be something. I feel I'm looking at a great blank."

"The trouble with you, Laura, is that for a straightforward, criminally honest, up-front sort of person you don't seem to be able to make up your mind. I suggest your cry from the heart means you want nothing more than to drink a bit too much, talk about nothing much and go home feeling glad you're not me and have a home to go to. Now isn't that about it?"

Laura's guilty look confirmed Melanie's theory. "Sorry," she mumbled.

"Don't be." Melanie gulped back her champagne and poured

them both more. "But don't think I don't know it and don't think I don't get fed up too."

"Fed up?"

"Of the gay single life."

"But you don't want to be married."

"Don't I? Why not? Because I like parties and dancing and holidaying more than working in a nine-to-five job? Because I'm lucky enough not to have to go out to work and so don't need to marry to escape the tedium of earning a living? Oh, I'm not saying that's why you married, but I know girls who do, who prefer company wife to office life. Don't be crass, Laura. Have you never noticed people marrying to escape not so much the endless rush-hour trips on the tube as the endless trips to yet another party? You just don't look."

"But you always laugh at me for my domesticity."

"Of course I do. And I do think it's quite funny that I have a best friend who's happier thinking about soufflés than where the next line or man or drink is coming from. I don't really think I'd be happy in your shoes, so it's not the shoes I envy. It's the ability to wear them, to make them fit. A sort of reverse Cinderella complex."

"You *envy* me!" For all her years of knowing Melanie, for all she had seen her wayward friend through, for all she believed herself to be a good judge of character, this idea had never occurred to Laura.

"In a way. And I worry. We all know what happened to the ugly sisters when they tried to fit into the glass slipper. They had to cut off their toes to do it. I don't think my feet will ever fit into those shoes without surgery, and sometimes I worry that I'll want that slipper so much I'll cut off my toes to get it."

"You can live without toes."

"But don't you lose your sense of balance? Oh, hell, I don't know."

The girls sat silently for a while as Laura thought about what Melanie had said.

"I'm ashamed," she finally said.

"Ashamed? Don't be ridiculous. You caught me sitting in a gloom watching *Neighbours* on my own. I probably don't mean a word of it, and if I do I'm glad I've covered up so well." Melanie was already regretting her speech, resenting the weakness that had made her feel Laura's telephone call was a result of unnecessary self-pity. "Anyway, I have news for you."

"Oh? a new man?"

"Not that kind of news. There aren't any new men left as far as I can see. No, it's about Sasha."

"Oh." Suddenly Laura did not want to know any more about Sasha. She wished she had not rung Melanie, wished she were at home with the cats waiting for Robert, wished she did not feel so selfish in her secure happiness – for she *was* happy. But she had asked Melanie to find out about Sasha and there was no reason to add cowardice to her sins.

"So what is it?"

"He's definitely not back on smack, which is good. But apparently before he left on honeymoon he was buying coke – good stuff and lots of it. He was partying like he did in the old days – but you know that. None of his friends can understand his marrying Camilla, but they all say the odd thing is that he really does seem to be totally in love. They're never apart, they're all over each other. They talk very seriously about the meaning of life and art and she seems to look up to him as a great brain. Which is odd as Robert's miles more intelligent than him."

"But he doesn't think much." Laura was surprised at the thought, and more so at uttering it. "I mean about the state of the world, or his soul or whatever," she added.

"Maybe not. But no one ever thought Camilla did either. Maybe it's the drugs."

"*Camilla*?" Laura, picturing smart, sophisticated Chelsea Camilla, was astounded. She fitted neither of the stereotypes Laura believed made up drug takers. She was not a rock-star groupie, nor a deprived child from an inner city. People like her did not take drugs, did they?

Melanie laughed at Laura's face. "I can't believe you're still so naive. Well, of course she joins in. I mean she'd have to, wouldn't she? Anyway it's only coke, it won't kill her."

"It might kill Robert," Laura muttered. She had at least been exposed to drug taking through Melanie. Robert had never been – except professionally in the days when he worked in criminal law.

"Don't be silly. It won't kill anybody. Most people can handle it better than I did, honestly. I wouldn't worry. I mean the children don't complain, do they? I doubt they even notice."

"That's hardly the point."

"I'm not going to argue about it. It seems to me that as long as children are clean and fed it doesn't matter what their parents do in the evening. You asked to know and I've told you, so that's that. What are you going to do about it?"

"I don't know. Talk to Camilla, I suppose."

"Fat lot of good that will do you. Of course, it's up to you, but I'd just keep a bit of an eye out and only do something if things get worse."

Laura was in a quandary. She wanted very badly to do what was best and right, but for once in her life her instinct was failing her. She was unsure whether she should believe third- or fourth-hand information and unsure too whether or not she wanted to believe it. Whether to keep quiet, tell Robert, talk to Camilla – she was only concerned for the children and knew that a false step would brand her as a busybody with no results.

In an ideal world she would confront Camilla who would either prove everything was all right or would see the error of her ways and reform at once. But Laura remembered Camilla's cool stare and knew she would be ignored, or laughed at, if she dared to approach her rival. If she told Robert, he would react, maybe overreact, immediately. Robert brooded about decisions, but he could think very quickly indeed if necessary. Laura did not want to risk Robert's disapproval, to put herself in the wrong.

Then she remembered when Julia had complained about an Alsatian that lived opposite her flat. "It spends its life on the first floor balcony, pacing back and forth like those wolves in Regent's Park," she had said. "It barks so much from anger and frustration that it sounds more like a Pekinese than an Alsatian. I keep thinking I should ring the RSPCA – it's never even taken for a walk – but each time I get ready to dial I can't make myself do anything so interfering and middle class." They had joked about the Alsatian every now and again for months until one day Julia rang almost in tears. "You remember the dog opposite? Yesterday it committed suicide. It just hurled itself off the balcony and broke its back. It had to be put down. It's lived there for months, it must have done it on purpose."

Laura had not been convinced by the idea of a suicidal dog, but now, wondering what to do about Camilla and Sasha, she remembered Julia's words. "I didn't ring because I was frightened. It's all my fault." Half of her said that she should remain silent and wait and see. The other half jeered that this was cowardly and that she should not mind about what people thought of her.

"So do you want to hear my own news?" Melanie interrupted her thoughts and Laura nodded.

"Dad's split up with Sue and is coming back to England at last. He wants to live with me while he finds himself a flat in London. He's taking early retirement and, as he puts it, wants to have fun. He thinks I'm the girl to show him how. My bet is that he's looking for a wife and reckons my age group will provide a racier one than the bridge-playing set."

"Are you looking forward to it?"

"I don't know. Yes, I suppose so. Although I won't be able to bear it if he does marry someone I know. I wouldn't put it past him – he's an old charmer and there are some pretty desperate girls around. I haven't decided how to play it yet. Either I go all demure and take him to lots of art exhibitions or I party so hard he begs me to stop. What do you think?"

"Oh, I expect he'll find his own feet before you're even aware he's there. Bring him to dinner with us if you like."

The invitation was automatic and Melanie laughed. "Your answer to any dilemma is to feed it. But thanks, I may well. Dinner with you is about halfway between exhibitions and partying, don't you think? Light relief in either case. My other news is—" she took a deep breath. "I'm going into business. Back into art."

She had been bracing herself to tell Laura about her new venture for some weeks but the time had never seemed right. But now her father was coming to live with her she would not be able to keep her own secrets, and she did want Laura's blessing.

For a while Laura completely forgot her own troubles as she

listened to Melanie's plans. At last Melanie had found something to harness her talents, and Laura was genuinely delighted for her. Melanie lost all her diffidence in the face of Laura's enthusiasm and the two sat and talked in the comforting glow of an old friendship.

In the end it was Laura who called for the bill and gathered herself together first. "Melanie, I'm sorry but I'd better go. Otherwise we'll have another bottle and I'll be very drunk and very late. But thanks for coming out at the drop of a hat. I feel much saner now."

They kissed and Laura left. Melanie prepared to follow, but thought better of it and ordered another large glass of champagne. Now she was out of the flat she could not face returning to it – or not for a while.

She thought about her father's imminent arrival, and wondered how they would survive together. Although she had been light-hearted enough about it to Laura, she was in fact very nervous indeed.

Melanie was not a very considerate person: despite her NA training she did not spend a great deal of time thinking about her relationships with other people. So it was not until her father announced his intention of coming to live with her that she had realised how little she knew him.

Her initial reaction had been to make any sort of excuse that would send him elsewhere, but her good nature overcame her hesitation. Apart from anything else, she survived on a trust fund set up by his mother and administered by him, as well as relying on the generous cheques that appeared through the post more or less regularly. If he wanted to call the debt in, she had little choice but to give in gracefully.

But that did not alter the fact that Melanie had never before lived with her father. School holidays barely counted as she had spent so much of them being shipped from one relation to another until, when she did finally touch down wherever her father was living, she was more of an honoured, if guilt-inducing, guest than a daughter. As a result she felt a long-distance affection for a father which was coloured by a tinge of dislike. No one can truly love a father they do not respect, and Melanie's father had not earned her respect.

Then there was the question of his new single status. Melanie had endured the fact that her father was an open womaniser while he was still married to Sue. Although his taste had not matured with his age, he was an embarrassment rather than a liability as long as Sue retained some kind of control. Now, with no holds barred, she knew he would be unstoppable. And what was charming and raffish in a forty-year-old father was, even to the liberal-minded Melanie, faintly disgusting in a man who was only a year short of collecting his bus pass.

Melanie drained her glass. There was no point in sitting and brooding herself into a stupor. She gave a quick look round the wine bar and caught the eye of a dark-haired man sitting alone at a corner table. He grinned and she smiled back. He rose and walked over to her. "Don't go. Let me buy you a drink."

Melanie hesitated. He was not bad-looking, hook-nosed, a pleasant smile. She had spent evenings with strangers often enough – sometimes knowing the evening would end in a one-night stand, sometimes fooling herself that it was the beginning of an adventure, sometimes just feeling like the company of someone who had no preconceptions about her, someone to whom she could be anything or anyone. Tonight she was bored and lonely. Drunk enough to take the challenge, sober enough to judge what the man wanted and make her decisions. But then she thought of her father. Who was she to be disgusted by her father when she behaved so very like him? If a man's charm loses its saving powers at sixty, a woman has many fewer years in which she can dally with impunity. The steps between good-time girl and old slag are few and close together when you are over thirty. Melanie was only just facing up to that; most of her girlfriends had begun their mid-life crises as they approached their thirtieth birthdays. Melanie had been slower off the mark but she always took life's ups and downs harder than most.

And who did this man think he was? If he was that wonderful what was he doing trying to pick up girls in Kensington wine bars? Suddenly furious and full of moral indignation, Melanie swung round, almost knocking the table candle to the ground.

"Absolutely not. You've misjudged your prey. Go back to your corner and wait a little longer, I'm sure someone will turn up. But I have somewhere to go."

She swept out on a high which lasted her until she arrived home. Then, looking blankly out of the kitchen window as she struggled with the ice-cube tray, she felt a little foolish. Perhaps he had just been lonely, or bored. That was no crime. Who, after all, was she to judge? Oh, hell.

Melanie was overcome with a wave of what as a child she had called Saturday Afternoon Feeling. It was a refined version of boredom, when the world seems grey and very, very exhausting. In one sense Saturday Afternoon Feeling had been to blame for her involvement with drugs – it had lasted too long to bear without some kind of stimulation. Now, as she stood with a glass of vodka in her hand she could see an unproductive evening of self-pity and drink stretching ahead of her. Unless . . .

Unless she took a grip on herself. She remembered the Steps System that had structured her recovery from drug addiction. Once cured, she had mocked them for their rigidity and simplicity. But they might yet help her. This evening was one of many such – meeting a friend or friends, having a drink or two, either going out to dinner or coming home to a piece of cheese and more drink. One thing she abhorred was routine, and she was not about to fall into one herself.

So tonight she would surprise herself. She threw the rest of her vodka down the sink and rinsed her hands under the tap. The flat was a mess. Her daily woman came twice a week, but by the time she had washed up the dirty cups and ashtrays, ironed and Hoovered round the place there was no time for anything more serious. Melanie was not at all sure how to set about spring-cleaning but she would work it out.

Four hours later the bathroom and kitchen were spotless, the sitting room and spare room neat and only her bedroom looked worse than before she had started, with piles of cloths for Oxfam, clothes for winter and books for sale stacked everywhere. Melanie looked at her watch – one o'clock, time maybe for a quick drink before bed.

She made for the drinks tray but stopped herself. What the hell, she was exhausted. She might as well go straight to bed.

9

Camilla and Sasha were due back from their honeymoon sometime during October. Robert allowed himself to hope secretly that they would never return, that the glories of the East would tempt them to stay for ever under the copper sky – that one day, in years to come, they would be found wandering down Freak Street in Kathmandu, hand in hand and blissfully happy, having forgotten all their materialistic past ... He knew better of course. Camilla would be in an air-conditioned hotel, running up bills at the hairdresser's and planning her next assault on Peter Jones and Harrods. She would return with no memories of the decorated temples, but a bag full of expensive silver souvenirs. She would return.

She soon made it clear that she would indeed be coming home, and that she expected the children to be on parade as soon as she arrived. They had barely heard from her until the beginning of September when she began sending telegrams almost weekly, changing her plans in each. She also made it clear that although the children had spent Christmas the year before with her, they were to do the same again this year. Robert was disappointed but realised that the unusual circumstances of the last few months meant he really had no claim. After half-term, life would go back to the old routine of weekdays and one weekend a month with Camilla.

Finally, by luck rather than good planning, Camilla was due to arrive during the children's half-term holiday. It was settled that Robert and Laura should drive them to their maternal grandparents in Herefordshire the evening before her return.

For some reason they thought that it would be less distressing for them to be left with their grandparents than handed over.

Laura packed their bags with a dreary soul. She had done nothing with her knowledge of Sasha's drug habit, telling herself that maybe he would come back from his long holiday a changed man. Something must have drawn him to Camilla, after all, and maybe it was a search for conventional stability. Camilla could not be the only one to change, marriage did not work like that.

Richard and Helen were looking forward to seeing their mother, but she had been away so long that their excitement was muted. Laura supposed she should be pleased or flattered that the children did at last think of their father's house as home, but she only worried. Maybe it meant life with Camilla was unstable, that they hated Sasha . . . Robert reassured her from his position of ignorance. "Children forget easily and are basically creatures of habit. Within a month of being back in the old routine they'll have forgotten this was ever their only home. Sad, but true. Still, at least they really know you now."

"Neither they nor I are ever on good behaviour with each other now."

"Exactly. And that can only be a good thing. They're at least stable with you, which puts them in a position of strength while they get used to having a stepfather. I must admit I'm not sure Camilla made her own life easier by leaving for so long, but that's her business. It's been a bonus for us."

Robert's phrase irritated Laura. Why should any father, particularly one as devoted and worthy as Robert, have to regard having his own children under his own roof as a bonus? Their mother was acting like a seventies' teenager, dumping her responsibilities and following the hippie trail, only to claim her rights as soon as it suited her, while Robert worked his heart out to earn money for and love from his children. Laura knew, although she had not discussed it with Robert, that Camilla had not suggested giving up her maintenance allowance while the children were in Parsons Green, and Robert was certainly too gentlemanly to stop it for those months. Laura wondered how much cocaine that money had bought the honeymooners on their travels, and how often Camilla had spared a thought for the children. Not often, if the post was anything to go by. There had been four or five postcards in as many months: it was no wonder the children had stopped missing her.

Laura was shocked at the way her thoughts were going: it was unlike her to be bitter, and was a trait she did not like to see in herself.

Robert and Laura decided they would drive the children to Herefordshire together, and after dropping them, would go on and spend a weekend at a comfortable hotel in the Welsh countryside. The thought was not spoken, but both wanted to act as though being alone together was a treat, although both suspected they would miss the children too much to enjoy themselves.

The drive to Herefordshire passed mostly in silence. Richard and Helen were looking forward to seeing their grandmother more than their mother whose aeroplane landed the next day and who would be in Herefordshire the day after. They discussed the pony their grandmother kept for them, the chocolate cake with which she always greeted them, the gardener's son who was their playmate despite their grandfather's disapproval, and then fell asleep. Laura brooded about the old Sasha/Camilla problem and Robert, always silent when he drove, tried to stop himself minding too much about the imminent separation from his children.

It was six o'clock when they turned into the long drive of Noakes House and Laura gently prodded the children awake. She had insisted that they arrive at that sort of time as she knew that offers of drinks, struggles with ice-cube trays, arguments about who had not screwed the top back on to the tonic bottle were good breakers of awkward silences between strangers. Dreading to meet Camilla's parents, who had been fed who knew what lies about herself, she quickly combed her hair and put on a touch of lipstick. She was not as pretty as their daughter, but she could at least look respectable. After all, it was only natural that they should be interested in their grandchildren's stepmother. And they would find her a darn sight more reassuring than the stepfather, she thought, and smiled to herself.

Noakes House was a large gabled William-and-Mary house, set in well-kept parkland and surrounded with a formal garden.

The children tumbled out of the car and into the house without a backward glance; Laura and Robert followed more slowly with the suitcases.

Robert had not seen the Christies since the divorce, so he too felt ill at ease as he stood with Laura in the large hall. They could hear the children giggling and shrieking in a room to the right, but neither thought it politic to follow them through.

Then Lady Christie appeared in the doorway, a grandchild holding each hand, and smiled warmly. "Robert, how nice to see you again." She came forward and kissed him, then disentangled herself from the children to shake Laura's hand. "Come on through, the hall's freezing." Leaving the luggage in the hall, they all walked into the drawing room where a huge fire heated the room more effectively than any state-of-the-art central heating could, and bowls of flowers and long red velvet curtains in three windows added to the warmth and welcoming aspect of the room.

Lady Christie was very obviously her daughter's mother: the same bold blue eyes, square chin and high cheekbones. Her good looks were marred by a too retroussé nose (which Laura presumed was how Camilla's had been before the appointment with the surgeon) but were enhanced by a grace and gentleness totally absent in her daughter. Richard and Helen plainly adored her and Robert, after his initial discomfort at the meeting, was happy to see her again.

Laura was introduced to Sir John, who briefly rose from the sofa to shake her hand and nod at his erstwhile son-in-law. He was a large man, big-boned, and big-nosed. He had the determined face of a stupid man who had reason to take himself seriously, and his manner to the new arrivals only just stopped short of rudeness. A full whisky glass was on a table at his elbow and he made no effort to help his wife with drinks for the guests.

Lady Christie poured drinks and chattered about the children, about neighbours and tenants on the estate Robert had known and finally, because it was inevitable, about Camilla.

"It all happened in such a rush," she said, checking quickly that the children were safely out of the room. "The children speak well of Sasha, but I must say I wish Camilla had brought him here before they set off on this holiday."

Laura and Robert looked at her, amazed.

"Haven't you met him, Corinna?" Robert asked.

"Well, no. John suggested that he take Sasha to lunch at his club before the wedding, but there didn't seem to be time. And then Camilla said she'd rather we didn't go to the registry office, that it wasn't that sort of wedding." She laughed edgily. "I'm rather nervous, to be honest. They're arriving the day after tomorrow and I won't even recognise him at the station."

"He's very good-looking," said Laura, remembering the vision she had first seen at Henley.

"So you've met him?" Sir John grunted. "What's he like then, Bedford?"

The pause lengthened into an embarrassing silence. Finally Robert said, "Unconventional," and looked at Laura for support.

"Well, he is a painter chappie after all. Quite successful by all accounts. Can't say I've seen anything of his, but I don't spend much time in Cork Street. Camilla promised she'd get us invited to his next show, suppose we ought to make the effort, although it seems to take the best part of a day to get to London with British Rail in the mess it's in . . ." he subsided into his whisky with a series of snorts.

"Do you see much of Camilla?" Lady Christie asked Robert.

"Not really, just with the children."

Lady Christie nodded. "Of course. I just wondered. Oh dear, Camilla is so very headstrong . . ."

Laura looked desperately at Robert. She could not bear the idea of a discussion about Camilla between her mother and ex-husband and for once Robert seemed to share her views.

"We must be going," he said, standing up and refusing the offer of dinner. "No, thank you. We've booked into a hotel an hour into Wales and really ought to get there before nine."

The children were called downstairs to kiss Robert and Laura goodbye, and both were uncharacteristically clingy. "We will see you soon, won't we?" Richard begged, holding Laura tightly by the waist.

"Of course. You know you'll be coming to us for the weekend after half-term – that's only two weeks away. Think how much you've got to tell Mummy – she doesn't even know about France yet."

"That's because she didn't ring us up," said Helen and Richard implored, "You won't forget to come and get us, will you?"

"Of course not, my darlings."

Laura knelt down and gathered both children into a bear hug. Richard gave a little sob and Laura felt tears coming into her own eyes.

"Come on, darling," Robert was brisk, eager to have the parting over.

"Go back up to Nanny, children, and I'll be up to tuck you in when you've had your baths." Lady Christie shooed the children upstairs with a smile, then walked out to the car with the Bedfords.

She shook Laura's hand but after kissing Robert did not let him go. "I know it's none of your business any more and I shouldn't ask it of you, but I do worry about Camilla. The children haven't said anything . . .?"

Robert shook his head and Lady Christie loosened her hold on him. "I hope everything's all right. It will be something to see her and meet her husband. Robert, you have my number, of course. Don't lose it, will you?" Robert shook his head again and Lady Christie stepped back. "I'm sure I'm being foolish. It was lovely to see you again, and to meet Laura." Lady Christie reverted to clichés, her eyes became blank. "Have a lovely weekend, and ring any time you want to talk to the children. Goodbye, goodbye."

She waved them off, the social mask back in place, but Laura was left with a strong impression that Lady Christie was no hidebound fool. Whether by intuition or not, she knew something was wrong with her daughter. Perhaps she was the person Laura should talk to – maybe she would have the answers.

Their weekend was not a great success. Although Laura had been expecting to feel a sense of loss after the children left, she had had no idea just how bad it would be. Friday dinner was late, but good, and they chatted contentedly about the Christies. Sir John was, according to Robert, no better and no worse than he had appeared that evening. "In all the years I was married to Camilla I never really knew him," said Robert. "He's always grunting and grumpy but never loses his temper. I think he's theoretically fond of the children but actually totally bored by them. His only weak spot is Camilla, whom he adores."

"What about the son?"

"Andrew is very conventional, quite friendly, married to a sweet girl. He's big in the city – much cleverer than the rest of them. You'd have thought John would worship him – heir to the baronetcy and all the land – got a baby boy to carry on after him. But they've never got on."

"Perhaps Sir John's jealous of him."

Robert looked surprised. "I suppose that could be it. I don't know. But poor Andrew can't do anything right. If he takes an interest in the estate he's accused of longing for John to die, if he keeps away he's told he doesn't care about his heritage and John's going to leave it to his old school."

"Is Andrew close to Camilla?"

"Yes, surprisingly so. I've always thought he's rather good for her. One of the few people she might, if it came down to it, be frightened of. Or at any rate respect."

Andrew Christie – another possible ally? Laura wondered as she looked at the pudding menu. Oh, hell, what was she to do?

They woke the next day to a grey, wet sky which mirrored their feelings. They could not walk or ride, so they played cards and moved into the bar as soon as it opened. After a huge lunch they fell grumpily asleep and woke up even more cross. It was that sort of a weekend.

Before too long, ridiculously soon, in fact, it was party season in London. Restaurants were full of grey men in silly hats, secretaries congaed down the street, giggling on high heels, pubs and motorcycles were festooned with tinsel and the shops played Cliff Richard over and over again.

Laura and Robert took to partying with a vengeance. They accepted every invitation, went to drinks parties from Richmond to Islington. None of them was particularly enjoyable, but it helped to pass the time and fill up the silences. Soon, Laura thought, she would begin to feel Christmassy and then everything would be all right.

Meanwhile, she brooded about Sasha, missed the children, and waited with increasing despair to become pregnant. Her initial rebuff from the gynaecologist made her nervous of approaching him again, but, she decided, once Christmas was over she would have to brave him. This had gone on too long: it was affecting the whole of the rest of her life; her relationship with Robert, her work, her concentration. And time was running out. Soon she would be too old even to adopt, not that she wanted to take that route. It was her own baby she wanted, not someone else's. She already had two of them. Maybe that was selfish, but that was how she felt.

The flat was orderly, the fake coals were glowing and ice was waiting in a small bowl on the drinks tray. Melanie had gone so far as to buy huge bunches of flowers and their smell was so far still stronger than that of Marlboro. Her father was due to arrive at any moment, and Melanie was chain-smoking in an attempt to blunt her nerves. She was frankly terrified.

She had invited her brother and his wife to dinner to break the tête à tête she dreaded between herself and her father, but now the prospect of a foursome with nothing to say seemed even bleaker than a twosome. She thought about cancelling them but knew she did not have the nerve, besides which, she had spent a fortune in Marks and Spencer on dinner.

At last the doorbell rang and Melanie moved slowly towards the intercom. "Hello?" His voice came up, unrecognisable across the wires and the years. "Melanie? It's me." She wondered by what right he could assume the "me" of long familiarity but banked down the thought. He was her father and she had resolved not only to take him in, but to do so with a good grace. She pressed the buzzer without a word.

When she opened the door she was amazed at how her father had aged in the three years since their last meeting. Alex Freeway's once magnificent nose was now a veined beak protruding from a fleshless face. His brown eyes had lost their former lustre and were red and rheumy. His hands were mottled with age spots. It was not so much that he looked old as that for the first time in her memory he looked his age. Melanie felt an unexpected wave of pity, but that too she set sternly aside.

She stood back and he crossed the threshold. There was an awkward moment: neither felt the urge to kiss but both were sure they should.

"Well, this is a lovely flat," he said at last.

"Thank you. I'll show you your room." By the time Alex returned to the sitting room Melanie had enough grip on herself to offer him a drink and ask about his journey. She wondered what other people talked about to their fathers, but with no family news – except for his divorce which she was shy of broaching – and a few memories in common, the silences became longer and more frequent.

"Adam's coming to dinner," she said at last.

Alex brightened feebly. "Ah, good. And – er – "

"Kim."

"Yes." He grinned at her and for a moment looked like his old self. "The little vegetarian." Melanie could not help but grin back. It was a moment of complicity and in it she was given hope for their future together.

The family evening did not begin a whole new way of life for Melanie but it did lay the foundations for the bridges that would have to be built before the Freeway family could be truly reunited. Kim tried hardest of all, and in doing so began to drive Melanie and Alex closer together. She was a type neither could hope to comprehend, but in their gentler moods both could appreciate her goodwill. In a way Adam was more difficult. Alex and Melanie found his conversation harder to stomach than the natural sweetness of his wife. Both father and sister knew too much about Adam's days of hedonism to accept entirely that this caring man, this modern father and born-again liberal exterior could possibly house Adam's soul.

However, they ate and drank and managed to keep conversation going. Finally they asked Alex about Sue.

"Well, do you know," he said, accepting a glass of whisky from his daughter, "I had always assumed that if she ever did leave me it would be over my – er – indiscretions. It was my fault, but I just couldn't resist a pretty woman and Sue – she lost her looks, poor girl, and the sun got to her . . ."

Adam and Melanie exchanged glances. Both remembered

Sue's early slide towards drink and tranquillisers and neither could hold their father entirely blameless.

"But I have to admit I was baffled when she left. I'd been entirely faithful – not even a flirtation, I can tell you – for more than two years. And off she went. Without a warning, just packed her bags and moved into the local hotel. I'd see her there sometimes – there we'd be, at separate tables, and we'd say hello and how was life – rum thing, really."

"So why did she go?" Kim looked concerned. "Is there any hope of your getting back together?"

"Good Lord, no!" His alarm made them all laugh. "No, I think we both like it this way. Do you know, I think we should have done it years ago. But it made me think. I'd been out in the sun long enough, it was time to come home. I've been a bad father, I know—"

"Dad, please. No sentiment." Melanie's embarrassment made her voice sharper than she had intended, but the last thing she wanted was a general display of manufactured emotion. Not after the evening had passed so much more smoothly than she had expected.

"No. Well, I'm back."

And we will see how it goes, Melanie thought. Maybe it would not be so hard after all.

Having her father to stay for an indefinite time would have been a great deal more difficult a year earlier. Melanie now had a purpose in life: at last she had a date for her first exhibition. She had agreed terms with two young painters and a sculptor, who were now aiming for a date in the middle of November. For the first time for many years Melanie had something to work towards.

One of the painters had never exhibited before and was in a raw state of nerves, Melanie found herself acting as his nursemaid, his cocktail waiter, his cook, his inspiration and almost (but just in time not) his lover in an effort to goad him into production. The second painter had exhibited once before and his bright paintings of West Indians having fun had sold well to the West London middle class, so he felt he was an old hand and tried to run the exhibition for Melanie. Only the sculptor, a shy and unassuming woman in her forties, left Melanie alone and quietly worked away at her abstracts.

So Melanie was out a lot and although at first she tried to be at home for dinner regularly, her father soon slotted into his own way of life without her. Gradually they began to be at ease with each other, even to feel real warmth for each other, and although neither gave much away, each realised that they did after all share a great deal. Both were frank to the point of brashness, both impatient with anything they could dismiss as pretension, and both had a sense of humour that verged on the malicious.

The major change wrought in Melanie's life by her father's arrival was over men. She was in her thirties, had lived alone all her adult life, was the daughter of an old libertine, but she could not bring herself to allow anyone to spend the night with her while her father slept under the same roof. Libidinous afternoons were equally out of the question as Alex had his own key and would usually be home for an afternoon nap ("I don't need it at all, it's just habit.")

At first this curtailment of her sex life worried Melanie, but after a while she found it a relief. She had more or less given up the brief affairs by the time Alex arrived, but Nicholas was still in her life. Try as she might, which was not very hard, she had not succeeding in breaking with him. He had been perfect for her: a married man whose demands on her were limited by his wife's on him. He made her laugh, he satisfied her sexually and he was not there enough to bore her.

He, however, was not too pleased when his long lunches and afternoon delight was brought abruptly to an end. Their affair had lasted too long for hotel rooms to be erotic; by now they seemed functional and distasteful. Melanie realised that their affair had degenerated into the purely sexual, and that now she had better things to do than provide Nicholas with escape from his marriage and his career. He began to whine. Like a displaced wife he asked her about her movements, her emotions, her lovers. This was not the point of their liaison, not to Melanie, who was feeling stronger in herself than at any time since leaving Broadway. She was amazed to discover that, far from relying on Nicholas, she could happily envisage life without him.

Telling him took some courage, but one night, sitting over *oeufs Florentines* in the Caprice, Melanie found herself saying in a calm, even sober, voice, that enough was enough, that it was time Nicholas returned to his wife and she cleaned her own slate.

To her surprise, he reached across the table and gripped her hand so hard she winced. "Don't do this, Melanie," he urged. "You'll miss me, I'll miss you. What we have is perfect, don't you see? We can't end it."

"We're not going anywhere, Nicholas," she said reasonably. "This has gone on for ages and we're getting stale with each other."

"We'll marry. I'll leave Angela and we'll marry."

This made Melanie cross. "Don't be ridiculous. You don't mean it and I don't want it. Nicholas, please, face the fact that it's over. It's not just that it's all too difficult at the moment – it's that I don't mind the difficulty. I don't want to make it any easier. It's over."

Two thoughts preoccupied Melanie as she sat alone in the back of a taxi after dinner. One was that it had not after all been she who had shed a tear as they parted. The other was the realisation that it had been Nicholas who had needed her so much more than she needed him.

The exhibition's preview was crowded. Melanie had invited everyone she knew and the art correspondents of every paper. A friend of Laura's who ran her own catering company handed out tiny tempting vol-au-vents and a huge toasted Brie. Friends, artists and dealers guzzled and slurped and talked and forgot to look at the pictures. More people poured in, signing the book at the door, until the crush was almost unbearable. Melanie feared for the sculptures but could only pray that they were secure. It was too late to do anything else now and besides she was insured.

Her head buzzed with adrenaline and vodka and she reached for an angel on horseback as it wafted by. She must keep a clear head. This was her big night.

Her father was there, chatting benignly to the excited first-time exhibitor. Adam and Kim stood together in a corner, baffled.

Melanie's old art friends crowded round one of the sculptures, drinking fast and noisily. She knew none of them would buy anything, but they could come in useful some other way. Dempster had sent one of his staff who Melanie hoped had noticed Sarah Armstrong Jones quietly eating a celery stick and actually looking at a picture. Laura was there and had brought her mother who was eyeing up a brightly coloured still life of yams and coconuts with a knowing eye. Two girls in velvet berets sat together giggling on a stair. Melanie had no idea who either of them was. The sculptress had not yet arrived and Melanie was worried that she would not come at all.

Melanie made her way through the crowd, nodding to people as she passed, discreetly passing a typed price list to anyone who looked remotely like a buyer, refusing a glass of Moët for the umpteenth time. She was very proud. She had not believed that she could really do it, that she could organise an exhibition and preview party and forget nothing. The invitations had gone out on time, the food and drink were delicious, the paintings were hung to their best advantage and the right people were there. She even saw a couple of red dots on pictures. The fantasy begun in London Zoo had become a reality at last. She had invented a label for herself. She was no longer a junkie or a recovering addict, she was Melanie Freeway, artists' agent. And that was something to talk about.

She was forced to double-take. Who should be arriving, glamorous blonde following a step behind, but Sasha Limpnakoff. Melanie looked at him amazed – he had certainly come on a treat since she had last seen him, on his back in a basement flat but looking at the stars. His face was no longer gaunt and his clothes were enough to encourage a second look without the draw of his amazing looks. The blonde could only be Laura's predecessor, Camilla. Melanie glanced quickly round the room. Laura was nowhere in view – maybe she had already left. Melanie, high on the feeling of her own success, decided that the way to crown the evening would be to carry out an unselfish act on Laura's behalf. Laura had not mentioned her fears about Sasha since the summer, but maybe Melanie could find out something now. Sasha had no reason to know the Bedfords were friends of hers.

She greeted him with two glasses of champagne which he and Camilla accepted.

"Sash, who'd have thought it? I haven't seen you for years."

"Melanie. I could say the same to you," he said, with no memory of their last meeting. "You've certainly changed your life," he nodded at someone in the crowd.

"If you can't do it, sell it," she answered. "I'd drifted for long enough. And you? I hear you're doing great things."

"Oh, interesting, I hope." Melanie had forgotten how much he drawled. Or maybe she had never known. "This is Camilla," he added, waving a hand vaguely in her direction. "My wife."

"Your wife?" Melanie tried to sound surprised but though she might have had an eye for good paintings, she was no Ellen Terry. "Congratulations."

Camilla nodded, her eye roving round the room eagerly. "I hope you don't mind our crashing. Sasha heard about the party and said you were an old friend, so we thought, why not?"

Why not, indeed? Melanie said to herself, pressing a price list into Camilla's hand to punish her for having called the exhibition a party. She wondered who or what Camilla was looking for, and decided to keep an eye on the pair. Sasha stayed chatting to Melanie as Camilla darted off into the crowd. They talked for a while of old times – without mentioning the pastime that had drawn them together all those years before – and Melanie told Sasha about her artists and asked him about his own work. She found him an easy companion, and liked him much more than she had expected. His drawl subsided a little as they talked and he seemed genuinely interested and knowledgeable about the current art scene. Not just a dauber with a private income, then, she thought, and was almost disappointed at the discovery.

Camilla reappeared and nodded briskly at Sasha. With barely a word, the two of them melted into the crowd. A couple of minutes later Melanie caught sight of them again, Sasha holding court to the ex-art student crowd, none of whom had had any of his success and all of whom hung on his every word. Camilla laughed first and longest and the others followed where she led behind Sasha. He seemed a different man in the space of those few minutes; his gestures quick and nervous, his nose carried high like a horn, his eyes now glittering and hard.

Ho hum, thought Melanie. So that's how it is after all. Well, lucky old Laura.

Laura had not left at all. She too had seen Sasha and Camilla arrive and had manoeuvred her mother to the back of the room to avoid a confrontation. The last thing she wanted was to make polite conversation to them; her suspicions were too deep-rooted now for her to feel capable of looking them guilelessly in the face, and besides what was there to talk about? She and Camilla could be civil to each other – just – but neither would want to establish a friendship. Laura cared for Robert too much, and Camilla not enough, for that to be a possibility.

Laura saw Melanie hand the Limpnakoffs their champagne and was annoyed at her friend's treachery. She could not throw them out, but need she offer them silver service? She watched Melanie talk to Sasha and saw she was at ease with him, and that too irritated her. Melanie and Sasha might be old friends, but Laura was of longer standing and better calibre. Melanie should remember where her loyalties lay.

Laura turned, slightly ashamed of her thoughts. This was, after all, business for Melanie and presumably everyone was a prospective buyer. Having given Melanie a mental lecture on loyalty, Laura felt she should buy something, but although the prices were not exorbitant, the pictures were so far from Laura's taste that she was very unwilling to spend much. Maybe the still life her mother had admired would be all right in the spare room. She turned to ask her mother's opinion and saw Adam and Kim exchanging "do you think we can go yet?" glances. Here was the answer to her loyalty dilemma. She had not seen Adam for years but he was clearly a man in need of a conversation. She only hoped Melanie saw them talking.

Her ploy was doubly unsuccessful. Melanie was beyond noticing anything so trivial as her brother's conversation. She had moved on from Camilla and Sasha and was (not entirely soberly) trying to sell one of the sculptures. And as Laura fumbled for some common ground with Adam, she was suddenly spun round by her shoulders to see Camilla grinning broadly at her. "Laura, well! Robert not here? No, he wouldn't be, I suppose. Art's not really his thing, is it? I meant to ring you but forgot, what with . . ." She stopped for a moment, her eye caught by some face or movement on the other side of the gallery. But a second later she was talking again, her eyes still roving round the crowd. Laura watched her, half horrified, half just interested. Camilla was not her normal self: either this was Camilla in party mode or, more sinister (and more likely) she was on something. And it did not look to Laura as though this glazed, flitting glance, this abrupt conversation, this lack of concentration was anything to do with champagne. She forced her attention back to Camilla's words – what was she saying?

"I'm afraid Christmas isn't on, after all. Of course, I wish I could have the children but it turns out to be rather inconvenient – for Sasha, I mean. So what I suggest is that we come and get them for New Year."

Laura was dumbfounded. Camilla had tried to change the children's plans at least once a month in the eighteenth months of Laura's marriage. But never before (the honeymoon had been an exception) had she rearranged their lives in the Bedfords' favour. "Well, you don't mind do you?" Camilla snapped. "If your parents can't fit them into their cottage you could stay in London." Laura tried to speak but Camilla's attention had wandered. "I'll ring Robert. *Ciao*," she said and with a wave was off. Laura was too amazed, and too pleased, even to be cross with the dismissive reference to her parents' "cottage". Now Christmas really would be Christmas.

Melanie woke feeling like death. Her head hurt, her eyes hurt, her mouth felt as though it stank and she was fairly sure her bank balance hurt.

She pulled on a jersey and wandered into the kitchen to find her father up and dapper and making coffee. He looked at her sympathetically, poured her some orange juice and waited until she had gulped it down before he spoke.

"Congratulations. I thought it went very well. Of course, I don't know if the right people were there, but I saw some red dots and everyone seemed to be having a good time."

"That's what's worrying me." Melanie held out her glass for more juice. "I've never deluded myself into thinking I'd do much business after the preview – not this time, anyway – and everyone was having far too much fun (and champagne) to

buy. You should have seen how many bottles we got through."
Melanie, knowing her own frailties, had preferred to clear up
the debris of the preview party after everyone left rather than
arriving early before the gallery opened in the morning. "Still,
let's hope we've got some coverage at least."

She slid behind the counter and pulled the pile of papers her
father had already been out to buy towards her.

"What are your plans today?" her father asked, too lightly.

"Oh, I'd better go to the gallery and I fixed lunch with Laura,
can't think why – yes, I can – and I must find Beth, my sculptress,
who never showed last night. We did manage to sell a couple of
her pieces, too. Why?"

"Oh, no reason." Alex poured two milky cups of coffee and
pushed one towards her. "Toast?" Melanie gave him a look.

"What have I done?"

"Nothing, why?"

"Why all this special treatment?"

"Special treatment? I just thought you looked a little worn."

Melanie sighed and accepted the coffee. If it was important it
would come to light, if not it really did not matter what Alex was
doing. And maybe he was just being kind. She was too hungover
to care. She would try to get through the day and leave worrying
about her father until tomorrow.

Melanie felt too ill to be able to face anything other than a curry
or a greasy spoon for lunch, so Laura, faintly disapproving,
followed her friend to a café. They sat down and ordered.
("Bacon, beans, fried slice, two eggs over easy, chips, strong
tea," recited Melanie. "Spaghetti bolognese and Coca-Cola,"
muttered Laura. "Big mistake," said Melanie, perking up.)

Then Laura moved in to the attack. "You could have cancelled
lunch if you felt this bad; it was your idea, you know," she said,
smoothing her paper napkin and looking aggressively healthy.
"Anyway, well done for last night. What were you and Sasha
so chummy about?"

"The same as you and Adam – opening the bidding for a
rip-roaring affair," countered Melanie, who had obviously been
keeping a sharper eye on her guests than Laura had thought.
"Actually we were just renewing acquaintance and swapping

useful addresses." Laura looked blank and Melanie gave up baiting her. It had always been a pointless exercise. "No, I remembered what you said in France and thought I'd see how the land lay. I've heard about him off and on, but haven't seen him for years. He seems a lot healthier these days – maybe it's the love of a good woman." Laura did not rise to that one and Melanie giggled, then apologised at once. She always did to Laura.

"So what did you think?" Laura hated Melanie in this mood, but could not disguise her curiosity.

"I think Camilla's very glam but not as pretty as you said and she's fraying a bit round the edges."

"And?"

"And Sasha's grown into his face and I wish I'd never let him get away."

"Don't be silly. What else?"

"I forgot to ask him who Flap's mother is but I'm pretty sure it's not me."

"*Melanie!*"

"Oh, all right. I think they're definitely on something, but oddly enough, I think she might be keener than he is. Not dope – not last night, anway."

"So, what?"

"Not Paracetamol either. I don't know, but it looked like coke to me. And that backs up what I'd heard on the grapevine."

"*Cocaine.*"

Melanie looked away from the naked gloating in Laura's eyes. When she looked back there was a more acceptable concern in its place.

"So what next?"

"So I make an appointment with a lawyer. If that's what's happening, my case is unanswerable. Thank you, Melanie."

"Hey, listen. I didn't see them take anything. I didn't even see them go in or out of the loos. I don't know of anyone that they could have scored from last night," (that irritated Melanie, it made her feel old) "all I know is that they did seem to be on something. But I don't even know Camilla – or Sasha any more. Maybe they were on a natural high, maybe they're just party people." Melanie, unsure of what she might have set in motion, felt herself back-pedalling furiously. But it made no difference. Laura was not even listening. She was calmly eating her filthy pasta and making conversation about Adam and Kim. She had heard what she needed to hear and was uninterested in anything more.

What Laura could not say to Melanie was how she remembered her friend during her drug-taking days. She had not been a girl anyone would put forward as an example to children. If there was any truth at all in Melanie's theory, Laura could not allow the children to spend one month, let alone most of the next fifteen years, with the Limpnakoffs. The slack eyes, the long nights and short days, the nervous and bitter arguments, abrupt changes of mood, veering between almost manic intolerance to an inane *laissez-faire* attitude, the inability to make any sort of decision: none of these would produce an atmosphere in any way healthy for small children or, later, adolescents.

Laura did not realise how much she had been thinking about the children recently. In France she had decided not to do anything about Sasha's past, afterwards she had come to the conclusion that there was nothing to be done. She had been able to push her worries into her subconscious. Every now and again the issue had come to the forefront of her mind, and each time she had decided that she was being hysterical, or that she was just trying to prove to herself how much better a step-parent she was than her rival.

Melanie's new news woke all the horrors, and Laura was now amazed at how many months she had wasted. If it were true that Sasha and Camilla were taking any drugs at all – even the occasional joint – she knew she must do all in her power to reverse the custody decision. It was necessary for the children. It would make Robert happier than anything else she could do for him.

And she would do it for him. He was too busy, he was involved with the law day and night. She would do the legwork and let Robert know later. She also knew from the jolt of happiness she had felt when Camilla had told her that the children were to stay with their father that Christmas that she missed the children herself. She wanted to live with them again. There was now no doubt in her mind that she was doing the right thing and that

Robert would be delighted. She was too excited to think any differently.

Melanie wearily let herself into her flat. The exhibition had four more days to run but most of her hard work was over. She had still not succeeded in finding her sculptress, but that would have to wait until the next day.

A sound caught her ear and she stopped, her hand still on the doorknob, and listened. It was unmistakably a woman's laugh – a *titter*, Melanie thought in disgust. She did not think she had ever before heard so definite a *titter*.

What was she to do? She could stride in and confront the titterer, and for a moment was sorely tempted. It was her flat, for heaven's sake, not a knocking shop for her father. She took a step forward and heard another noise, from the sitting room, not, as she had feared at first, from her father's room. And this time it seemed less of a titter and more of a laugh – a warm, chuckly laugh. And Melanie, with a flush of shame, realised that she had not been angry, but jealous.

She quietly turned and left the flat. She wanted a drink. When would her life ever be in order?

The old man was courteous but his suit was a little shabby. Perhaps she had made a dreadful mistake, Laura thought as she took a seat and accepted the offer of a cup of coffee more to put off the discussion than because she needed cold filter coffee. The office was also tired-looking, the books old, even for a law firm, and the secretary a cheerless frump with a part-time air about her. But here Laura was. Working secretly as she had been, she had had no choice but to look in Yellow Pages for a solicitor with a reputable-sounding name in an accessible part of the City.

Mr Chisolm scratched his neck and cleared his throat. Laura wondered if he were ill and crossed her legs. Both waited for the other to speak.

"So how can I help you, Mrs Bedford?" It was a gentle reminder that it was she who had instigated the meeting and that his time at least was valuable.

Laura had prepared her speech but it had fled from her. All she could think of was Sasha's handsome, mocking face. It was her turn to clear her throat.

"It's a question of custody, Mr Chisolm. Of children, I mean. I'm wondering how to get an order changed."

"Ah." Chisolm switched gear. He had obviously been expecting something else. Divorce, perhaps, or a shoplifting defence. "Custody," he mused a little theatrically, and pulled a pad of paper towards him. "Very well, tell me the facts. How often do your children see their father at the moment."

"I don't have any children," Laura began, and the door opened to the secretary with the predictably undrinkable coffee. "They're not my children," Laura tried again after biscuits, milk and all the paraphernalia attendant on office coffee had been dealt with. "They're my husband's. They live with their mother and come to us for three or four weekends and half of the holidays. She has care and control, but the custody is joint."

Chisolm nodded. "Perfectly normal arrangement. So what is the problem? Do you want less of the children or more?"

"More!" Laura was impatient for everything to be explained and sorted out and the children to be back in Parson's Green Lane. "My husband and I have been married for a year and a half; his first wife has recently remarried. We don't like – don't trust her husband. He's – I don't know, he's odd – wild . . . She tailed off, knowing she would have to do better than this. But how could she explain Camilla, her total change in character and way of life? How could Chisolm ever understand about Sasha and Henley and Kathmandu? How could she put across how much better off the children were at home with her – how much she needed them there?

Perhaps it was only now, as she sat in this dingy office struggling with her words, that she realised how much she wanted the children back for herself, not just for Robert. She knew she had grown to love them, but now she saw that without them there was a gap in her life. She felt – wrongly – that Robert's love for her grew with the children's. She was not Helen's and Richard's mother and knew she could never fill that place, she had not yet given up hope of having her own child, but none of this mattered. She wanted them home, wanted to be a family again.

She made another effort. "Mr Chisolm, my husband is a lawyer. His first wife is from a – wealthy – and conventional family. Until she met this man she was happiest shopping, lunching and going to charity dances. She looked like a well-off professional wife and behaved as she looked. Then she met this man. They go out all night together and leave Richard and Helen (my stepchildren) with his thirteen-year-old daughter. He's a painter, though that's not the point. They marry, dump the children and honeymoon for almost *five months* in Kathmandu. *Kathmandu!* She was always irrational but now she's more – I don't know, jumpy, nervy. The children know me and think we are properly married (Helen's words, not mine). We can offer them security, continuity, comfort – everything. Can't we have them?"

There was a silence. Laura feared she had given away her feelings. She waited. The telephone rang outside the office and she heard the Frump answering.

"Why isn't your husband here?"

The question was so unexpected Laura did not at first understand it. Then she mumbled, "Oh, he was busy, it seemed better . . ."

Chisolm nodded as though this confirmed a theory. "Forgive my asking, but does he know you're here?" Laura did not need to answer. "You said he was a lawyer himself, you see," Chisolm's voice was surprisingly gentle. "It would have been more usual for him to consult a colleague if he did not know about family law himself. Now, Mrs Bedford, it occurs to me that if you are here without your husband's knowledge you must have a very good reason. Maybe your husband does not share your desire for a larger part of the custody—"

"No! He'd love it, more than anything else he would want that. It's just – he doesn't like to make waves – he wouldn't want to risk upsetting the children again now that they're used to the way things are."

Laura began to panic. Oh, dear God, had she been right and sensible or was the whole plan just crazy? Perhaps she should have told Robert first, maybe surprises weren't always such a good idea. She had felt so sure she was wise and helpful – had she acted secretly because she was subconsciously worried that she was wrong? It was too late. She sat waiting for Chisolm to break the silence and trying to calm her scurrying thoughts.

Chisolm nodded and scratched his neck again. "So there's something else. From what you've told me, Mrs Bedford, you would not have much chance of changing the court order. So the first Mrs Bedford goes to a few parties, marries again. And didn't Mr Bedford do the same thing himself? So she is a little nervy, upset – maybe you were when you first married? The thirteen-year-old baby-sitter, that's not good, a little careless maybe – but no, that wouldn't be enough to warrant care and control passing to your husband. Are the children clean and well fed?" Laura nodded and Chisolm continued, marking each point on a stubby finger. "Are they kept back from school unnecessarily? Does she prevent your husband seeing them? Do they complain about the stepfather? Have any unexplained bruises appeared on their bodies? Have they regressed in their behaviour? Begun bed-wetting, become overtimid or overaffectionate? You shake your head, Mrs Bedford, and I confess I am at a loss as to why you feel the order should be changed."

For some reason Laura had been loath to play her trump card, but under this insistent probing she grew bold. "Drugs," she said, looking him full in the face.

"Ah." His wrinkled eyes opened a little and he let his hands fall to the desk. "Ah. Drugs. Very well." He turned over the virtually untouched pad of paper and started a new sheet. This encouraged Laura.

Now more confident of having Chisolm's full attention, she quickly told him about Sasha's past and the rumours she had heard about his present. She mentioned the possibility that Camilla was also experimenting with drugs, if in a minor way, and ended by describing her own life, her own suitability as a stepmother, and the fact that she was now full time at home. And a churchgoer. "They're only four and seven, you see. So very impressionable," she finished, almost pleading with Mr Chisolm to make everything better.

He looked more impressed, nodding seriously as he wrote a few notes. "Now, of course, we have something," he concluded. "Although you'll agree it's all a little circumstantial at the moment. The past, it's not good, no. But a public schoolboy? A good background? Yes, of course. And a sign of the times, drugs – dangerous, and so sad."

Laura was not prepared to weep for Sasha. But she would go along with Chisolm. For today at least. "Their lawyers would play with all of this," Chisolm added unnecessarily. "So we must play with it also. Now, when and how did he stop the heroin?"

"I don't know exactly – Broadway Lodge and quite a few years ago."

"That's good for them, the longer the better, of course . . ." The neck-scratching began again.

"But now! That can't be good! If they're taking drugs *now*."

"*If.* If, Mrs Bedford. There is the dangerous word. And that is what we must discover."

Laura felt very, very tired. She had come here to be advised, not to play verbal pat-a-cake with a tired old man from Central Casting. And he was right, she had a husband who was a perfectly good lawyer and who, even if he was not up to date in the nuances of family law, would know a man who was. But she was paying this man and he might as well earn his money.

"So what do you say, Mr Chisolm?" she asked, pushing the half-full cup of scummy coffee away from her. "Putting aside your views on the drug culture in general, what do you think?"

He looked taken aback at Laura's rudeness, but it did make him sit a little straighter and stop scratching his neck.

"If you would like my professional view, Mrs Bedford, I would say this: do I think the children would be better off with you? Almost certainly, yes. Do I think we could change the court order? Taking the information you have given me as factually correct, yes, I do. *But* we must be able to establish that the young man's past is spilling over into his present and that it will materially affect the children's future." He paused a second, looking pleased with his pronouncement. "Past, present, future. Yes," he muttered, ticking the words. off on his fingers again. "Now where shall we take it from here?" he concluded, pretending not to notice that Laura was standing up and shrugging into her raincoat. "Well, I can give you one very good piece of advice which will help your case a great deal."

Laura looked at him again. "Yes?"

"Tell your husband your plans, my dear. Don't keep him in the dark." Chuckling at his small triumph, he patted Laura's hands and delivered her to the Frump.

Laura was furious. Furious with Chisolm ("Chisolm, indeed!"), with herself, and with the person next to her on the tube whose fat thighs were spilling over onto her share of the seat.

Chisolm was right, of course. Robert would have to be told and indeed should already have been. They were his children and if Sasha and Camilla were druggies – if, if, there was that irritating if again.

Very well, she would tell Robert tonight. The whole story. Including her visit to the ridiculous Chisolm. She would apologise for having acted behind his back, explain her worries, and from then on they would work together. It was, after all, very simple.

A part of her that suggested there might in fact be a few difficulties ahead prompted her to get off the tube at the next stop and ring Melanie. She was not in, probably still out to lunch somewhere, Laura thought crossly. (In fact she was visiting a painter of tribal art whose career was not going too well. Probably because he came from Kent, had studied anthropology at Sussex University and visited Kenya once for a couple of months.) Laura hesitated and decided against ringing Julia. She was so wrapped up in herself these days. (In fact she was wrapped up in thoughts of the new baby, due any day now.) Charlotte, though . . . she was sensible. Laura very much wanted to talk this through with someone before Robert. For practice really.

She rang Charlotte's office which was in Wright's Lane and so not too much out of her way home. "Charlotte? Are you very busy? No, no, I'm in a call box, that's why – yes. Listen, if I came by your office in about ten minutes, would you be able to sneak out for a quick cup of tea? Honestly? You're a real friend. I'll explain when I get there. Yes, ten minutes. Bye."

Charlotte did listen. She drank her tea and crumbled a muffin and waited until Laura arrived at the end of her tale. Finally, she asked one question. "Why didn't you tell Robert?"

"I don't know. I didn't know what to do and didn't want to upset him and was cowardly, I suppose. I thought I was preparing a wonderful surprise. Babyish, really. But then I realised how important it was. I don't know, things changed."

"Everything you've said seems clear cut and yet you seem in an awful muddle."

"I was. I am. But you do think it's clear cut then?"

Charlotte nodded. "I don't know anything about law but if Camilla and Sasha are taking drugs, of course the children shouldn't be there. What about the stepdaughter?"

"Flap? We don't want her," Laura said nervously.

"Laura! I didn't mean that, but . . ."

"Yes, sorry. I don't know anything about her, or where her mother is – I presume she still exists. But honestly, she's not our responsibility. It's Richard and Helen I'm worried about. They should be home with us."

She spoke so fiercely that Charlotte said nothing, just looked. "Is anything else the matter?" she asked after a moment. Laura looked down at her plate and shook her head. But she could not stop the tears welling up and Charlotte waited in silence. "Don't tell me if you don't want to," she said after a while. "Is it Robert?" Laura shook her head so emphatically that a big tear sploshed onto her hand. It stayed there, glinting for the moment more brightly than the emerald on her finger.

"No, it's not Robert. It's everything else. The worry about the children, and that I didn't tell Robert when I should have and . . ."

"And?"

Laura looked up and meeting Charlotte's clam, sensible gaze, weakened. She had to tell someone.

"I've been trying to have a baby and getting nowhere. It's not been much more than a year, but – I don't know. I just can't see the point of anything if I don't have children. So then I thought – well, if Richard and Helen *are* in trouble we should have them and I know how happy Robert would be and I knew that I'd love it too – I do love them, honestly, and then it wouldn't be so bad not having my own, but maybe it would help me to have my own, you know the gynaecologist said relax but how can I when all this is happening and maybe I shouldn't have left work . . ." she tailed off in soggy whimpers. Charlotte handed her a crumpled paper napkin and thought for a moment.

"Is that why you want the children so much? And if it is, are you absolutely sure of your facts about Sasha? You'll have to be careful, you know."

Laura pulled herself together. "Yes, I do know. And that's partly why I haven't said anything to Robert. But it's getting out of hand."

"I should say." Charlotte looked furtively at her watch.

Laura caught the movement and huffily gathered her things together. "Sorry, sorry, I know you're working."

Charlotte sighed. Laura was getting impossible these days. "Calm down. I've got a bit longer. Now why don't you tackle these things one at a time? First, tell Robert what's happened so far – including your Mr Chisley. He'll know about the legal side and what must be done if the drugs thing is real. Then go back to your doctor, ask about the baby problem. He'll reassure you and say everything's all right. A year's no time, Laura. I've read stories . . . anyway. Then wait for the weekend and see if you notice anything wrong or different about the children. Don't alert them, whatever you do. You know how children say what they think grown-ups want to hear. And finally, see if you can find anyone more – responsible – than Melanie to corroborate what she says. how about that for a plan of action?"

Laura smiled. "Thank you. I'm sorry I got into such a state."

"Don't worry. And now that I've been so wise I really must get back to work." She stood and kissed Laura. "Let's have a drink one evening."

"OK." Laura wanted Charlotte to stay longer but did not dare ask.

"And Laura – please tell Robert about it. Tonight."

Laura cooked Robert's favourite dinner, but her hand was not as light as usual and the pancakes were leaden, the pork-and-nut stuffing bland and tasteless. She tried to open the conversation several times during the course of the evening but always managed to put it off. Robert watched and gave her no help. He had known something was brewing for some time but, tied up with work, he had let the problem slide. Laura would tell him in her own good time.

Finally she had put on the coffee machine, cleared the table and poured the last of the wine into her glass. With one more gulp for courage she sat down and told Robert all that had happened in the last few months.

As was his wont, he heard her out in total silence (a habit that had always irritated Laura, more used to the noisy question-and-answer sessions of a large family). He gave no sign at all as to what his reaction might be until Laura finished. She finally reached the description of Chisolm and the interview with him and for the first time for some minutes she turned her eyes to his.

He was looking at her with a cold anger she had never thought to see in his face.

"Do you realise what you have been doing?" he asked at last.

"I thought—"

"You did *not* think. Had you thought for one instant you would have come to me at once. As soon as Melanie even hinted anything was up. Had you thought, you would not have taken Melanie, with her past, as a reliable witness. But if you do persist in having faith in her – for no reason that I can understand – you would have come straight to me. If you did believe her – and I don't believe you did until it suited you – we should never have allowed the children to go back to Sasha."

"Robert—"

"Let me finish." Robert did not know where to begin, let alone end, he was so angry. He could not believe it of Laura, that she should go behind his back like this. And to Melanie of all people – to Melanie and some second-rate lawyer out of a telephone book. Neither could he understand her motivation. Why had she not trusted him? Because she was not sure if she trusted herself?

It was not only Laura he was angry with; he was livid with himself. Part of his denial of what Laura had told him was because he did not want to believe he had been so blind. He was the children's father, for God's sake. He should have noticed something was amiss – if indeed it was. He took a breath, wishing he could clear his head.

"I know you care for Richard and Helen and I'm grateful to you for that. *Grateful!*, Laura thought. *How can he be so cold as to talk about gratitude?* They love you and are certainly happier now than they ever were, even when Camilla and I were married. I cannot believe that that would be the case if their life at their other home were not entirely normal."

"But Sasha—" Laura wanted to defend herself, but did not know where to start, what was making Robert most angry.

Robert meanwhile was trying to go back to the beginning, to exonerate himself. "You told me yourself not to judge by appearances. We met him, he seemed all right. Stupid, affected, all that – but basically all right.'

''Camilla—''

''Camilla is my business. And she does seem to have settled down since she married. You must grant that.'' *Hadn't she?* he asked himself. *She's certainly been more reasonable about access arrangements* . . .

Laura had at first been abject under the force of Robert's cold anger. She felt guilty enough at her silence to take his wrath as her just deserts, but now she began to respond in kind.

''All right, Camilla is your business. Lucky you. And so are the children. But remember what I've said. I know what you think of Melanie, but she's been a good friend to me. She could be being a good friend to you now, if only you'd listen. I'm sorry I went behind your back, but now it's up to you. I took too long to tell you: I was stupid, maybe a coward. But if you feel comfortable next Sunday when you take the children back to Camilla's you're tougher than I am.''

Robert stalked into the kitchen without answering. Laura heard him smashing about looking for cups and saucers. He came back in with a mollified expression and two cups of coffee. He handed her one and poured himself a whisky. Perhaps he had been too severe. Oh God, he needed to *think*. Despite his confusion, his anger, he had already begun to feel the first flickering of hope. He tried to damp it down: he knew only too well how long the odds were against him. He would not be able to bear the pain of hoping and being disappointed.

Meanwhile, Laura had turned on the television and was furiously watching the end of the news. His anger had swept away her doubts and left her feeling profoundly in the right.

''I'm sorry if I overreacted,'' Robert said tightly. ''You must admit it was a shock. We must go into these – allegations – thoroughly. And, of course, we must act upon what we find. Meanwhile give me Mr Chisolm's bill when it comes and I will settle it. We don't need his type involved in this. You're not to say anything to the children about this. Nothing at all. Or ask them any odd questions.'' He softened at last, although too late for Laura ever to forget his bitter anger. ''We should hope you're wrong,'' he said sadly. ''But I can't help – Laura, if you are wrong, I don't know if I'll be able to forgive you."

She looked at him through puffy eyes. "And if I'm right?"

"If you're right? Even your friend Mr Chisolm warned you against relying on if," he said, and left her alone with Peter Sissons.

12 ∫

The worst was over once Robert had been told. Laura felt as though the problem had entirely vanished and lived for a few days barely thinking of custody or babies. After all, Christmas was approaching, and the children would be with them for a fortnight. After that came the New Year and Laura still believed in new beginnings.

At first, Robert made no mention of the problem or what was to be done: but he was by nature a brooder and Laura knew it would not be long before he came to a decision. A few days later, he broached the subject.

"To be quite honest, I'm not entirely sure how we should go about this all," he began, starting to open a bottle of wine while closing the fridge door with his bottom. "Custody has been awarded, and although circumstances have changed, they have in theory changed for the better. Camilla is now married to someone with money and as far as we know a fairly responsible attitude to his own child. At any rate he appears to support her financially and make his home open to her. Which is more than many unmarried fathers do. So the problem is the drug-taking allegations. I want to know how we can collect satisfactory evidence of that. And fast," he added with a frown. "If it's all true we must get the children away."

"Melanie—"

'Melanie would not make a good witness. Camilla's lawyers would only ask one or two questions about her past and her friendship with you for her to be destroyed as an objective viewer."

155 •

Laura took the stew and baked potatoes from the oven. Her heart was racing. "What about Camilla's friends?"

"I don't know. What do I do? Ring them up and ask if she's taking drugs? They'd cover up for her if they knew and most would not know. If she's changed her life as completely as you imply then she's probably lost touch with most of them." He looked amused for a moment. "I can't imagine Sarah or John taking drugs, I must say."

"But wouldn't that help, then?" Laura sat down and helped Robert to a plateful. She was thinking too hard to watch what she was doing and dropped a Brussels sprout on the table. "I mean isn't it a bit odd to dump all your friends? If all her good, respectable, middle-class friends say she's disappeared out of their lives, wouldn't that tell its own tale?"

Robert thought as he mashed butter into his potato. "Only if they said they'd given up on her because of drugs, or her new drug-taking friends. After all, new marriages often mean new friends and when a marriage breaks up friends often drift apart." Robert was trying hard to remain objective, to think like a lawyer, but the father in him kept panicking – awful images of Camilla and Sasha in a drug-induced coma, the children left for days before anyone found them, flashing through his head. "Laura, you've got to realise that a judge won't change a custody order without a very good reason. They take the view that the status quo is better for the children unless there is abuse or neglect. I just don't know if this is the right thing to do. It will be hell for the children, and if it all backfires, God knows Camilla will have good reason to bitch up our lives then."

"But if we win—"

"Yes, and if we lose? Laura, I want my children to live with me. But I could not stand it if through some half-cock idea we end up with them coming to us less often. I don't think you understand the risks. I can't see how we can be sure." He paused to chew his meat, but his thoughts were not with the food. "And what are Camilla and Sasha supposed to be taking? That will make a difference too. I don't think we'd be given custody if they're just smoking marijuana. They'd be given a slap on the wrist and have an eye kept on them. If they're taking cocaine they'll be in more trouble – we'd get the children for sure if they're taking heroin." The thought made him sick with fear, made him want to go roaring out of the house and seize his children without further ado. But that was not the way.

Laura pushed a piece of beef round her plate. Robert's wavering irritated her. Knowing him, she was sure he would be unable to let matters stand as they were. But neither would his inherent caution allow him to declare himself and, pennants flying, spur himself into action. He could dilly-dally for weeks, but if she pushed him too hard his stubbornness would only make him balk more. Laura would never have thought of herself as manipulative, but a year and a half of marriage had taught her a few tricks about getting her own way.

"What about a detective?" she suggested, knowing full well how Robert would receive that idea.

"Of course not. This isn't a B-movie, it's Helen and Richard's life." And ours, she thought, but wisely held her peace. "Maybe I should have it out with Camilla," Robert went on, abstractedly helping himself to more food – a good sign, as he always ate a lot when he was working on an important case.

"I don't think that would help," said Laura, thinking that if Camilla were to be declared an enemy it would be better to keep her at a distance from the start.

They went to bed that night with nothing decided except Robert's promise to talk to Melanie and listen himself to what she had to say. That in itself was an improvement.

As she had feared, Melanie had made a substantial loss on her exhibition. But she felt it had been worthwhile. She had sold a respectable amount of work and the press reports, though scarce, were favourable. She must just remember to have cheaper champagne and fewer waitresses at the next preview. Aside from the financial loss, the exhibition had also changed her life for the better. Those young artists who had not been sure of her now paid court to her, and gallery owners wooed her to place her next exhibition in their rooms. She had made the move from knowledgeable and agreeable outsider to insider in one step. Her telephone rang constantly and she no longer ever found herself alone in a wine bar wondering how to spend the evening ahead. She did not miss Nicholas at all, but neither was she on the hunt for a replacement. Not yet, anyway. And her new happiness made her more tolerant towards her brother and father. Theirs would never be a normal family, but at least they could now pass muster. For the first time in very many years Melanie did nothing of which she should be ashamed. Oh, she still drank too much and wore too much lipstick, still swore and was too frank, but there was something about her that was more open and relaxed than for many years.

Laura was too preoccupied to notice all these changes in her friend. If she saw that Melanie was more relaxed, she assumed it was drink. She was pleased at Melanie's moderate success but not really all that interested in it. Melanie did not allow herself to be hurt by Laura's distance: she had expected it to come with her friend's marriage and she realised that it was unhappiness, not happiness, that was drawing Laura away.

They did not talk much any more – their conversation had become platitudinous and almost polite. Melanie knew Laura wanted a baby and knew she was worried about Helen and Richard. She could do nothing to help with the first problem and was at a loss as to any part she could play in the second.

So when one day she picked up the telephone to Sasha Limpnakoff, her first thought was for Laura.

"Sash," she was genuinely surprised. But wary – he was speaking with a full drawl.

"Melanie. Just thought I'd say hi." There was a silence. Melanie was sure he was after something, but could not think what. And, after all, so was she.

"Well, that's great, yes, hi. It was good to see you the other day." Nearly a month had passed since the preview but in their lives that came to the same thing.

"Yah, well I'd been meaning to get in touch. How about a drink?" They fixed a day and place and Melanie hung up feeling fairly bewildered. Well, well. What next?

Laura was furious when Melanie told her about the date. To her, Melanie was going over to the enemy. Finally she accepted that Melanie was not so much visiting her own past as investigating Laura's future. Then she was excited. "Robert wants to talk to you about all this – actually that was why I was ringing you –

but let's fix a date for after you've seen Sasha. We may have more to go on. Come to supper the day after, yes, that'll be fine. Good. Oh, and Melanie – thanks.''

Melanie and Sasha met in a Kensington Church Street wine bar and drank Australian Chardonnay alongside journalists drinking champagne on expenses. At first, conversation was awkward and Melanie wondered why Sasha had rung her. But as the bottle emptied Sasha's drawl retreated and they began to talk properly. The subject of Camilla came up. Sasha admitted that he had been almost surprised into marriage but insisted that Camilla was ''a laugh'' and not at all to type. ''She's got two children which can be a bit of a drag, but then Flap's around a lot as well and she helps out.''

''Flap?''

''My daughter.''

''Tell me about her.''

''Well, you know she's that age, but she's all right really.''

''No, I mean, who's her mother? I never knew you had a daughter.''

Sasha shifted a little and poured more wine. ''Yah, well I wasn't very cool about her then, and her mother – you don't know her, just a girl – wasn't that cool about me seeing her anyway. But after Broadway, I thought, well, she was my daughter and it would help my growth to be able to interact with her properly, take responsibility for my actions . . .'' he tailed off and grinned uneasily. ''All that Broadway shit. And anyway, I liked her.''

Melanie gestured at the bottle. ''And we're both back on the pop.''

''Yah, well, what the hell. I'm in control.'' He ordered another bottle to prove it while Melanie considered how to broach the subject of drugs. In the end she was direct.

''Sash, do you know where to score these days – or has Camilla put a stop to all that?''

Sasha looked surprised but answered readily. ''Thought you were still clean? Yah, I know – I could get you something for old times' sake. I don't do much now, just parties, you know. Not smack, though. I've done with that.''

Melanie nodded. "Me too. But sometimes – like my preview – I do wish I could have just a couple of lines of coke, just to get me going."

She watched him closely and hooray! he rose. "You should have said. We got some that night. Camilla's taken to it – you know she'd never tried it before she met me? I suppose I should watch her," he added, "don't want her getting too keen."

Their eyes met and Melanie felt suddenly uncomfortable. Even in his most drug-crazy days, Sasha had always had compelling eyes, eyes that made it hard to lie. She had met him as a friend and was in fact a spy. She wondered how much she was going to like herself for this. But there was another reason for her discomfort. She still found him very attractive. And it crossed her mind for the first time that maybe he had not rung her for a chat, or to ask her to represent his work (if she were honest she knew he did not need her), but because he also found her attractive.

Melanie, Melanie, please be careful.

Melanie found Laura more like her old self than she had been for months. Her new worry lines had smoothed out, her sitting room smelt of Floris-burning essence and her hair had been cut and even highlighted. The affection between her and Robert was almost tangible, so that Melanie, although invited and warmly welcomed by both, felt an intruder.

Robert too was relaxed and jokey. He poured Melanie a vodka and apologised for having missed her show, but from his comments he had clearly read the press coverage and Melanie was touched by his interest.

They sat down to chicken breasts in cognac and slightly overcooked broccoli. They talked about family and friends, gossiping without malice and drinking Robert's wine slightly too fast.

"So what about Christmas?" Laura asked, producing the season's first mince pies from the bottom of the oven. "Any plans?"

Melanie was unsure how to answer. She hated Christmas and this year, despite her rapprochement with her family, boded no better than the last ten. "Well Adam and Kim are going to her family's in Surrey, so Dad and I were going to go to the Ritz or something for lunch. But you know he's got this girlfriend – she's invited him (and me as an afterthought) to lunch with her family in Belsize Park. I suppose I've got to go – Dad won't unless I do – but I must admit it doesn't sound very wacky." She caught the tiny look between Robert and Laura and the infinitesimal nod he gave.

"Well, don't if you don't want to, but why don't you come here for the day?" Laura offered. "We've decided on a London Christmas. Mummy and Daddy are going to Aunt Mary in Fife and Oriana and James are off to Norfolk. We'll have the children and possibly Ferdy's lot – it depends. If his in-laws are here they'll just come for supper – but why don't you?"

Robert seconded the invitation. "Do come, Melanie. Your father can go off to Belsize Park if he wants and you're almost family, after all."

Melanie was amazed and very grateful. She knew that she and Robert had become something approaching friends in France, but knew too how precious his time with his children was to him. And Christmas – well, no one had to welcome outsiders in on that day.

"Thank you both. If you mean it, I think I'd love to. I'll have to talk to Dad first, so tell me if you change your minds. Thank you." Oh, hell, there were actually tears in her eyes.

They moved into the sitting room for coffee, and as Robert lit the gas fire and the flames began to flicker around the coals, the atmosphere shifted. Despite all the jolly camaraderie of supper they knew there was business to be done, and not for the first time, Melanie wished she had not become involved.

Laura fussed with coffee cups and Robert with whisky until there was no more putting off to be done. In the end it was Robert who opened the bidding.

"Well, Melanie," he said. "Laura says I should listen to some things you have to say."

And so Melanie told him the whole sorry tale. How she first knew Sasha, how she had left him almost ten years ago, the rumours she had heard since, her surprise at his marriage to Camilla, his behaviour at her preview and the admissions he had made at their meeting the day before. She spoke uninterrupted for almost twenty minutes while Laura stared into the blue flames and Robert looked gravely at Melanie. Sometimes she could meet his eyes, sometimes not. As she told of the wine bar rendezvous her colour rose slightly and she looked down at her elaborately buckled shoes.

At last she finished and Robert began to question her, gently but determinedly. He double-checked every aspect of her story and probed into the drug-taking past all those years before. He asked about Sasha: his background, his education, his character. And finally he made an apology. "I'm sorry about this, Melanie, but there's one thing I must ask you."

Melanie looked at him and nodded. "Could you swear, on oath, that since the day you left Broadway you've never taken another drug?"

She answered without hesitation. "I gave Broadway a couple of shots as you know, but since I left for the last time, no, nothing. On the other hand you should know that NA takes a very dim view of those of us who drink again."

Laura had been silent throughout the speech and the questioning. Now when she spoke her voice was gentle. "Melanie, I'm truly sorry about this. Thank you."

Melanie shrugged. "Oh, in NA I got quite used to soul-baring. Some of the stories I heard . . ." but her flip answer belied the strain in her twisting fingers. She stood abruptly. "Look, I'd better go. It's getting late and – I'd better go. Thank you both very much for supper. I enjoyed it."

They all stood, but the tension was not so easily broken. They hurried the parting on as fast as they decently could, but Melanie and Laura hugged and Robert said as he kissed Melanie goodbye, "Do think seriously about Christmas. We did mean it."

As the door closed behind her Robert and Laura were left looking at each other.

"Well?" she said at last.

"I think we have no choice left but to go for it. My children should not be with him. Nor, I fear, her. We'll have to take our chances with Melanie. I believe her, and I think if she tells her story as she did just now, a judge will too."

This was not a moment for congratulations, but for comfort. Laura had never seen Robert look so sad.

*　　*　　*

Christmas was perfect: a fairy-tale day in a storybook week. Laura went to Midnight Mass at the Oratory with Ferdy and Aimée and the next morning took the children to a special service with carols and a real donkey. Melanie did go to the Bedfords and found herself enjoying Christmas for the first time in her adult life. The Sawyers came to early supper and the children played noisy card games while the grown-ups lolled like cats on sofas.

With the children back under their roof for the next fortnight, Laura and Robert succeeded in putting all thoughts of custody cases out of their minds. For now, at least, they were safe and their arrival, with shining hair and neatly packed suitcases, showed that at least their bodily comforts were well looked after. On Boxing Day only did an unpleasant incident sour the flavour of the holiday for Laura.

"Can I ring Flap?" asked Helen, who had been mooching about the house the whole morning in a very Boxing Day-like way.

Laura paused in opening a tin of cat food and Whiskas butted her hand impatiently with his head. "Flap?"

"My sister," said Helen, as though to someone very stupid or foreign or both. "I'm missing her."

Laura put the tin down and turned her full attention on the child. "Your *what*?" she asked carefully, knowing she should let it ride.

"My sister." Helen was eyeing her, watching for an effect, and this made Laura pull herself back into action. Helen watched as her stepmother briskly fed the cat and snapped a plastic cover on to the tin. Disappointed, Helen continued. "Well, my almost sister. I've always wanted a sister," she whined. "Flap lets me play with her make-up and she brushes my hair and she helped me and Richard pack our suitcases and she lets us play a long time in the bath if we want and sometimes she takes us shopping." She waited again. "Anyway, can I ring her?"

"Yes. If you know where she is." Laura began unloading the washing-up machine. Her movements were measured but crash bang wallop went the plates and ting went a glass as it shattered into a hundred pieces. A gleam came into Helen's eye which Laura wished she had not seen.

"She's with Mummy and Sasha of course," said Helen, reaching for the telephone.

"Not with her mother?"

"No, she's in hospital. She kept crying and she needed a special sleep."

Laura swept up the glass while the child stood by the telephone, hand on the receiver.

"Do you need help with the number?" she asked, straightening.

"No, thank you. Only it's a private conversation," said Helen.

Laura slammed out of the kitchen with excusable but ill-advised annoyance. She knew Helen could have nothing of importance to say to Flap, but the manoeuvre had succeeded in its aim.

It had also raised some questions in her mind about the roles played by Camilla and Flap in that house in Chelsea. When she was calmer, that was what she would think about very hard.

Melanie had seen Sasha again before Christmas, but did not find it necessary to pass this on to the Bedfords. They had sat in the same wine bar, drinking another two bottles of white wine, and Melanie had decided that much as she would like to reheat that particular soufflé it would be too dangerous. Now both were clean from drugs (more or less, in his case) they discovered they really did have a lot more in common than a needle and a pair of dirty sheets. Melanie was sure they could enjoy a flirtatious friendship without anyone being the worse for it. On the other hand, she did feel (maybe because of Sasha's eyes) that she must come clean about Laura. She could warn him where she stood without being too disloyal to her older friend, couldn't she?

She waited until he brought Camilla up in coversation. "What did you say she was called before?" she asked, jumping into a sentence. Sasha looked surprised. "I don't think I did. But Christie originally, then Bedford."

"Yes, it did ring a bell. One of my oldest friends married her husband. What a small world." She giggled sillily, but Sasha barely reacted. "Oh? That quiet girl with straight hair is your friend? I wouldn't have thought it."

"Yes, well." Melanie waved her hand. "We all go against type sometimes." And *that* was both bitchy and disloyal, she thought, nevertheless relieved to have told Sasha the truth. Now it was up to him to guard his tongue.

After a silence in which they both sipped wine fairly morosely, Sasha put a few ideas together. "Oh, Mel, you'd better do me a favour and not say anything about Camilla and her new hobby," he said. "Her ex didn't look the type who would be too relaxed about it. And to be honest I'm not sure she shouldn't be easing off a bit myself. I've barely painted for months and what I have done . . ."

"That can't be Camilla's fault."

"No, but we're on the party circuit. You know . . ."

Melanie did, only too well, but she was unprepared for Sasha's awareness of the dangers.

"Do you still want some stuff?" Sasha asked. "I've got some at home I wouldn't mind shifting."

Melanie had told Robert the truth when she had said she had been clean since leaving Broadway: she could have added that after the first few months she had not even been tempted. She could look at people, knowing they were high as kites, with neither envy nor bitterness. Yet now, for some reason, she felt a yearning for the high cocaine could give her so intense it almost hurt. She had allowed herself to drink alcohol again, but that was because it was not the same enemy as drugs. Drink blurred the edges of her life when its delineations were too harsh to be faced. It brought her a numbing sort of peace. Heroin had been a little like that, but the peace it offered was more dreamy, even more unreal. She knew she should never go back there.

But what Sasha offered was different again. She ached for the high that nothing but cocaine could give her. Melanie had never been a girl whose spirits could suddenly rise and whose whole body could buzz with a joy of a moment. She knew some people had that capacity and envied them. She needed help, and remembered the zing, the confidence given by cocaine with longing. With that help she could sort out her life, control her whims, be a success.

She met Sasha's eyes and they exchanged a silent conversation. "I'd better not," she said sadly. And he nodded.

*　　*　　*

Laura told Melanie about her conversation with Helen, but found her friend surprisingly reticent. She pressed for more information, but Melanie had nothing to tell. "Melanie, please," she begged. "Camilla's coming the day after tomorrow to pick up the children and we're meant to be going to the Pughs for the New Year. We can't go if we don't know what's happening with the children."

"You do, you know they're going to their grandparents and they must be safe there. Anyway," she added cruelly, "it sounds like Flap's doing a good job with them. I shouldn't worry."

"Melanie!"

"Listen, I'm sorry, but I don't think there's much more I can do. I'm not cut out to be a spy, you know that. I'd open my big mouth before I'd earned the fur coat. And Sash is an old friend too. I owe him some loyalty." Laura gaped. She was terrified that her ally was deserting her. She realised how much she needed Melanie on her side. "Look, I absolutely swear that if I hear anything at all which makes it look bad for the children, I'll tell you. I'll do everything I can. I'll even help kidnap them. But I can't report back every time I see Sash. We're in the same world again, a different world from last time. Please understand."

Laura tried, she really tried hard. But all she could see was her dream recede just as it had begun to form into a reality. She had spent a calm and happy month, was probably the only woman in England who had grown calmer as Christmas approached and stayed sane under its tumult, but Christmas was the sort of thing Laura had always been able to cope with. This was something else. Panicky images of a future without children overwhelmed her. Christmas had after all been a false peace, a mirage not even an oasis. For the first time Laura was terrified – terrified at what she had started, at the possible outcomes. She was scared she had hurt Robert with her secrecy, would hurt the children with the inevitable battle ahead. She was also genuinely frightened for the children, did not know how she could faced handing them back to Camilla and Sasha in a few days' time. While the grown-ups were thinking, what sights were the children witnessing? Never before had she lost her self-control as she did now, and she broke down entirely.

Huge tears rolled slowly down her cheeks, plopping fatly onto the oiled tablecloth. They gathered momentum, turned from a stream to a torrent. Her mouth opened wet and square like a child's. Her shoulders heaved, her mascara ran. She laid her head on the table and wept.

Melanie looked on, then silently went to the cupboard and poured Laura a large whisky.

Camilla burst through the door, smelling expensive first and slightly stale second. Behind her was Sasha, hanging back and faintly apologetic. Camilla was all mouth and hard bright eyes; Sasha all cheekbones and compressed lips. Helen and Richard had run downstairs when the doorbell rang but now both hung back and Laura saw on Richard's face the wary, watching look she associated with Helen but had never seen in him. Camilla was still talking but Laura had not heard a word she said. Her first reaction was to get them all out of the house as quickly as possible, but then something told her to hold them there until Robert came back. She led the way into the sitting room assuming, rightly, that they would follow.

''Robert's just gone to the supermarket for me,'' she said, ignoring the look of contempt Camilla flashed her. ''I can't think what's kept him so long. He'll want to see the children off – why don't you both have some tea?''

Camilla laughed. ''What do you think, Sasha? Tea or Scotch?''

''Tea,'' he said firmly, but Camilla had not paused. ''Straight please, no ice,'' she said, plonking herself onto the sofa. Laura noticed her hem was coming down and stood fascinated, staring at the loose thread and hanging lining. What was up with Camilla? She went meekly to the drinks tray and poured them both whisky. When Sasha refused his, asking for wine instead, she decided to drink his whisky. Why not, it seemed that they were well ahead of her already. Laura and Sasha sat in silence while Camilla talked about their Christmas, their plans for the New Year, asking questions but not pausing to hear the answers. When Laura noticed the children had not come in, not even to greet their mother, she went to find them and coaxed them downstairs. Reluctantly, they kissed Camilla and Sasha, but then both crept back out of the room. Laura did not try to stop them.

When Robert returned, flustered and cross at being late, they were all on their second drink. Camilla was still talking, the children still upstairs. It took him a minute or two to understand quite what was going on: he shook hands with Sasha, poured himself a glass of whisky (with only the tiniest glance at his watch), sat down and prepared to join in what he thought was a civilised social. But as he watched Camilla, Laura saw surprise, then awareness come over his face. He looked at Laura and quietly asked her where the children were. When told they were up in their rooms, he rose and shut the sitting-room door.

"Are you all right, Camilla?" he asked, standing in front of her and looking down at her. Something in his voice shut her up effectively for the first time since her arrival.

"Of course." She tried to stand up but Robert was too near to her and she half-fell back onto the sofa cushions.

"Sasha," Robert turned to his wife's husband and both women were silent as the green eyes met the brown in a cold challenge. Sasha dropped his look first. "Yeah, she's fine. A bit tired."

"She doesn't seem tired to me." His look at Camilla made even Laura nervous for the consequences and Robert stood, dominating the room while the others waited for his verdict.

"Sasha, I think you'd better take Camilla home now," he said, leaning forward and taking both their glasses. "I hope you both enjoy New Year." Sasha and Camilla stood, then Laura stirred herself. "I'll get the children."

"Don't be ridiculous, Laura." At last Robert's voice was sharp. "Where do you think they're going?"

"Now just a minute," Camilla was shrill. "What do you think we're here for? Not pleasure."

"Not ours, nor yours, I'm sure. But you've wasted your time. The children won't be going with you tonight."

Then hell broke loose. Camilla screamed and ranted, Sasha's drawl rose in counterpoint to her yells, Laura wept. Robert stood in the middle of them all, unmoved by the cacophony, not even bothering to try and calm everyone down. Finally, when his silence had dampened their noise, he walked to the sitting-room door. With his hand on the knob, he said, "I'm sure you'll ring me tomorrow. I'll tell the children you were ill."

Sulkily, Camilla gathered herself together. She gave Laura a filthy look as she passed her but said nothing more. Robert opened the door for her and stood back. Laura was the first to see Richard and Helen, sitting together at the bottom of the stairs. Richard's face was wet with tears, but Helen's eyes were dry. She looked at each of the adults in turn with a cold, scornful stare. Then, her face tight, she stood, pulling Richard up with her. Her parents and step-parents watched as she and her brother walked slowly up the stairs. When her bedroom door shut behind them with a quiet click, Camilla and Sasha turned and left the house.

So that was how the last week of the year was spent. Angry telephone calls, confrontations, the children tight with misery, Robert and Laura talking in tense voices behind closed doors. Robert had made up his mind.

First he rang the Pughs. Yes, of course it was all right for the children to come too. They could ride the pony, other children would be asked over to entertain them, the pointer had just had puppies, what *fun*. The children looked as though nothing would ever be fun again but crept silently about, asking no questions. Robert had simply told them that their mother was unwell and they would not be returning to her for a while. Helen had nodded dumbly, neither child had cried.

Then Robert rang the Christies. It was only fair, as they were inevitably to be drawn into the discussion, that he should tell them himself that he believed Camilla to be incapable of looking after the children properly. He told them he was worried about her drinking, and said that he feared she had also been drawn into a bad set of friends and was probably taking "some kind of" drugs.

Lady Christie was surprisingly calm. "Oh, dear, I've been worried sick about her. But can't they come here?" Robert explained that he did not want Camilla driving the children anywhere, that her state of mind was not normal and he was not even sure whether she would actually take them to Herefordshire anyway now that this row had blown up. He asked Lady Christie why she was worried about her daughter, but the mother was deliberately vague and noncommittal.

Then Sir John rang up in a fury, blustering and shouting,

roaring about his and his daughter's rights, custody orders and kidnap. "I'm afraid we're going to try and have the custody order changed, John," said Robert, who remained totally unprovoked throughout the conversation. Sir John roared again and hung up.

Camilla rang, subdued but unrepentant. "For goodness' sake, Robert, we'd been out for a long lunch and I'd drunk a little too much. Sasha was sober and driving."

"That was not drink, Camilla," Robert answered. "I've seen you drunk and that was not drink."

So Camilla rang Laura and tried a sprightly, best-friends, frightfully civilised tone. "I'm sorry, Camilla, it's not for me to discuss," said Laura politely, although after Camilla turned into a hissing hellcat she hung up and cried.

Next Melanie rang, saying Sasha had rung her asking what the hell was going on and she had told him nothing except that Robert was worried by Camilla's apparent character change. "He's in a frightful state. Says Flap's mother's had a nervous breakdown and is sleeping it off at some incredibly expensive rest home and it looks as though Camilla'll be in the next bed."

Ten minutes later, Sasha rang. "Laura, I wondered – do you think we ought to talk about all this?"

Laura was very tempted, but knew that once lawyers were involved it was safer to do nothing. "I can't, Sasha. It's not really to do with us."

"You know that's not true. If it does come to court, you know that you and I will be just as important as Robert and Camilla. Can't you at least tell me what's going on?"

Laura thought for a second. "Robert didn't like how Camilla was when you came to pick up the children. He says he wants to know what you're up to before he lets them back. Maybe you can tell me something. None of us wants to go to court," she added, lying badly.

Now it was Sasha's turn to pause. "Maybe you're right. Maybe we have nothing to say to each other. But, Laura, are the children all right?"

"They're fine, of course."

"I wondered – would you mind very much if Flap came over one day? She's missing them."

Laura was astounded. "I'd have to ask Robert. We're going away for a few days now, but maybe . . . I'll ask Robert." Perhaps it was not such a bad idea.

The last of the telephone calls was between Laura and Camilla's brother Andrew Christie. She had been considering the move for a long time, ever since the Welsh weekend after she had met the Christies. Then she had hoped that maybe he could be enlisted on to her side. He might have listened to her then, but she had left it too late. He was polite but cold.

"I'm Richard and Helen's stepmother."

"Yes."

"I'm been worried about Camilla, and I wondered . . ."

"Yes?"

"I wondered . . ."

"I know what you wondered. I can't enter into this. Of course, I'm concerned for the children's welfare, but I'm also concerned about my sister. She is very unhappy at the moment."

As Laura hung up she knew she had blown it. Maybe if she had rung Andrew earlier, months earlier, it would have been different. She could even have asked him and his wife to dinner – Robert and he had always been friendly in the past. But now she had made another enemy. What a fool she was.

On New Year's Eve, the Bedfords packed up the car and crawled into it with a sense of exhaustion. Laura had left the answer phone unplugged and no one knew where they were going. As they drove out of London the children began to perk up a little. There were the puppies to look forward to, and a change of scene.

For the adults there were a few days of reprieve before solicitors' offices opened and the battle was engaged in earnest.

Laura and the children all enjoyed themselves at the Pughs, who were expansive and generous and unpunctual in their hospitality. Robert tried to relax for the children's sake as much as out of politeness to his hosts, but found it impossible. He was incapable of putting the struggle that lay ahead out of his thoughts: he could only marvel at his wife's apparent tranquillity.

Each morning he woke feeling as though he had not closed his eyes all night – he supposed he must have dozed off occasionally,

but when he did he was persecuted by dreams of law courts, of
Laura leering in a judge's wig, of the young Camilla he had loved
coming to claim the children while the new drug-crazed Camilla
tore his eyes out so he could not see. He dreamed that the judge,
like Solomon, ordered the children to be cut not in two but in
three – one part each for himself Camilla and Laura. He dreamed
of the children as hippies, dancing in tie-dyed chiffon away from
him, laughing and waving, with enormous joints in their hands.
When he woke he paced the room, trying not to wake Laura, or
he would sit on the edge of the bed, head in hands, stifling his
groans.

After breakfast the next day, with food and strong coffee
inside him, he would look at his children brightening under the
influence of the country air and the exuberance of the puppies
and be sure that he was doing the right thing for them, but he
feared for the future.

Laura returned to London refreshed and confident. Her struggle had been in bringing Robert to the point where he would
agree to reopen the fight for the children. Then she had worried
that they would lose the battle, or if they won, the children
would resent her for having removed them from their mother.
Seeing how a few days in the country had relaxed some of
Richard and Helen's tension, she remembered how adaptable
children are. She felt certain that nothing could go wrong. Now,
she thought, it was just a matter of the formalities. Before many
months were out the children would be officially theirs, to live
in Parson's Green Lane with them for evermore.

Two days after their return to London, when even Robert's
strained voice and expressionless face had not succeeded in
dampening Laura's happiness, Viv rang late and unexpectedly
at the Bedfords' door.

"It's Julia. She's had a girl," he told them, blinking in the
light which flooded on him from the hall. For a tiny moment,
Laura felt physically sick. She had not seen much of Julia in
the past few months, making various excuses to herself and
her friend but knowing that she could not face Julia's growing
stomach and excited plans. She loved Julia as much as ever (of
course she did) but told people that recently Julia had become

– well, just a bit *boring*. She was as excited as anyone about the baby (of course she was) but honestly there *was* more to talk about than swelling ankles and the price of prams at Peter Jones. Every now and then she could not help but feel a twinge of guilt about her desertion of Julia, but then – well, she was busy with the children and her work and the house and she just seemed to run out of time these days . . .

All this went through her mind as she stood looking at Viv's bemused face, and then she just felt honestly and wholly glad for her friend.

"I'm sorry to call so late, but I was on my way home and – didn't know what to do next," Viv said, still on the doorstep. From behind her Laura heard Robert's laugh, and realised it was for the first time since the Great Debacle.

"I remember that feeling," he said, shaking Viv's hand and ushering him in past Laura. "What you need now is a stiff drink and an opportunity to tell us how you are the first person who really understands the mysteries of fatherhood. Come in, come in."

"Are you sure it's not too late?"

Although Robert and Laura had been on the point of going upstairs, they assured Viv that on the contrary all they felt like was whisky and a social and the three of them settled down with drinks in hand.

Robert and Viv did most of the talking; Laura could not share these experiences. She felt no resentment, though: she could never be a father. Julia was well but tired, the baby was the most beautiful ever born, the father the proudest.

"And I should probably wait for Julia to ask you, but we'd love you to be a godmother, and her middle name is to be Laura – Rose Laura, pretty don't you think – and we're going to be married in three months' time." Viv tried to drop this last piece of information casually but he could not keep the foolish grin from spreading across his face.

"Viv!" Laura sprang from her chair, wholehearted in her happiness. Marriage she could understand. Marriage, she knew was a Good Thing. "At last."

"Well might you say it. She's only just agreed – but to

everything. She'll even do it in a church as long as we don't ask too many people."

"I knew she would come round in the end."

"I hoped so. My word, I hoped. So everything's going to be all right."

Viv left late, slightly the worse for wear. Robert and Laura were physically and emotionally exhausted, but Robert was calmer and more relaxed than he had been for weeks. Whether it was the whisky or relief at someone's luck turning, Laura did not analyse, but, although she had blocked awareness of his coldness from her mind she welcomed back his return. "It'll be all right for us too," she whispered as they lay under their feather-filled duvet, separated by two feet, two cats and too many unspoken words.

"I wish I had Viv's faith," answered Robert, but there was no bitterness in his voice. A few moments later Laura felt his arm reach out to her and heard two disgruntled cats squeak as they were pushed from the bed. "Of course, we'll be all right – better than that," he said as he pulled her to him. And for a while at least they were.

The next day, Laura and Robert paid two important visits. The first was to the solicitor Robert had chosen to handle their case. Laura realised the difference between Mr Vavasour and Mr Chisolm as soon as she saw the entrance to the office. While she had been impressed by the dusty air of learning in Mr Chisolm's waiting room, she now saw it for the shoddy pretence it really was. Mr Vavasour was a lawyer who meant business, and he earned enough money to keep his offices bright and comfortable. While they were waiting, Laura and Robert were offered tea, chocolate or coffee by an impressive-looking young secretary. The coffee when it came was freshly made and surprisingly good.

Mr Vavasour, too, was a more impressive spectacle than had been the stooped Chisolm. Everything about him said he was a solicitor of the old school, gentlemanly, professional, with, it became clear, not only a good brain but also a Cambridge Blue of which he was inordinately proud. Robert had chosen his lawyer with informed care and it was clear the two men respected each other. Laura felt relaxed and unthreatened. She sat back, waiting for the exchange of pleasantries to be over and business to begin.

"So, as I understand it, you are applying to vary the custody order of the children," Mr Vavasour began. "The children are how old?"

Laura said nothing while Robert, in precise and uncluttered sentences, told Vavasour the outlines of the case. Vavasour listened, making notes, flicking quick glances at Laura and reminding her very much of her husband. At the end he referred to Laura for a few details concerning Melanie, then he nodded and stood. Laura and Robert watched him for a moment as he walked to the window where he paused, looking down onto the street.

"Very quiet, London, at this time of year," he said. "Of course you, Mr Bedford, will be aware that keeping the children against their mother's wishes will not look good. On the other hand they were already on your premises, you did not seize them from her." He looked over to Laura and said, "You must know, Mrs Bedford, that the judge's only consideration will be for the welfare of the children." She nodded. That was what she was fighting about, too. "What are you hoping for, Mr Bedford?"

"Custody, care and control. Defined access to Camilla, but only when we can be sure her – habit – is under control. Well?"

"Well, we must make an affidavit. I suspect Mrs – ah – Limpnakoff is applying for an order enforcing the return of the children. If we can substantiate the drug-taking evidence we should be all right. I can certainly advise you to go ahead with the case. We will prepare the affidavits now if you have the time." He smiled at Laura, his face sympathetic for the first time. "You will be surprised at how fast everything happens from now on."

On the way home from the City, Robert and Laura dropped in at St Mary's Paddington. Julia was in a tiny cubicle, surrounded by flowers, pale-faced in a white lace nightdress. Her baby lay in a plastic cradle beside her and looked, to Laura, much like any other baby. Each woman was too full of her own concerns to pay much attention to the other, but both felt drawn together again after the months of unacknowledged coolness. Laura was sincere in her delight at the forthcoming wedding and her own role as godmother to the baby. She held Rose awkwardly, making Julia, an old hand after fewer than twenty-four hours, laugh in delight.

Robert frowned when Laura began telling Julia their own news, and as Julia was only half-listening anyway, Laura stopped talking, but with no feeling of hurt.

That night, with the children both in cheerful mood, supper to cook, Helen helpful – everything just as television films portrayed middle-class family life – Laura raised the question of Flap coming to see the children for a day. Robert looked puzzled.

"Who suggested this?"

"Sasha."

"Do you think he's up to anything?"

Laura hesitated. For months now her instinct had been to undermine anything said or done by Sasha and Camilla, but something prompted her to be truthful.

"I don't think so. He asked after the children, seemed almost embarrassed to do so. And when he asked if Flap could come . . . No, I don't think he expected us to say yes, but I do think he asked for the children's sake – all three of them."

"Have the children asked to see Flap?"

"No. Helen hasn't mentioned her once; Richard talks about her sometimes but I don't think it occurs to him that she might come here."

"It would be better to keep it that way, don't you think? Ring Sasha and tell him no, we don't want to disrupt the children's routine any more than necessary. Of course, when all this is settled . . ."

Laura nodded and with a quick glance through the sitting-room door at the children, who were now settled in front of a Walt Disney video, she reached for the telephone. Robert's voice stopped her just as she was dialling. "Laura, be friendly to him, won't you? If he's been kind to the children . . ."

Mr Vavasour had been right. From the moment of their visit to him the legal men moved swiftly.

On the same day that Robert and Laura had visited Vavasour, Camilla and Sasha had indeed gone to their solicitor to make an application for the return of the children. "He's good, her solicitor," Robert said ruefully. "Especially at this kind of thing."

"Well, he did get Camilla custody in the first place," Laura agreed, "but it must have been more straightforward then."

"Not just the custody, though . . ." Robert reminded her, and Laura realised that he was thinking of the more than generous financial settlement Camilla had been awarded. For the first time she was faintly worried.

Nine days after the visit to Vavasour – only just over a fortnight after Robert's refusal to allow the children to return to Camilla – the Bedfords and the Limpnakoffs found themselves facing each other across a small West London courtroom. Robert nodded to his ex-wife and her husband: Sasha nodded back, Camilla, drawn and pale, stared straight ahead. Laura did not even try to meet Camilla's eye, but she and Sasha exchanged half-hearted smiles. Vavasour and Russell, Camilla's solicitor, were brisk and (to Laura's mind) heartlessly businesslike.

Laura wondered how the four of them appeared to outsiders. She herself was quietly but not too formally dressed in a red skirt and black jacket; flat shoes and minimal make-up made her appear, she thought, concerned without any claims to earth-motherhood. She felt relaxed and confident, sure that their claim was well founded and everything would be sorted out in their favour.

Camilla's suit was much more expensive than anything Laura owned. In a warm coral pink, it made the best of Camilla's pallor and should have given the air of a smart but relaxed mother dressing slightly up out of deference to the court. However, a button was missing on the jacket, and there was a stain on the front of the skirt. Her fixed gaze seemed frightened rather than bold and her fingers were never still. By her side, Sasha looked far more at home in his surroundings: his hair was tied back with a black ribbon and if his unstructured suit was purple it was so dark as to appear almost black. Every now and again he touched Camilla, or talked to her quietly as though she were a nervous horse. He always seemed to succeed in calming her for a moment or two at least. Robert, so used to appearing in court, was not as at ease as Laura had expected of him, but his experience led him to cover his feelings well. To any but Laura – and, she supposed, Camilla – he looked like a lawyer on a routine job. Laura sighed and sneaked a look at her watch. Not long to go now.

There was a noise at the back of the court and Laura turned to see Melanie arriving just in time. She looked pale and nervous, but managed a wan smile and quickly sat down. The judge, when he arrived, gave the parents and step-parents only the briefest of once-overs before settling into business. Laura found it hard to accept that he should be so matter-of-fact on so important an issue. Six people's lives were at stake: did that mean so little to him?

Of course it did not. The affidavits were read, giving each side in the sorry state of affairs and then the judge looked fiercely from Camilla and Robert and back again.

"I find it hard to understand how a custody arrangement, agreed between two parties and approved under the law, should so soon go awry," he remarked to no one in particular. "However, the allegations are very serious."

There followed half-an-hour of intense questioning by the judge. The Limpnakoffs denied any drug-taking, admitted to Camilla having been slightly the worse for wear (Christmas week, tired, too much to drink – it sounded plausible if lame) on the day of what Camilla emotionally (and foolishly, both Bedfords were sure) referred to as "the kidnap'" and insisted on their right to have the children returned forthwith and the custody order to remain unchanged. Melanie was called and made a surprisingly good witness. She came across as subdued but frank, admitting that as Laura's friend she was likely to be biased, but adding "Wouldn't any friend be worried?" with such innocent sincerity that she could not be doubted. Sasha looked at her with a stony face, failing to respond to her small shrug of apology as she walked past him.

Vavasour admitted that the children remained in good health, attended school and were clean and clothed. However, he, and Robert, insisted that Richard in particular had of late become withdrawn and that his recent regression into bed-wetting could only prove that all was not well. They held firm to their statement that they had had no choice but to keep the children from Camilla and that proof positive of a change in her was necessary before they could think of the children being well looked after. Neither Sasha nor Laura was called to give evidence.

Finally, when nothing more could be said, the judge paused, looked over his notes and the past history once more and sighed.

"It would be normal for me to insist on Richard and – uh – Helen being returned to their mother at once while the welfare officers undertook their enquiries into this matter," he said. "But," and here he looked very fierce, "the allegations made by the children's father are very serious. While I wholly disapprove of any breach of custody agreement such as that made by Mr Bedford in retaining the children, it has been noted that the children were at that time under his care and there was no such force as a – uh – snatch involved. I also note that the children spent a considerable span of time with Mr and Mrs Bedford while Mr and Mrs Limpnakoff were on an extended – uh – honeymoon. This breach of the strict terms of the custody agreement was made with the approval of all parties involved, and all are agreed that the children suffered no distress during or because of this period. Therefore I intend to make an interim order varying the custody. The children will stay where they are – with their father – while court welfare officers prepare their reports. Mr and Mrs Limpnakoff will be allowed access every other weekend, but only during the daytime. The children must be returned to their father at night. I shall look on any breach of this with the greatest severity. The case is adjourned for six weeks."

Outside the courtroom the four of them stood, dazed. Even Robert seemed uncertain of how to behave next. Then the solicitors chivvied them away for a further conference.

'I thought it was all going to be settled," Laura moaned.

"I did explain," Robert said tetchily, and was interrupted by Mr Vavasour.

"You're on the right road, Mrs Bedford. Judge Edwards does not approve of divorce at all – old-fashioned as you probably realised. The fact that it was Camilla who originally sought the divorce will have counted against her with him. Then there was

the honeymoon, admitted drinking, and the fact that she did
not seek to change the order herself. It's normal under these
circumstances for the second party to retaliate by trying to vary
the order herself – to block you entirely. They haven't, which I
would have thought was a tactical mistake. It was very unusual
to vary the order in your favour, and a good sign. Now you
will be visited by the welfare officers, and I must urge you to
be totally frank with them. You have nothing to hide; if they
want to look inside your Marmite jar, let them. They will want
to know everything about you how you live, will want to talk to
the children as well as you." He looked at Laura sympathetically.
"It may be difficult, but it won't be long. Now it's just a matter
of time."

14 ∫

Laura had taken to going to church again in the past month, but she no longer patronised Reverend Fraser. She no longer felt anything in that church, even much respect. There was too much a sense of half-hearted duty, of going to church because that was the thing to do before having a dry sherry. She also could not face discussing her private life with the old women who had so little else to discuss.

Instead, she began moving around, trying different churches in the hope of finding something that would move her the way she had been moved in Venice. But try as she might, burying her head in her hands, kneeling on the most uncomfortable kneelers, saying her prayers as best she knew how, she never felt a spark of emotion. Occasionally, she wondered why she kept on trying. She was still unsure about the very existence of God, feeling as she said her prayers that they were dry words echoing around a silent, scientific universe. She muttered thanks for the good in her life, asked God to bless her nearest and dearest, recited the Lord's Prayer and the Creed. Sometimes, more heartfelt, she would beg God, or whoever, to grant her wish, to bring her a baby, to bring her Richard and Helen, but as she did so she felt almost ashamed. Should she not be praying this fervently for the children of Bosnia rather than for well-scrubbed Fulham darlings?

Laura did not tell Robert quite how often she was going to church, nor did she take his children. It was not that he was hostile to the Church, more that he seemed worried, almost antipathetic, to the idea of her going. They never discussed it, but Laura knew that to Robert her churchgoing was a mixture of the search for a strong crutch and the hope that fairy tales really did come true. Laura denied this to herself, but was not wholly convinced.

One thing Laura did not do, although she had quite freely in earlier years, was go to church with Aimée and her children. She shied away from the thought of Catholicism, although it had been in a Catholic church that she had felt that strong sweep of spirituality which had lured her back towards Christianity. Away from the magnificence of Venice, she rationalised her emotions as being brought on by the beauty of the place, the Christmas spirit, her exhaustion at the time. There was too much going on in her life for her to face the possibility that maybe the Roman Church had the answers to her questions.

Meanwhile, the divorce court welfare officer, in the shape of one Miss Sharon Dedrick, moved in. As Vavasour had promised, there seemed to be no area of their lives which she did not see fit to invade. Miss Dedrick rang and announced that she wished to spend two days with the family. She would not stay the night, but would come on Saturday morning before the children were awake, leave after they were in bed and repeat the visit the next day. They were, of course, to "behave as though she were not there". As though that were possible, Laura thought bitterly as she cleaned the house with a vicious attention on Friday.

She and Robert decided to tell the children nothing about Miss Dedrick or the astoundingly important part she was to play so briefly in their lives. Neither could they quite bring themselves to call her a friend, so Laura just muttered to the children in passing that "someone" was to spend the weekend with them and would they be good.

"Oh, is that Sharon?" Helen asked. "She came to Mummy's last time we were there. She's boring."

"Why?" asked Laura, angry that Camilla's visit had taken place first.

"I don't know; she's really nosy. She asks questions all the time. And she holds her knife wrong."

It was not much of a clue, but Laura did not press the child any further. She longed to know what had happened when Miss Dedrick had met Sasha, but knew better than to ask.

Miss Dedrick arrived at eight o'clock, at a time when the

children were normally playing in their bedrooms while Laura and Robert slept. Nothing could be normal today, though, so Laura and Robert were up and dressed and the children were asking why they could not get up too if the grown-ups were. Miss Dedrick arrived to find Helen whining, Richard whining and Laura trying very hard not to snap. How could Miss Dedrick not realise that it would be impossible to be there before the children were awake? The pretence at normality was already ridiculous.

Breakfast was eaten calmly enough, although Richard did ask why they were having sausages when it wasn't anyone's birthday. Then there was the rest of the day to be faced. While the Bedfords slowly, slowly, wore away a day supposedly like any other, Miss Dedrick inspected every room, looked at the children's wardrobes, their toys, even their hairbrushes. She read their schoolbooks, looked on their bookshelves, discussed their menus. She appeared to approve of the cats once she knew they did not have a litter tray, but wondered aloud whether the *Beano* would really *stretch* Helen enough. Laura rather tartly pointed out the "Mrs Pepperpot" book that was by Helen's bedside, then regretted that she had spoken. Miss Dedrick was not like the welfare officer that reading the *Daily Mail* had led Laura to expect. She was gentle and considerate to a fault, yet more irritating than anyone any of them had ever met before. There was absolutely nothing wrong with her, nor was there anything right. She made it clear, without actually "verbalising", as she would have expressed it, that she had not entered welfare work to sort out squabbles between rich professionals. She did not think she allowed her prejudices to cloud her judgment, but Robert and Laura were soon aware of her true feelings.

The children bickered more than normal that day, and Laura could feel Miss Dedrick noticing the spats with metaphorically raised eyebrows. For heaven's sake, had the woman never met children before? Didn't she know that they all fought, that it meant nothing? Laura realised that Miss Dedrick, like the Queen, probably had a rather artificial view of life. As far as the Queen was concerned, every house was full of fresh flowers and newly laundered curtains. As far as Miss Dedrick was concerned, every house was full of bickering children, edgy parents and perfectly

balanced meals. Laura was sure that Miss Dedrick did not have
the imagination to make allowances for the tensions her visit was
bound to cause. Even Rebecca of Sunnybrook Farm might have
been tetchy with her homestead under such close and critical
surveillance.

After lunch, while Laura was making coffee for the grown-ups,
Miss Dedrick followed the children upstairs. "For God's sake,
what's she doing?" Laura said, wondering if she could run up
the stairs and eavesdrop under cover of grinding coffee.

"She's perfectly within her rights," Robert said wearily. "She's
probably asking them where they want to live."

"She *can't* be. They're far too young."

"Oh, yes she can. She probably won't ask Richard, but she'll
certainly ask Helen."

"So that's it, is it? Whatever Helen feels like saying in that
split second goes?"

"Of course not. But she'll certainly take it into consideration
when making her report. Oh, God, I wish this was over."

Laura made the coffee in silence. Nothing could be said when
Miss Dedrick might wander back in at any moment. At the
moment they were united in their desperate attempt to please
a woman to whom they would normally have done no more
than smile politely in a bus queue.

By the end of Saturday, Laura felt that Miss Dedrick knew
more about the insides of their lives than even they did. She
did not quite open the Marmite jar, never quite squeezed out
the toothpaste tubes, but Laura would have been unsurprised if
she had suggested it and would probably have offered to help.

Laura found it all very difficult to understand. She knew that
she had set the domino chain tumbling, but could not see why
there had to be this interim period of questioning and intrusion.
The longer she looked at the problem, the simpler it became.
The children would be better off with Robert and her than with
the Limpnakoffs, and that was an end to it. Her logical mind
understood that the law made this process necessary, even
desirable, but her emotional self could not allow it to be either
useful or wise.

Robert and she were not getting on at all well either. Again,
Laura knew this was almost inevitable, and was sure that as

soon as the case was settled their relationship would return to its easy pattern. But in the meantime they were polite to each other, never arguing or even bickering, but speaking with a quiet tension that never quite snapped. Laura ran the house as smoothly as ever, Robert's work continued in its normal routine, they went out together to friends and the cinema and no one ever whispered, "Pity about the Bedfords, do you think they're all right?" But Robert at least knew that they were balancing on a very thin edge indeed.

Robert was becoming more and more resentful in the face of Laura's serenity. He tried to understand her, supposed that her way of coping with the stress of the inquisition into their lives was to block it out of her mind. Her apparent ability to do this drove him almost to breaking point. He was consumed with worry; how could she ask him such banal questions as whether he wanted pork or lamb chops for supper? He did not want to discuss the problem with her – there was very little to say – but there was no other conversation of any interest either. He tried to keep control of himself for the children's sake – for all of their sakes – but he could hardly bear to be in the room with Laura now. If they could get through this (for the first time the "if" appeared in his mind) he would take the whole family away on holiday. They all lived together now, but no one was at ease. Something would have to be done to break the atmosphere.

That evening they were going to dinner with Julia and Viv. They had thought about cancelling when Miss Dedrick's weekend coincided with the invitation but decided that would be no help. Miss Dedrick would have left the house by then, so the children were left with a baby-sitter, and the Bedfords hoped that an evening out of the house might do them both good.

Julia's baby, only a few weeks old, held court in a Moses basket at the end of the table and all agreed that she was the sweetest, most well-behaved, most beautiful baby that had ever been born. But although Rose was the centre of attention, it was Julia that Laura was watching. Her friend had changed almost beyond recognition, yet without losing any of the charm and gaiety that had always made her so attractive. It was hard to pinpoint anything different in Julia or her house, but Laura saw the alterations, and looking at Viv knew that he too had noticed.

Julia had managed to achieve a new level of domesticity, yet there was still the same slapdash element that was so totally like the old Julia. The food was not delicious nor particularly ambitious – smoked salmon, roast chicken and vegetables, chocolate mousse – but it was home-made. Neither Marks and Spencer nor some Sloaney out-of-work girlfriend had played any part in the meal. Baby mobiles and soft toys were lying around the edges of the room, but it was not that they were there so much as the effort had been made to tidy them up that marked the difference in the atmosphere.

Viv was also different. For the first time since Laura had known him there was no trace of worry in his eyes. And with the worry had gone the faintly feeble, apologetic air which some women found attractive but which had always irritated Laura. At last he had become a match for Julia, but it had been through his growth rather than her dwindling. Julia had stopped fighting against domestic happiness, and having accepted it, having admitted to herself that there was something to be said for the old way, had shed her protective shell and become gentler.

Neither was she a bore about the baby, even Laura had to admit that. She clearly adored Rose, leapt up if the baby murmured, breast-fed her tactfully but openly after dinner. But her conversation was as wide-ranging and jokey, she was as brisk and unfanciful as she had ever been. In finding a centre for her life, she had not made it the focus.

The Bedfords did not stay late, Robert had too many memories of sleepless nights and a tearful Camilla to allow them to outstay their welcome, but they climbed into their Golf feeling warmer towards each other and the world in general than they had for weeks.

"I'm glad to see that there's some sanity left in this world," Robert remarked as he plugged in his seat belt and switched on the ignition.

"I know. I'm so glad it's worked out for them. Mind you, she'd have been mad to throw Viv away. She's one of my best friends but at times I wondered if he wasn't too good for her."

"He isn't at all. It's just that she took so long to realise it herself," said Robert.

They drove in silence for a while. Then, "It's only a couple more weeks, Laura," Robert said gently. "And it'll be all over."

"I know." Again, silence, but Laura felt she should say more and was struggling for the words. "Robert, you know what we're doing is right, don't you?"

"Yes, I do now. And I think we'll win."

"It's just that – I'm frightened at what this is doing to us."

Robert was relieved she had noticed, but was giving no quarter. "And the children," he reminded her.

"And the children," she agreed wearily. Richard was still wetting his bed and both children were silent and moody. Robert and Laura had done everything they could to protect the children from the implications of Miss Dedrick and not staying the night with their mother, but the children, though small, were not fools, and their antennae of self-preservation were twitching manically.

"They'll be all right," Laura added. "It's tough for them now, but children are tough themselves. Soon it'll just be a perplexing memory."

"I suppose."

"And us?" she tried to speak lightly, but her tone was dead.

"Oh, we'll be all right as soon as the Dreaded Dedrick is out of our hair."

Helped by the darkness in the car, Laura managed a very small "I love you, Robert, and the children."

"I know. I'm just sometimes – just a bit – worried where it's going to leave us. Sometimes I think you think that love is the answer to everything. It isn't, you know."

"Oh, but it is!" Laura was horrified at what he had said. "Yes, Robert, it is! Don't you see that?" If he did not understand that he understood nothing, nothing at all. "That's what's going to save us – all of us, you and me and the children. Even Camilla and Sasha. Of course it is. That's why the children will be all right at the end of all this. They know they're loved. That's why you'll be all right. It's love. Love's made us do this, nothing else. Before I loved the children I wouldn't have bothered. Not to this extent. You know that. If love isn't the answer—"

"What is? You sound like an evangelical Christian, Laura. But I loved Camilla, you see, and where did that leave me? High and dry without my children, whom I also loved. You, after all, loved Frankie, and then what happened? Love can help, but it can also get in the way. I see it all the time in court. Love can be a pernicious thing. Oh, it can be pure and cleansing but it can also be very selfish. And that can cause the most hurt of all."

There was nothing Laura could say to defend herself. She rebelled against what he had said but a part of her knew he was right. And, although she did not think he had been trying to get at her, his words struck horribly close to home. She did love the children, she did want the best for them. But perhaps what she really loved was having something to love. Perhaps her love was the most selfish of all. And if that was the case, dear Lord, what had she done? She felt the tears, uncomfortably hot, painful rather than easing, forcing themselves into her eyes. She began, for the first time in her life, to feel that maybe she had been wrong in a major decision. But she was not yet ready to make such an admission, even to herself. She could not be wrong. Everyone knew she was not wrong. She was honourable in a wicked world, she had old-fashioned values in a society with no values. She was motivated by love and concern. With those motives, could she possibly be wrong? Of course not.

Robert, silent beside her, said nothing to break her thoughts. He was partly aware of what was happening inside her, and although he sympathised with her agony, he was almost glad that she could feel it. He did not want to punish her for the upturn she had caused, but he was not going to stop her punishing herself. How he would feel towards her if their case failed, he did not know. But he did know that he would find it very hard to deal with her if they were once again left childless. If only she had turned to him at the very beginning; if he had been involved right from the start, he might not be blaming her so much. He felt an outsider in one of the most important events of his own life.

The next morning Laura woke feeling distinctly odd. Now that she thought about it, she had been feeling odd for days, but with the panic of Miss Dedrick's approaching visit she had not allowed herself to examine her illness. It was nothing serious, just an appalling lassitude that she had put down to worry. This morning she felt worse, though, sick and heavy and tired. She knew she could not succumb to flu until the next day. With Miss Dedrick arriving again she could not – would not – leave Robert in charge.

It was only as she was being sick (she had realised on leaving bed there was no alternative but to head for the lavatory as fast as she could move) that she wondered. As soon as she had cleaned up and brushed her teeth, she looked for her diary. She could not find it. Roaring around the house, begging the children to help her find it, she presented an unorthodox sight to Miss Dedrick as Robert opened the door to her. She pulled herself together, apologised, but continued her search, rummaging behind the sofa cushions and in the cutlery drawer until at last she found it. She ran upstairs and pored over the pages, turning back and back until she found the pages marked with a small cross. Seven weeks – could it really be seven weeks? She, who had so carefully counted each day for so long had allowed three weeks to go by without noticing? She felt sick again, but this time with fear. Oh God, could it really be? She had had so many false hopes ... but *seven* weeks!

She ran down the stairs. "Robert, darling, I'm sorry but I have to go out. I won't be long."

"Laura?" he looked worried as he turned from making coffee for Miss Dedrick.

"I've just got to go to the chemist. The one on the other side of the green is open on Sunday mornings, isn't it? Will you give Miss Dedrick some coffee? Oh, yes, good, you are. OK, I'll be back in a second." And she was off, slamming the door behind her. She ran to the chemist, using the technique she had read of in a children's book years before and had never forgotten – walk twenty paces, run twenty paces, walk twenty paces. It could be kept up for hours.

Back home she rushed upstairs to the bathroom. Five minutes later she was weeping, almost hysterical, clutching the ridiculous plastic pen which had confirmed her almost forgotten hopes. At last, at last. She was pregnant.

Laura decided almost at once to keep her secret for a little longer. She could not resist telling someone, but knew better than to trust her mother or sister with the news, so she told Melanie. She made her promise not to say anything in front of Robert, explaining that he had too much to think about now, and that she was saving the news for after the court case. Laura did not think Robert would rejoice enough right now, when all his energies were concentrated on Richard and Helen, but was sure of his happy response when the case was over. She spent a great deal of time imagining the moment she would tell him. She could not decide whether to whisper it to him as soon as the judge found in their favour, whether to wait until they had left the courtroom, or maybe later still, as they drank the champagne she would buy, letting him think it was to celebrate being able to keep Richard and Helen.

Melanie heard Laura's news with interest, with pleasure for her friend, but with only half an ear. Melanie had news of her own, news that she did not really want to tell anyone, even under such strictures of secrecy as Laura was making. In fact she had two pieces of news, and because she knew Laura would be so much more interested in the second, she kept it back.

"I wasn't going to tell you, but as you're on the phone," she began coolly, after having made all the right noises about the baby. Then she wondered how to say it. Such announcements always sounded feeble, whether from an overexcited teenager or a respectable widow. "I've got a new boyfriend," was in the end the best she could manage.

"Oh, good," Laura tried to sound enthusiastic, but her mind was too much on her baby and, if she had spared a thought for her friend at all in recent weeks she had noticed how well she was doing without a man and wondered whether in the end she was not better off on her own. If that was what she wanted, of course . . .

"Aren't you interested in him? Usually you ask all those what-does-he-do questions and invite us to dinner before we've even finished the first date." Melanie was nettled. After all, it was rare that she could answer all those questions so satisfactorily.

"Of *course* I am. Tell me – is he good looking?" Melanie's nearly always were, so Laura felt on safe ground.

"Not really, but what he looks like works. You know what I mean?"

"Yes." She didn't really, but was not up to imagining men right now.

"Well, if you're not going to ask me I'm just going to tell you. He's French, his family comes from somewhere in the south-east of France and makes glass, I think. Anyway it's a big factory, and he's doing the learning-the-ropes bit. He's in London for a year working for the company in some minor way with a big expense account. Taking out the buyers at Asprey and all that stuff. He's taken a house – a *house*, take that in, in the Boltons and he's really good fun. Really good fun."

"How's his English?"

"Oh, fluent. He's lived in New York for three years before the family reclaimed him. Then he was back in France, but got bored with provincial life, so although he's not really in love with the factory, he was dead pleased to be sent here. He's going to try and spin it out a bit, but it all depends on the father."

Laura was becoming more interested, it sounded as though Melanie had done rather better for herself than normal. "Any catches?" she asked, trying to make the question sound light-hearted.

"That's what so amazing. I don't think so. No wife, no ex-wife even (sorry, I didn't think). Doesn't take drugs, although I gather in New York . . . Plenty of money. Good prospects. Doesn't seem to lie, spends a lot of money . . ."

"A man after your own heart."

"Well, yes."

Something in Melanie's voice, in the silence that followed, made Laura pay attention. "Really?"

"Maybe. Yes, maybe really."

"Melanie!" (she did not say "at last!" but it was in her voice). "That's brilliant. Why don't you bring him to dinner?"

Melanie laughed. "Now that's more like it. Yes, I'd love to. Thanks."

They fixed a date, then just as they were saying goodbye, Melanie remembered the second piece of news she had for Laura. "Laura, have you heard about Camilla?"

"No, what?" All Laura's well-being vanished and her voice was panic-filled.

"I don't know how it will affect your case, but, well, apparently she's gone into a home."

"A home?" Laura was bewildered for a moment.

"Yes. She's gone to Farm Place. For a cure. For the coke. She's booked in for three weeks, although it may be longer. Probably will."

More than three weeks! Laura's mind raced. That meant Camilla would still be drying out when the court re-met. She would not be able to be there. And that must be good. The mother of the children not there to hear the fate of her children. That could only make a dreadful impression on the judge. Laura was jubilant. She could not believe there could be so much good news in one week.

She finished the conversation with Melanie, impatient to talk to Robert and tell him the news. Melanie and her new lover were to come to dinner three days later, and they would talk then. Sorry it had been so long. Yes, what good news. Lots of love. See you Friday then.

Robert was in court when she rang, so Laura did not have a chance to talk to him until evening. To her dismay, she saw that he did not think the news was as good as she had believed. "It proves it was true about the drugs," she said.

"Yes, but it's more complicated than you think. It proves she was taking cocaine, but the question now is whether she was sectioned or whether she went in voluntarily. It's much more likely that she is a voluntary patient than not. Although she hadn't been behaving properly as a mother, we know nothing that says she was in any danger or endangering anyone else."

"But even if she went in of her own accord, she's still admitting fault by going in."

"Exactly. She's admitting fault and she's trying to rectify that fault. I'm afraid whether it's genuine or not it's a very clever move."

"But she can't possibly be out by the time of the second hearing."

"I know. But that might do no more than give us a few weeks' grace. Oh God, this really changes the whole thing." Suddenly Robert looked frightened.

"They won't let them go to Sasha on his own." Laura caught his fear, but tried to reassure him.

"No, but it will only be a matter of weeks before Camilla is out – a new clean Camilla, back to the old Camilla who was so obviously a good mother but with the added advantage of a husband."

"Sasha!" Laura managed scorn, but was uncomfortably aware that he was not necessarily deserving of it.

"Sasha. Who has looked after his own daughter while her mother was ill, although he did not even know her until she was eight. Who has a not insubstantial private income. Who is even moderately successful at his own game. Oh God." Robert sank his head in his hands while Laura looked on, with no idea what to say.

Then she was filled with a bitter anger. Just as life was about to become perfect. Just as they were about to be given custody of the children. Just as she was pregnant, once again everything was going to go wrong. Robert looked more wretched than she had ever seen him. It crossed her mind to tell him about the new baby now, but she still wanted the news to come at a glad time, not one of more worry. Everything was spoiled again, and by Camilla. She felt more jealous of Camilla than she ever had before: not of her looks or her money or even her history with Robert, but of the power she still seemed to have over him. Maybe having her own child would give her the same hold over her husband, but somehow Laura doubted it. And she was aware for the first time that no matter what the outcome of the case might be, Camilla would always be there. She would always be a third in their marriage. Laura turned her head from Robert so that he would not see the hatred in her face. Her time would come, please God. The battle was not over yet.

Melanie produced Rémy de Vincent with an uncharacteristic shyness. He, however, appeared totally at ease with her, with Laura and with life in general. He was almost too much at ease, almost too friendly, almost too relaxed. Yet, somehow, Laura could not help but like him. There was about him that indefinable air of too much money and too much leisure. His clothes were almost too well cut, too expensively understated. His charm was almost, but not quite, too overpowering. As Melanie had said, he had no looks to speak of, yet somehow his was the sort of face that bore a lot of looking at.

Robert, making the right sort of polite conversation, was given the right sort of replies and yet both he and Laura found Rémy very difficult to place. "Eurotrash," Julia whispered to Laura in the kitchen, "but the best sort."

Eurotrash was a word Laura had heard used, but Rémy was her first experience of the type. On balance, she decided that it was a type worth occasionally entertaining but not really the sort with which she wanted to spend too many daylight (or moonlight she suspected was more to the point) hours. As the evening wore on, she began to see "where he was at", as Melanie would say. He clearly had a misspent youth: too many hours in nightclubs, too many pounds (or dollars or francs) on drugs. However, he enjoyed dancing and champagne as much as snorting and had been clean for some years. He also seemed to be genuinely funny and genuinely (and this was the real surprise) kind. And although he and Melanie barely touched, barely glanced at each other Laura (still, despite everything, a schoolgirl romantic) became increasingly convinced that there really was something serious between them. That despite the raillery and the bantering and what appeared to be a distance between them, they were very close.

Laura had not grown so selfish that she was not pleased. She had never expected Melanie to find a man who could put up with her mood swings, her flippancy and her past. Perhaps here at last was someone who fitted her. His own past was clearly unorthodox, although he had had more money than Melanie to cushion him. His future was mapped out for him – an important post in his family's firm, eventually taking full control; a life spent between France and England and New York; the family château in the country, a bolt hole in Paris and maybe (if he took an English wife) one in London. Melanie would not immediately fit in to the ordered, formal life of the French aristocracy, but Rémy did not seem the man to marry one of his own type, and if he was marrying out, it would be easier by far to muddle his relations with a foreigner with whom they would be forced to make an effort than confront them with a *petite bourgeoise* or a *pied-noir* whom they would know instinctively how to despise.

The evening went well, Rémy complimenting Laura on the food (watercress soup, chicken with sun-dried tomatoes and olives, lemon mousse), but eating little; Melanie on her best form; Julia laughing as she told of her mother's panic at the wedding preparations; Viv trying to discuss the difference between the Roman Catholic and Orthodox Churches with a bemused Rémy. Even Robert seemed to be lifted for a while out of the gloom into which he had sunk since hearing of Camilla's treatment. And Laura? Laura was wholly happy for the first time for months. She had her closest friends around her and felt no pressure of competition or comparison. Julia was to be married and had her baby – and Laura had been the most eager to press her to take on both; Melanie looked set at last for a fair future; and she – well she had her baby, she had her husband and soon, she remained stubbornly convinced, within a very few days now, she would have Helen and Richard under their roof for good. Her pregnancy had not made her any the less committed to the fight for Robert's children. She would not have believed it on her wedding day, but she wanted them home almost as fiercely as did he.

A new year had begun and with it a whole new future. She was now free to discuss Julia's wedding and her baby's christening (they were to have a joint ceremony) with as whole a heart as any friend could wish. When Rémy went to the lavatory, Laura could even murmur "Go for it!" to Melanie with a fervour that amazed her friend.

So it was with a truly light heart that she left the table carrying the remains of the mousse, refusing offers of help, asking Robert if he would just reach for the cheeseboard on the sideboard while she went for the plates. For a while that evening both Laura and Robert managed to forget the traumas that the next day would bring. The evening broke up early, but they cleared up and went to bed chatting as easily and happily as in the old days before their troubles began.

Their calmness could not last them through the night, though. They both lay awake with that ghastly stillness which comes from the effort not to wake a bedfellow. Both thought the other lay awake too but neither was sure enough to ask. And both wanted to be alone with their thoughts.

Laura was not so confident of the outcome of the case now she was in the dark. What if the judge fell for Camilla's conversion, if Helen had told Miss Dedrick she wanted to be with Sasha and Flap and Camilla, if the judge was so against changing the status quo that nothing would sway him? And what if they did fail? What would Robert think? How much would he blame her? She had been right to bring the case, but had she done so in the right way?

Through that long, sleepless night, Laura thought hard about the trail of incidents that had made her set this whole thing in motion. She went through the events step by step, and was sure she could not have acted differently (except for the secret visit to Chisolm; she could not clear her conscience of that). She asked herself if she had been interfering and decided no, not really. Either she was involved with the children or she was not, and Robert had always sought her involvement. Had she looked for trouble? No, although she had to admit that she had not been disappointed when she met it. And if trouble was there, it must be better to seek it out and destroy it than wait for it to destroy her family. On and on, round and round, went her thoughts. Until at last she fell into a deep and unrefreshing sleep.

Robert beside her was following much the same trail. He too asked himself what he felt about Laura's role in the conflict, but although he could not see what else she could have done (except for the secret visit to Chisolm; he could not entirely forgive her for that) he did not know what she should have done differently. He asked himself if he believed in Camilla's conversion, and decided that he did. She had on the whole always been a good, if overflighty mother. He did not believe she would willingly damage the children, only that sometimes her selfishness might put them second where they should be first. He believed that Laura always put them first – after him – and admired her for that. She was not even their mother, after all. No, she was not their mother. That was all the judge would see. That Laura was not Richard and Helen's mother. Robert too at last fell asleep, as deeply and unsatisfactorily as Laura beside him.

The courtroom was almost empty on the morning the case was reopened. Sasha sat on one side with his lawyer, Robert and Laura on the other with theirs. It was almost like a wedding, his 'n' hers on each side of the aisle, Laura thought, and a nervous smile flicked cross her face. Miss Dedrick sat waiting her turn, an implacable witness towards the back of the room. A few other people were scattered in the back seats. Laura was surprised to see the Christies, but followed Robert's lead in acknowledging them with a nod and a weak smile.

Once the judge had taken his seat everything seemed to happen very quickly. After a few introductory comments from the judge, Miss Dedrick was the first witness to be called. Laura could not afterwards claim that her report was unfair: she said that the children were loved in both households and clearly emotionally attached to both their parents and their step-parents. She acknowledged that the Bedfords clearly understood their educational as well as emotional responsibility towards the children and that they were involved in the children's schoolwork and in their wider education as a whole maybe more than the Limpnakoffs. She said there had been a certain amount of trouble with the Limpnakoffs, but that she believed that after Mrs Limpnakoff's course of treatment at Farm Place she would be able fully to take on her role as mother. She said she believed that had the case not been brought, Mrs Limpnakoff would probably not have realised the extent of her problem but that she (Miss Dedrick) believed the seeking of a cure was genuine. She added that, although this might have no bearing on the present custody case, she had been most impressed with the way Mr Limpnakoff had taken care of his older daughter by a different woman. Finally, she said that her main concern with the Bedfords was the strength of their marriage, that from her viewpoint they seemed a couple under strain and the worst thing of all that could happen to the children would be if they went to live with their father and his second marriage broke up. (Laura hung her head in misery and shame, remembering the tetchiness during Miss Dedrick's visits, her manic rushing to look for her diary and disappearance without warning, slamming the door behind her.) Finally, Miss Dedrick said that the older child had expressed a wish to stay with her father, but had given no very good reasons for this preference and had made no complaints about her mother. On Miss Dedrick's visits she had thought the child seemed happier at the Limpnakoffs than at the Bedfords.

Then Sasha was called, speaking for his wife. He repeated all Miss Dedrick had said about Camilla's drug addiction, taking the blame fairly on his shoulders but somehow managing to come out of it with credit. He, after all, was a man with a drug addiction behind him and he had, after all, persuaded Camilla to see the evil of her ways for the sake of her children. He accepted responsibility for his share in his wife's problem but said he had not realised the stress she was under, had not understood that to her the perhaps slightly bohemian world he moved in was foreign and exciting. He spoke of the children with an affection that even Robert conceded was genuinely felt, and hoped very much that the court would not punish Camilla further than she had punished herself.

The other witnesses called were Lady Christie, who confirmed much that had been said before, but gave strength to Camilla's case with her respectability and trust in a wayward daughter.

The surprise witness was Karen, Flap's mother. She turned out to be a tiny, fey-looking creature from the North-East of England. Sasha had met her years before when on a trip ("more than a journey, if you ask me," said Robert) through County Durham and Northumberland and had been taken with her accent and sparrow-like looks. She had followed him, uninvited, to London where they had conceived Flap. He had wanted no part in his baby at the time, and she had returned to her parents in Durham, an out-of-work miner and his Catholic wife. They had given her a frosty reception, her mother in particular, who cleaned students' bedrooms in Aidan's College and told her she was no better than one of those sluts from the south. After the baby's birth, Karen had come back south and found a series of jobs. Eight years later Sasha tracked her down, said he wanted to meet the baby and from then had taken a large part in her upbringing. He had given Karen a lump sum to compensate for the years he had missed, and from then on had paid her regularly and generously. More than that, he had, through his efforts rather than Karen's and Flap's, become a real father to the girl. Since his marriage, Karen had had a nervous breakdown and Sasha had paid for her treatment in a private clinic. During this time and indeed for some time before, Flap had lived with Sasha and Camilla. Flap was very fond of Richard and Helen and also of Camilla. Under cross-questioning Karen admitted that Flap had often baby-sat for the children, that maybe she was officially too young, but that that was what families were for, wasn't it?

Then it was Robert's turn, although he was questioned only briefly. There was little he needed to say, except why he had brought the case. The evidence already given explained that, and its implications had already been softened.

And that was it. There was nothing left to do but listen to the judge's decision. And he decided, without seeming even to hesitate, in favour of Camilla and Sasha. He ruled that, although the children had spent a great deal of time in the past year with their father, their home had been and should remain with their mother, "a child's natural home". He hoped and believed that the regrettable events of the last months had shocked Camilla into realising where her priorities lay. So Richard and Helen were to stay with Robert and Laura until after Camilla's return from Farm Place. There was then to be one more report on Camilla's state of mind and health and if, as was to be fully expected, she was considered by the doctors treating her to be in recovery, the children would then return to the Limpnakoffs and the access remain as hitherto defined. Finally, he sympathised with all parties for the anguish caused, commended Robert and Laura for their concern for the children and mouthed a few platitudes about the dangers of modern life.

Robert and Laura walked away from the courtroom together, without meeting anyone's eyes or talking to anyone. They were side by side, but they did not talk nor did they touch each other. Only when they were alone in the car together did they turn and look at each other. There was a long, long moment in which each waited for the other to say something, make some kind of move. Laura saw in Robert's eyes misery and despair but also a cold dislike which frightened her almost to the grave. Then she stretched out her hands to take Robert's and at last said, "I'm sorry." Not just for the outcome, but sorry for the whole mess, sorry for her madness, her determination, her utter sureness that she was right. She hoped that Robert understood all that, knew that one day she would have to say it in full, but prayed for now that one "sorry" would be enough.

Robert looked at her and nodded. But still he did not speak. He just turned away and turned the key in the ignition. They drove home in complete silence, Laura numb and dumb, Robert bitter and angry.

It was left to Robert to tell the children that they would be moving back to live with their mother as soon as she was better. He, of course, made the best of it, said wasn't it good that she was getting better so fast, wouldn't it be fun to be back with Flap, told them that Sasha was missing them and had sent his love, did not tell them where they had seen him. Neither Robert nor Laura was prepared for the children's reaction. Both, but particularly Helen, were wild with anger and grief, wept that they wanted to stay with Daddy and Laura, that they could see Flap at the weekends, that it wasn't any fun at Mummy's any more. Robert tried to explain that that was because their mother had been ill, that all would be well again now.

After the first day the children withdrew into themselves entirely, moving silently around the house. Occasional outbursts of aggression were all that varied the deathly hush that hung over the family. Both Robert and Laura tried, but neither really knew how to cope. Robert could not bring himself to ask Sasha to visit, but did go so far as to ask Flap. Even this seemed to cause more trouble than it laid to rest. Helen just announced that Flap should move into Parson's Green Lane with them. "Her mummy's ill too quite a lot."

The worst of it all was that the only time the children relaxed out of their angry misery at all was when they were alone with Laura. They blamed their father entirely for all that had happened – although of course their grasp of events was necessarily vague and muddled – and clung to Laura as their only lifeline. This did not help them to come to terms with their move back to Chelsea (for which a date was still not set), nor did it help relations between Robert and Laura.

One day, Laura tried to have it out with Robert. As usual, she began by cooking, trying to break through his coldness with some of his favourite food. But he did not even comment on the herb dumplings and refused the syllabub outright. Daunted but determined, Laura finally said,

"Robert, we must talk to each other. We're not making things any better—"

"No, we tried that and cocked up, didn't we?"

"—and we're not making them any easier for the children," she persisted, and he nodded sadly. "I feel this – wall – coldness from you." Robert would not look at her and she ploughed on, increasingly incoherent. "Of course, the whole thing's a disaster, but on the plus side, at least Camilla is going straight, the thing we were worried about has been removed even if we haven't got the children."

"Yes, and at what cost to the children?"

Laura realised with pain that Robert was still blaming her, that the hurt of the failed fight had gone much deeper than she would ever have imagined. She sat in silence, fiddling with her coffee spoon.

"What else could I have done?" she burst out. "Do you wish I had ignored the whole problem? Or waited until it got so bad that Camilla OD'd and forgot about the children entirely? Is that what you wish? Then you'd have been sure of getting the children, wouldn't you? There'd have been no question of a court case even – the little orphans would have come straight back to you." She stopped, horrified by what she had said and by the disgust on his face.

He stood up, carefully pushed his chair into the table, and very steadily walked to the door – too steadily. *He's drinking too much*, Laura thought as she watched him, but felt neither worry nor compassion, just a cold detachment. "Perhaps I am unreasonable, probably I am. I don't know what the fuck we should have done – you, or me, or us both. But I only know that two years ago everything was in order and now—"

"Stop blaming me!" she shouted. "You will have the children no less often than before – it's not my fault." But the door between them was shut and there was no one to see her tears.

After three weeks, when it became certain that Camilla would be at least another fortnight in Farm Place, Robert told Laura that he was sorry but that after the children left them he too would leave. He hoped it was not for ever, but he could not live with her now. The more the children blamed him, the more he blamed her. He was sure this was illogical, he was deeply sorry, but that was it.

Laura had still not told him about the baby. She was only ten weeks pregnant, no one would notice for a while. To tell him now would only add to his angst. She wanted him to make any decision he had to make about their future without the emotional blackmail a future child would hold out. When Laura's father rang saying that Rosalind still had not shaken off her flu after two weeks, Laura decided to use the excuse to leave the house for a while. Maybe if the children were alone with Robert, their relationship would improve. Maybe if she were away from him, hers would too. So after a tearful scene (Laura and the children cried: Robert was cold) Laura left Parson's Green for Paddington and the west.

Two weeks later Robert rang saying the children would be leaving at the weekend. He did not ask her, but she sensed his appeal for her to return to see the children off. So back to London she went and began the dreary task of packing the children's lives away. The same dead silence hung between her and Robert, although they remained civil to each other, the same dead silence hung from the children except when they were alone with Laura. When Camilla and Sasha arrived to fetch them, they left without the tears Robert and Laura had dreaded, just kissed them both with no warmth and turned to walk out of the door. Tears would have been a deal less painful.

That night Robert took Laura out to the local Italian restaurant. He wanted to talk to her without distraction, he said. On neutral ground, she thought.

"I can't live with you now, Laura. Not now, maybe not ever. I'm sorry. I don't know how much of all this is my fault, but wherever the fault lies we clearly can't go on as we are. I'm sorry."

Laura nodded, poked at her avocado, blinked hard. It was not unexpected. But it hurt.

"I'll pack up my things tomorrow and be out by the evening."

"No." Laura was surprised at how firm her voice was. She had been afraid it would wobble into tears. "It's obvious I should go, Robert. The children will be back next weekend and they must come home. You can't start having them in a rented flat. You've done all that once before, they don't need that again. I'll go to Charlotte or someone and then rent a flat as soon as I can." Robert looked as though he were about to protest, but Laura waved him to silence.

After a few moments in which they stared at the bottle of Chianti in silence, Robert said, "If you need to use your study there's no reason why you shouldn't come back for work."

Somehow, this hurt Laura more than anything. "Oh, Robert, has it really come to this? To sneaking in and out avoiding each other, being polite about the telephone bill? Can't you at least shout at me, give me a really good *bollocking* for Christ's sake?" Robert looked alarmed. Laura did not as a rule swear much. "Oh, I'm not going to make a scene, Robert, you know me better than that, I just wish you'd say what you mean. Can't you do that?"

"No. You're right of course. Perhaps if I could it would be easier. But I can't. Not yet. I don't know what I think yet, that's the problem. And I don't want to get Californian about it, but maybe if we were separate for a while I could sort it out." He poured them both some more wine (so much for Laura's resolutions, but she was not in a mood to turn down drink this evening) and when he spoke again he sounded gloomy. "I don't suppose I'm being fair to the children. I suppose your not being there will only muddle them more. But I want to be fair to you too."

They decided against a main course as neither had really touched their first dish, so they paid and left, walking home in silence. There were too many silences these days, Laura thought as she followed Robert into the house. Too much pain, too many secrets.

Robert slept in Richard's bed that night and Laura lay awake for hours, her hands on her stomach, trying to find it possible to believe that there was a baby growing under her still flat belly. She would have to tell Robert one day, but the moment had hardly arisen. She supposed she must wait until his final decision about their future. She tried to imagine life as a single mother, but the words meant nothing to her. Holding her belly, hoping her baby could not understand her misery, trying to pray for them both, she cried herself to sleep.

Robert, on the other side of the corridor, did not have that release. Richard's bed was too small for him, the room strangely bare and tidy now that most of the toys and boy's clobber had gone. The shadows were different on this side of the house; an orange streetlamp shone through the gap in the curtains and Robert lay amazed that his son had ever managed to close his eyes in this hellhole of a bedroom. After tossing and turning, trying to read, trying to sleep without reading, trying even the old trick of counting sheep, Robert at last got out of bed and went downstairs to make himself a hot drink. As he opened the fridge for the milk he saw the bottle of soda water beside it. "Oh, what the hell," he muttered to himself and poured himself a whisky and soda instead. Whisky and soda at one in the morning – well, he'd had a bitch of a day. He wandered through to the sitting room and turned on the television. A film, noisy, violent and incomprehensible, screamed away and he looked at it without watching. No part of his body seemed to work, not his eyes or brain, not his ears or heart. All that was left was the hand that lifted the glass and the mouth that sucked the bitter yellow liquid down.

At last, Robert slept, slumped on the sofa, the television a shouting blank.

For Melanie at least, life was grand. She did not like to think too much about "relationships" – usually brooding on her new love affairs only made her realise quite how hopeless they were – but in so far as she did think about this one, she felt at ease. Much to her surprise, she found herself contemplating the possibility of marriage with optimism. She was not dead set on it, absolutely not, but she began to see its charm. She quite liked waking up in the morning with Rémy, missed him when he was not there. When he stayed in her flat he did not seem to be in the way, as so many men were. For him she could remember to take off her mascara last thing at night and keep enough coffee in the cupboard for them all.

Her father had at first been a difficulty, but finally Melanie decided that she was a grown-up living in her own flat, that she was introducing a boyfriend rather than a row of one-night stands and if her father did not like it he could lump it. He was not always there any more himself: the Chuckle had become a permanent fixture. In fact when Rémy first stayed the night Alex happened to be away, and when he let himself in at ten in the morning to find an ugly Frenchman dressed in his daughter's towelling dressing gown, he merely nodded good morning and made himself scarce. From then on it was easy, and the two men even seemed to like each other. Melanie was unnerved to discover how alike they were, despite their apparent differences, until she decided that it was the differences which made Rémy attractive to her, not the similarities.

Her new-found romance did not stop Melanie from working at her next exhibition. After all Rémy went to an office (although he could hardly be said to be an office slave) and she had to do something during the day while he was away. There were three new artists to promote, a new exhibition to plan. Alex had started muttering about giving Melanie some backing, and although she wanted her work to remain her own venture, the idea of taking a lease on a gallery was very tempting. She decided to wait until after the next exhibition before committing herself, but meanwhile she was gathering more artists and one of her painters was being commissioned to do book jackets (particularly lucrative, as he was paid for the work but kept the painting which could then be sold). Melanie knew it would take time before she would be making much money, but felt confident that she would one day make a living. If she was selling anything at all in these hard times, there was hope for a larger market "after the recovery".

One day, Alex said he wanted to take Melanie and Rémy out to dinner. Later he said perhaps Adam and Kim should come too, and although Melanie groaned and wondered why, she suspected nothing. The Chuckle of course came too: she loved a meal out. Her hair was newly set, she wore a becoming blue number and she talked and chuckled even more than normal. Melanie had yet to meet Rémy's family, but he had assured her he thought other people's familes were *amusantes* and although she wished he didn't have to meet Kim and Adam at a peculiar family dinner, she brushed her hair and put on more mascara with a perfectly good spirit.

Adam and Rémy took one look at each other and knew they would never be friends. Both were civil, though; Adam longed for Melanie to be married (only then would the final traces of guilt leave him) and immediately decided that her marrying a Frenchman would be just the thing to take her away from her still dodgy friends and stop this art lark which was certain to ruin her, possibly taking their father down too. Kim loved the idea of a Frenchman as she thought they were romantic, so she tried very hard to make the evening go with a swing.

They dined in a fish restaurant (in deference to the vegetarians in the company) in Covent Garden. Alex declared that this was a treat and everyone was to have everything they wanted (Melanie and Rémy knew no other way of eating in a restaurant, but the

Chuckle and Kim squealed with delight and ordered kir royale).
After everyone had ordered Alex began to talk, and to Melanie's
despair she realised he was making something of a speech.

"Well, here we all are," he said pointlessly. "Um, I just wanted
to say how glad I am that I came back to England and how
pleased I am to be seeing my children again more often."

"Dad," pleaded Melanie.

"All right. Well, the news is – I'm divorced!"

His words were greeted in silence. Melanie and Adam had
presumed he had returned to England divorced, so did not react
with quite the enthusiasm their father had hoped. He ploughed
on nevertheless. "But you know your old dad – it's out of the
frying pan and into the fire and Stella and I are engaged to be
married."

Again, a silence. But one soon broken by congratulations
and kisses and questions. Melanie thought it a little unfair to
expect Rémy to take part in family celebrations so soon, was a
little worried in case he thought he was expected to cap their
announcement with one of his own, but Rémy's manners were
impeccable as always. He could not help looking slightly amused,
but he gravely offered his congratulations to Alex and kissed the
Chuckle's hand with a Gallic formality which she declared sent
shivers up her spine.

Adam, continually searching for peace, was genuinely pleased
that his father was happy and would no longer be a responsibility. The cheerful Stella was fifteen years younger than Alex,
and although he played tennis in the summer and was fairly fit,
the likelihood was that she would outlive him. Then she would
become a responsibility herself, he thought gloomily, but put that
thought behind him. Kim, who thought any marriage was lovely,
was unselfishly pleased. She had come to like her father-in-law
although she found him hard to understand. Sometimes, she
even, disloyally she knew, found herself wishing that Adam
were a little (just a little) more like his father.

And Melanie? Melanie had been so angry when she had found
out about Stella, but that had been when she had nothing to do
but whip her passions up for no reason. Looking back on the
year since her father's return, she realised that her life had
changed, and only for the better. A great deal of her anger had

been diffused: anger against her brother, her father, the world. It was increasingly directed at more impersonal targets. She could now become furious over subjects like teenage drug-runners, date rape, politicians' double-speak. Perhaps she was enjoying a late adolescence, the adolescence she had missed out on the first time round. Whatever the reason, Melanie was now able to be happy for her father, happy for Stella and happy that her family was now normal enough to get together in a restaurant and talk and celebrate like other people's families. She poured another glass of champagne and kissed Stella's cheek. She would give them Delia Smith in wheelbarrows and a send-off from her flat. The thought that her flat would be her own again did cross her mind, and did please her, but her joy was firstly for them and only secondly for herself.

Needless to say, as the evening wore on and the glasses were refilled, Stella could not resist asking Rémy how long it would be before he and Melanie met at the altar and, giggling, suggested that a double wedding might be the thing. Rémy, who had certainly drunk more than his share of the wine, kept his head rather more clear than Stella and answered carelessly without being rude. But what gave Melanie most hope for her future with him was that he did not appear to be put off by her family; seemed almost to enjoy the evening, even if he was entertained by the Freeways.

After dinner, Rémy and Melanie returned to her flat – he was definitely not living there, but he did seem to be there more often than not – and Alex went home with Stella. One advantage of going home with Rémy was that Melanie was capable of going straight to bed, no longer sat up drinking another drink she did not need and did not even really want. She supposed this was domesticity, found she even liked it. She spent ten minutes in the bathroom, wiping off the make-up with cold cream and inspecting her face which, although it was no longer young and fresh, although it showed some signs of the life she had lived was not that bad really. Then she slipped between the sheets – she even made her bed in the mornings these days which was a life-enhancing change in her habits – and, head slightly fuzzy (but only slightly), waited for Rémy.

He followed her in just as she was falling asleep and, rather than going straight to the bathroom, sat on the edge of the bed. "Are you asleep?"

"No," she said, but only just. He began taking off his shoes (he always unlaced them, never just eased them off with the toes of his other foot) and Melanie, with an effort, woke up a little more and propped herself on her elbows. "No," she said again.

"I was thinking," he said, and something in his tone made Melanie's heart begin to thump. "I was thinking. Would you like to come to France with me for a week? It would be nice if you met my parents."

Melanie lay down again. For a few seconds she had been expecting something quite different. But she was not disappointed. From the way Rémy had asked her, Melanie knew this was not an invitation given easily, and that he was not asking her just for a week's holiday eating foie gras and going to nightclubs. This was important, and it felt very good.

"Yes, please," she said. "That would be lovely." And she did not fall straight back to sleep.

Laura's flat in Earl's Court was tiny and ugly and expensive. It was all she could find at short notice, but it had the advantage that she need only rent it for a month at a time. It was in no sense a home, nor did she wish it to become one. She was at the moment living in an emotional limbo, and it suited her that her surroundings should be as meaningless and impersonal as her soul had become. Luckily, Laura had her work. She had fallen behind with her schedules during the last weeks before the case, and she now forced some discipline back into her life. Although sitting at a small table in the tiny, dark room where she spent most of her working hours, she behaved as though she were in an office. Each morning, she left the flat at a quarter to nine, walked round the block, and was sitting down at the table by nine. She broke for lunch for half-an-hour, which she usually spent eating a nasty sandwich in front of *Neighbours*.

Occasionally, she met one of her friends for a wine-bar lunch, but she knew that she was not good company at the moment and was genuinely busy with her manuscripts so avoided social life as much as possible. Occasionally, she went to the cinema with Charlotte, but she had told her too much in the first few days after she left Robert and now felt almost uncomfortable with her old friend.

She became closer to Aimée. She had always liked her sister-in-law, always found her easy to get along with and good company, but was surprised to realise that Aimée was the only person she could really talk to about the last year. Before her troubles, she might have assumed that Melanie's would be the shoulder she would choose to cry on when times were bad. She had performed that service for Melanie often enough, after all. But she discovered that the two roles – listener and talker – were so very different that a friendship could not work both ways. She knew that Melanie would do her best, but knew too that her kind lack of comprehension would be hurtful. Julia might have been more understanding, but Julia was so wrapped up in her baby and the plans for the wedding that Laura did not want to spoil her happiness. Laura was no longer resentful of Julia, she knew that it was pointless. On the contrary, she enjoyed seeing her friend and was genuinely pleased that her life was at last working out. Laura could dandle Rosie, nursing her own secret, and look forward to the days when she would take Rosie and her own child out for spoiling, godmotherly treats. If she were honest, she knew she loved Rosie much more than she loved any of Oriana's children.

Aimée, though, was a perfect confidante. She had been in the family long enough to understand all the silences that Laura did not care to fill in, her children were old enough for her to be occasionally free of their demands, and she was an excellent listener. She did not let Laura descend into self-pity or self-loathing, she made her laugh, she was always relaxed and cheerful.

She also took Laura to church.

In later years, Laura would always defend Aimée from any charges of proselytising. But if Laura turned up at their house as they were leaving for church, she just put all the children into the back of the car and held open the passenger seat for Laura. She never asked her if she would be coming, or commented whether she did or not. Laura, of course, did not go to communion, nor did she consider taking any instruction. She was not thinking of converting, but she had not found a church she felt at home in yet and preferred going with Aimée and her family to being alone. Laura liked the huge congregations that the Catholic Church seemed to be able to command, liked that children were taken as a matter of course rather than a mild embarrassment, liked the mix of age and class that she saw in the Catholic Church. She missed the old prayer book, still occasionally went to matins or communion at some other Anglican church, but found no new church that she liked half so much as the Oratory.

The only active move Aimée made towards bringing her sister-in-law towards the Catholic Church was in introducing her to Alexander Lane, a friend of many years' standing who had recently become a priest. In fact, Laura had met him before, while he had been a banker, and had liked him then (although not as much as a matchmaking Aimée had hoped), so there was no reason why he should not one night be at a dinner party given by Ferdy and Aimée. Father Lane became a real friend to Laura, unthreatening and as prepared to talk about books or the news as theology or church politics.

Of course, Laura spent a great deal of time in thought during the long lonely evenings in front of pulp television in Earl's Court. She still hoped that Robert would ask her back, realised more and more how much she loved Robert the man, not just Robert the husband, the provider, the companion. She wanted to be with him again, to drink cocktails and laugh, to cook him a good dinner and sit and talk. She wanted the past back and feared it was impossible. If he took her back, she thought, she would never complain again about his habit of emptying his electric shaver into the basin and leaving the bits there for her to find. She knew her only hope was to wait and give him time. But would he still want her? How could he? She had failed him utterly. He had delivered all he had promised in his marriage vows. She had married a man with two part-time children in the hope of having some of her own. He had fathered a child, had helped her to give up her office job and work for herself, had made her comfortable materially and emotionally. She, on the other hand, had upset the status quo to no effect at all. He had accepted that he was not to live with his children, and she had forced a false hope on him. At last Laura realised what she had done. Now, in her introspective, morally weakened state, she had the humility to accept responsibility for her actions. But now it might be too late.

She thought too much and came up with the wrong conclusions. Now she was taking all the blame for events which had not been entirely her fault, would be prepared to admit to anything, apologise for anything if only Robert would take her back.

At last Robert rang her. Only to ask her to come back for lunch on a day the children were with him, but nevertheless it was something. Laura was not sure how wise she was in accepting his invitation, but she did. She missed him. She missed the children as much. The thought that, having learned to love them, she was now going to have to learn to live without them, had often kept her awake and weeping at night.

So, one Sunday, Laura rang the doorbell at Parson's Green Lane and, hating to be made to feel a visitor, waited. She heard the children's feet running to the door and saw the letterbox wiggle as Richard tried to look through it. Then she heard a wail as Helen, pulling open the door, banged her brother on the nose. Soon both children were hugging her legs so tightly that she could not even bend to kiss them back. She was not sure she wanted to at once, anyway. Her eyes strained to the door at the end of the corridor through which Robert must come.

Then there he was, wiping his hand on a drying-up cloth, smiling apologetically for the noise the children were making – as though she were just another guest, Laura thought sadly. He hesitated, then came forward and kissed her. Laura resisted the impulse to cling to him as the children were clinging to her. They made stilted, polite conversation for a while as Robert poured her a gin and tonic and Richard and Helen squabbled over who should sit next to her on the small sofa. It was, of course, thanks to Richard and Helen that the conversation began to ease, become less formal. Within half-an-hour Laura could almost have pretended to herself that everything was back to normal, that soon they would all go out for a walk, come back, bicker over toast . . .

After lunch (Robert had always cooked a good joint, had often taken over Sunday lunch entirely to give Laura a break from cooking), they did indeed go for a walk in the park, and then, as the children raced ahead to the swings and slides, Robert and Laura could talk freely for a while. They did not discuss themselves, only the children, but even this seemed to Laura to be an advance.

Robert told Laura that Richard and Helen had found it very difficult to adapt back to living with their mother and Sasha. Although neither Robert nor Laura had wanted to bring them into the custody battle, they of course knew what was happening and had come to their own conclusions. They had liked the slightly more ordered way of life with their father, in the end even liked the formality of sitting at the kitchen table for half-an-hour after tea, Helen doing her homework, Richard doing his reading. In the first weeks back with Camilla they had run a little wild and she, trying to repair the damage she had done, mistakenly let them. Sasha had in the end proved the calming ingredient, and had gradually established a routine – different from Laura's, but nevertheless a routine – reinvented a bedtime, even sat down and played board games with them.

Laura, listening to Robert in sympathetic silence, did not lose the irony of the situation. Sasha had been her reason for bringing the case and Sasha turned out to be the children's saving grace. Camilla had returned from Farm Place a different person. She was neither the wild, party-going, slightly dishevelled woman of the early days of her second marriage, nor was she the conventional, flip, rather bitchy girl who had married and deserted Robert. She had entered into the Narcotics Anonymous world with gusto, never missing a meeting and bringing home a succession of girls with whom she earnestly discussed the step system and the damage their parents had done them. But she never went out without organising that either Sasha or a proper baby-sitter (from an agency, not Flap) should be with the children.

Robert, sounding amused now – for the first time in how many months? – told Laura that for the first time in her life Camilla was even considering finding a job, but was balked by her counsellors who had told her that an addict in recovery should make no major life-changing decisions for at least a year. Robert and Laura laughed together as he wondered how reluctant she had in fact been to drop that particular craze. Now she was apparently very interested in the idea of becoming a psychotherapist herself, and was even thinking about training for "some sort of heroes of ex-junkiedom diploma".

"That explains it," Laura said quietly.

"What?"

"I wasn't sure I was going to tell you, but Camilla rang me a few days ago – heaven alone knows how she found my number. She said she wanted to meet up, but when I said I wasn't sure that was a good idea, she started to go on anyway. She said her counsellor had said that it was a good idea she should talk to me, told me a lot of stuff about confrontation and personal growth."

"So what did you say to her?"

"I was perfectly polite but I was not very interested. Honestly, Robert, I've been there already with Melanie and I can't be fagged to get into all that ex-junkie stuff again. I feel as though I'm an ex-junkie myself sometimes, and I didn't even get the fun of it. Whatever the fun is."

She had ended bitterly, but Robert chuckled. "Fair enough. She is taking herself tremendously seriously these days, but as far as I'm concerned that's to the good. I don't have to live with it after all, and it does mean that she sticks to plans about weekends. She's gone further – she's told me not to worry if I want to take them away sometime, as long as they don't miss school. She's overcompensating, I suppose, but I do think she means it, I really do."

"Good." Laura did not quite know where to go from there; it had always been dangerous to discuss Camilla in too much depth, and she did not want to spoil the friendly atmosphere which was now between them.

Robert watched the children arguing with a strange boy over the swings for a moment, then said, "It does mean that some good has come of all this mess. Give the children time, and I'm sure they'll settle down. They're young, they're adaptable."

"Good," Laura said again, but more softly. Robert called the children and as they turned to walk back to the car, he offered Laura his arm. Without a word, she took it and they strolled back in silence together, the children exchanging glances behind them.

Robert sadly closed the door behind Laura and called to the children to tidy up their toys and collect together anything they wanted to take back to Camilla's (he could not use the word "home" about their mother's house, doubted he ever would). He had almost asked Laura to stay on, to wait until the children left. But he had known that if she had, he would have wanted her to stay the night, and he knew that it was unfair to expect her to stay until he was prepared to ask her back for ever. After the initial unease between them the day had gone so well; he had not imagined it could be so easy. He had asked her chiefly for the children's sake – or so he had told himself – but now they had spent the day together again he knew he had been lying to himself.

He wondered if he had been foolish in asking her to leave, knew suddenly that he wanted her home, wanted her to be there with him to help him forget the mess of the last months. But would she come back? Would she want him? He had spurned her when she was at her most vulnerable, had held her to blame for the fiasco that was not entirely her fault. For what else could she have done? He had accused her of meddling, but she had done so only for his children – his, not hers. It was chance that she had learned of Sasha's past, and she had been right in saying that neither Sasha nor Camilla was at that time capable of looking after the children properly. She had handled it all wrong, that was sure, but only through muddle-headed incompetence, through a goofy sense of doing the right thing. Robert began to see that he had been unjust to Laura, that he had been directing all his pain at her behaviour, not facing up to the central issue which was his children's betrayal by their mother. Could the conclusion have been any different if Laura had told him her suspicions as soon as she had heard the rumours from Melanie? And just when she had seen the damage done, just when she had turned to him for understanding and forgiveness, he had sunk into his own sorrow and shaken her off. History had shown him that he could find another wife, but now he realised properly that he would never find another Laura.

As he organised the children into readiness for their mother, opened a tin of baked beans and fed them, all he could think about was Laura. Maybe these weeks apart had done them some good after all. Maybe without them he would have continued to blame her, to hold her accountable for the separation from his children – which after all had happened long before she even met him – and would have forgotten to see her worth.

He loved her. It was as simple as that.

As he kissed the children, waved goodbye to them from the open door and turned back into his silent house, he realised that he probably loved her more now that he had forced himself to live without her than he had at any other time. He missed her. He missed her companionship, he missed her cooking, he missed her presence, he missed her in his bed. He knew the children missed her, knew now that they loved her and she loved them with a real and uncomplicated love, but at last he put the children second in his thoughts. He did not want her back for the children's sake, he wanted her back for his sake. But would she have him? Would she forgive him?

He walked stiffly down the narrow corridor, looked at the mess in the kitchen and poured himself a whisky and soda. Then he went to the small desk in the sitting room and, after a brief and incompetent search for paper and pens, sat down to write a letter.

Laura woke in the night with a dull ache in her lower belly. She lay in bed for a while, then felt it recede. That was all right then. She had not eaten such a big lunch for weeks, her stomach was probably complaining (*but it wasn't that, was it? This was not indigestion*). A few minutes later she felt the ache again, felt it mount and increase and peak before it died away again. Perhaps is was diarrhoea (*of course it wasn't, this was a different kind of bellyache entirely*). She lay in the dark, waiting to fall asleep again (*waiting for the next pain, for they were going to keep coming, weren't they?*). She laid her hands on her belly, beginning to swell a little now, and whispered to her baby. "Hold steady there, it's just a tummy bug, don't let it upset you." (*of course it wasn't, she was never ill*). And then there came the next pain, holding her in its grip for a few seconds before dying away again.

Laura had never been more frightened. She lay there, not daring even to turn the light on, willing the pain away, willing away any thoughts which dared to suggest that the baby . . .

She could not last out for long. She switched on her bedside light and lay, looking at the ceiling, waiting for the next pain to pass. Then she sat up, and pulled her duvet back, feeling around for the dressing gown that should be at the end of the bed.

She went dizzy for a moment in panic. The bottom sheet and her nightdress were soaked in blood. She must find a doctor, she must ring now, she must not move. *Oh, the baby, dear God, the baby.*

Sunday

My darling Laura,

All I can say is sorry. I'm sorry I blamed you, sorry I lost you, sorry I sent you away. These weeks have made me see more clearly. Darling Laura, I love you, and more than anything in the world I want you home. Yes, more than anything. I think I went mad for a while, but seeing you today has restored my senses. Please come home. Please give me – and us – another chance. Seeing you and the children together made me realise how much we all belong together, but it is more than that. This has nothing to do with the children. My sweet girl, I am being entirely selfish when I ask you to come home. I want you here for my sake – dare I say our sake after my behaviour?

I am not very good at this sort of letter – luckily I have not had much practice and hope never to have to try again. But I remember something you said to me once, when we were driving back from dinner somewhere together. You said that love would make everything all right, and I said you were wrong, that there was more to life than love. You looked horrified. You were right and I was wrong. Love does matter more than anything. I know now that you acted out of love, and I ask your forgiveness and for you to come home out of love. This is your home, I don't know what I was thinking of, and seeing you leave for Earl's Court this afternoon felt so wrong and sad.

Darling Laura, we can talk, we can resolve everything. If you still love me.

With unchanged love,
Robert

He put on his overcoat and walked up the road to the postbox. The letter would arrive in Earl's Court on Tuesday. Only one more day alone and then, please God, she would be back.

"Robert?"

"Yes, hello, Aimée."

Robert, hurt and perplexed that he had heard nothing from Laura – she must have forgiven him enough to give him a reply, she had come to lunch after all, she could not be too bitter about him – was pleased to hear Aimée's voice. He had always liked her and thought of her as a firm and solid friend to Laura.

"I think you should know that Laura is in hospital – the Charing Cross. She's been there since Sunday night and didn't want me to tell you, but I'm afraid Ferdy and I thought you should know."

"*Of course.* Was there an accident? I'll go straightaway."

"No, there was no accident. Robert, she's had a miscarriage."

Robert's silence was total. He was numb with shock. Aimée went on gently. "She was nearly four months pregnant. She found out just before the court case but was waiting until after it was settled to tell you. And then . . ."

"Yes. And then. Oh, God, I thought she'd put on a bit of weight."

Aimée registered that they must have met recently and felt relieved. So they were not at daggers drawn after all. It had been so hard to get anything out of Laura since she had gone into hospital. She, too, was in shock, white and silent and despairing, sure she was being punished by some malign spirit – not God. He would not do that, He must just have been looking elsewhere for a moment, just have let her slip His mind.

"Robert?"

"Yes. Thank you, Aimée, of course you were right to let me know. Which hospital did you say? And the ward? Thank you. I'm going straight there." And with the briefest of words to his clerk, Robert left his office and hailed a taxi.

* * *

Nothing Robert said could change her mind. Laura, weak and miserable, sent her mother away from her bedside at his request, but would do nothing else for him. It was no use, she said. No use at all. And she wept. Convinced that he was there out of pity, out of sorrow not for her but for their dead baby, she remained deaf to his pleas and finally he kissed her on the forehead and left. She loved him, but she would not go back to him now. She had ruined his life once, but would not take the chance to ruin it again. She did not hear him at all, only saw his face mouthing at her. He did not mention his letter, but if he had, she would not have heard him, would not have realised that he had already appealed to her. She did not listen as he begged her to come home, wishing only that he had asked a few days earlier, before the baby had died. Although they said the baby had been dead for three weeks, that it had just taken some time to abort spontaneously. How could they use the word abort about this baby, this longed-for, cherished baby?

After Robert left, Laura turned on to her side and ignoring her mother looked blankly at her lonely future until, worn out with pain and drugs and disappointment, she slept.

After Laura was released from hospital she agreed to go to Devon for a few days. Although she found her mother's concern exhausting, she supposed that at least she would be looked after in the country, would be able to eat and sleep at will and without effort. She did not think she would spend another night in the Earl's Court flat, the place where her baby had died.

Aimée took her from hospital back to the flat so that she could pack for the ten days she was to be away. Afterwards, she would stay with Ferdy and Aimée until she had decided where to go next. She must ring the publishers on whose manuscripts she was working, and hope that she would be well enough soon to pick up the threads of her work.

When she walked into the flat she scooped up the pile of waiting letters and put them on the kitchen table without another glance. Avoiding looking at the bed (although Aimée had cleaned up all traces of that dreadful night) she quickly packed some trousers, jerseys, a skirt or two, without really thinking about the task. In the sitting room she collected together

her Filofax and two manuscripts then, remembering to check the fridge and ruthlessly throwing all food into the bin, said she was ready to go. The two women were halfway down the stairs when Aimée remembered the post. Laura, weighed down with her luggage and looking at Aimée who was carrying the rubbish bag and a few books said there would be nothing which could not wait a week or so. Aimée, disliking any sign of apathy or depression, gently sent her back.

As Aimée negotiated her way through the traffic in Laura's car, Laura sat reading through her post. Aimée was to give her lunch at her house in Islington before Rosalind and Laura set off. Rosalind hoped that they would thus avoid the worst of the traffic, remarking idiotically that by Saturday afternoons half the people were on their way back from their weekends so the rush to the West would not be too bad.

Suddenly Laura shouted "Stop" and Aimée just avoided hitting a cyclist who was overtaking on the inside. "What day did I go into hospital?"

"Early Monday morning." Aimée looked bemused.

"And when did you ring Robert?"

"Wednesday morning."

Still Aimée did not understand, but her eyes followed Laura's to the letter she held in her shaking hands and she sensed a glimmer of the truth.

"Oh, Aimée, do you mind terribly, would you turn round and drive me to Parson's Green Lane instead?"

And Aimée was only too happy to be helpful.

A cold wind made its way into every corner of the church, so that those who had woken to a feeble sun and gambled on an early spring day sat huddled in their festive finery. Julia had been wiser and came up the aisle in a fine wool suit, cut as though she were to spend the day in a side-saddle rather than in a church. Green suited her best, but in a surprising fit of superstition she had decided against her favourite and wore a purply-grey colour trimmed with dark purple. It was the baby who wore white lace which bubbled down almost to her mother's knees.

Viv had chosen the service from the 1662 Prayer Book and with only a couple of hymns the wedding was soon over, followed almost as swiftly by the christening. Afterwards, the company gathered in Mrs Sinclair's drawing room – no marquee or hotel for her, Julia had decreed, and her mother was so relieved that her daughter was finally marrying that she allowed her her own way in everything. Laura, watching her, remembering her own mother, wondered if she were disappointed. But at least, she thought with a trace of malice, Mrs Sinclair had been allowed the comfort of the Church.

Laura's main emotion today was not bitterness: bitterness seemed finally to have left her. Sometimes she felt nothing at all, only a blankness, and on those days she just lived, following through each day as calmly and thoroughly as she followed a recipe. But for the most part she survived with the sense that no matter what would happen her marriage was going to survive, with or without children of her own. Father Lane was helping her, and Robert no longer seemed so set against the Catholic Church. Maybe there would come a time when she would ask Father Lane for more: it was becoming increasingly likely. Now that they were reunited, Laura found Robert's understanding and lack of accusation astounding. He endured her silences, left her alone when she needed solitude, held her when she needed reassurance. His love, and his example, helped her over her self-pity. After all, he had lost three children.

He stood beside her in the church, straight-backed as normal, looking straight ahead, singing loudly and not entirely tunefully as Julia and Viv and Rosie came back down the aisle, and Laura felt a rush of love for him. She slid her hand into the crook of his arm and squeezed and he looked down at her with a smile.

Afterwards, over champagne and canapés, Laura watched the crowd, feeling quite happily, mildly drunk and oddly detached. Julia really was the belle of the ball, frankly and unashamedly pleased with herself, with Viv, with Rosie, with her friends. Pretending that she had always wanted just this and had only been joking when she had threatened to throw it all away. In a sense that was true, of course. Julia as much as Laura had been made for fidelity and maternity and domesticity.

Mrs Sinclair joined Laura and kissed her warmly. "So who'd have thought we'd see this day?" she said, probably for the hundredth time.

"Oh, I knew," Laura said. "Although I admit there were moments when I was worried . . ." The two women laughed, united in their pleasure at a marriage, at being matrons at the feast.

"I was sorry to hear about your baby," Mrs Sinclair said. "I know it's not really the moment to talk about it but I wanted you to know how I felt for you."

"Thank you," Laura said, hoping that would be the end of the conversation.

"I know you had a bad year last year – it didn't seem fair at all – just as things were going so well for Julia too."

"I was not very nice to her," Laura mused, but was hurt by the implicit agreement in Mrs Sinclair's reply.

"She understood." There was a pause for a moment, and Laura began to wonder about moving away from her hostess when Mrs Sinclair said, "Laura, it's none of my business, but . . . did you know that Julia was adopted?"

"Julia! No." Laura was genuinely astounded.

Mrs Sinclair smiled. "I take that as a great compliment, to us, I mean. She was two when we adopted her, and I think she has no memory at all of life before us. But you know, she never tells people – after all you are one of her oldest friends. I asked her once why she didn't and she said it didn't matter, we were her family. I wondered why she had no curiosity about her natural family, but she said she had worked all that out. She knows the outline of course, and she did say once that she was tempted to look for her real parents, but had looked at her life and decided against it."

Laura wondered why Mrs Sinclair was telling her this if Julia had decided not to for so long. Maybe the woman was slightly drunk.

"I wonder sometimes if that wasn't why she seemed so set against marriage, against having children. Maybe I worried too much, maybe that was just Julia being Julia. In any case, it seems to be sorted out now, doesn't it? I know we're not allowed to think of marriages as happy endings any more, but this looks like one to me, even if Rosie arrived a little soon for my old-fashioned ways." *Better early than not at all*, thought Laura, but she said nothing. "Anyway I really don't know why I'm telling you all this," said Mrs Sinclair with a laugh which did not ring quite true. "You're an old friend, and I suppose people always behave oddly at weddings. How's your drink? Oh, there's my sister-in-law; I haven't even said hello to her yet. Will you excuse me?"

Laura watched Mrs Sinclair's neat, pale blue back disappear into the crowd and thought she should really stop standing here in a daze and talk to some of the guests. She supposed she ought not to tell anyone else about Julia, although her head was full of the news. Luckily, the next person she bumped into was Charlotte, who was certainly, but not offensively, a little drunk.

"Laura, hi. I'm glad to see you. Who's that man Robert's been talking to for about ten minutes – over there by the cake?"

Laura told her and led her over to be introduced. Poor Charlotte, still looking, still hoping. Still believing that old lie that women meet their future husbands at other people's weddings, when in fact weddings are celebrated most by those already in the club. Nothing, Laura remembered, was more desperate for a single woman than a wedding. Nothing was more reassuring for those already married. If your friends see your marriage and it hasn't put them off, you must be doing the right thing. If your friends are getting married, you must have done the right thing. If your friends are all married and you are not, you must be doing the wrong thing. Desperate, desperate.

For the second time that day Laura felt a great rush of love for Robert. As Charlotte and John were introduced, Laura and Robert's eyes met in a moment of joking complicity, and with it came the realisation that life was running almost back on track.

The wedding was soon over after that. After the speeches (short) and the cake (chocolate), Julia and Rosie and Viv disappeared to change and set off for their holiday in the Lake District. The company gathered in front of the house to wave and cheer in celebratory style.

Laura was one of the last that Julia hugged. The hug was fierce, concentrated, not at all social. "Bye, Laura, see you soon. Laura, did Mummy tell you?" Laura did not answer but her look said enough. "Good. I'll ring you when we're back. Have you seen Rosie's going-away outfit? Isn't it chic?" And she had moved on.

Robert turned to Laura: "Are you ready to go? Or we'll stay longer if you want – I'm in your hands."

Laura took his arm. "No, I think that's it. I'll say goodbye to Mrs Sinclair and then we'll make our way home. It'll take us a couple of hours."

They made their way to the car through the bitter wind, Laura thinking hard. Of course Mrs Sinclair had not been drunk. Julia had put her up to it. The whole conversation had been planned. And with a reason. Of course. Earlier in her marriage she had been set against the idea, but wouldn't it be better to help another baby than to long hopelessly for her own? And if her own came afterwards, no harm would be done . . .

As they reached the car, arms linked, Laura turned to Robert. "Robert," she said, "Robert, I've had an idea."

Cupid's Tears

PEGGY WOODFORD

When I think of my sister I think of nets, of mesh, of toils in its old sense: a netted space into which a quarry is driven and ensnared . . .

Natalie Harper could not feel any emotion other than relief when her younger sister Jane followed their father out to Australia. Now, at the start of a promising career as a barrister, Nat is about to marry her Head of Chambers, Freddie Mentieth QC, a widower fourteen years older. After much indecision, she sends her father and sister an invitation, never expecting them to come. But Jane arrives unannounced the week before the wedding, and it is soon clear to Nat that her younger sister hasn't changed, and that the pushing, hustling force that stormed her in childhood is back to damage and demoralise her all over again.

Jane is beautiful, intelligent, charming – particularly to Freddie. And Natalie is about to be faced with an agonising dilemma.

Perceptive, sympathetic, always cute, CUPID'S TEARS is an examination of the delicate, complex ties that bind together sisters and lovers.

'An extremely clever and original book . . . I was full of admiration. *Cupid's Tears* will be a great success – it so well fits our times'
Rumer Godden

SCEPTRE

Walls of Glass

AMANDA BROOKFIELD

While many regard her marriage with admiration and a trace of envy, Jane Lytton quietly reaches the shocking conclusion that her relationship with Michael, a successful banker with little time for the nitty-gritty of family life, has failed.

Jane's decision to leave a man who does not love her, but who has shown no obvious signs of abuse or neglect of her or their children, is greeted with a mixture of vitriol and measured, uncomprehending sympathy by family and friends. Mattie, Jane's needy younger sister, is walking her own tightrope of depression. Even her oldest friend, while recognising the courage of Jane's action, becomes impatient with her difficulties in adjusting to a new life.

Sympathy and strength come from the most unlikely direction, but just as the seeds of trust have been sown, an unfortunate coincidence of events and human failing throws Jane off balance once more. When her vision at last clears to reveal her best chance of happiness, it seems she may have left it too late.

∫

SCEPTRE